I0690935

THE OBESITY PANDEMIC

MARK SARNEY

The Obesity Pandemic

Copyright (C) 2017 by Mark Sarney All rights reserved.

First Ebook and Print Edition: June 2017

Print ISBN: 978-1-941188-08-8

Ebook ISBN: 978-1-941188-09-5

Cover: Streetlight Graphics

❀ Created with Vellum

[1]

I am part of a vast corporate conspiracy to make America obese. It's our best hope to save the world from an environmental collapse. But I couldn't admit this to my son's high school biology class. I had my standard talk ready to go, full of the comforting lies and disingenuous half-truths we all have heard over and over again.

The teacher, Mrs. Paris, said to the class, "Our visitor today is Dr. Elaine Cassano, Charlie's mother. She has a PhD in systems biology and has worked on nutrition and human health in research labs in the government and private sector. She is the director of the AgSol research lab. She's here today to talk about the obesity epidemic."

"Oh my God, Charlie, she's your *mom*?" It was a guy in the back row who had long, greasy hair. He was sitting right behind a morbidly-obese girl who was studiously ignoring me. "I hope you were breastfed."

Long-forgotten high school reflexes sprang to life. I wanted to run from the room and cry but at the same time I wanted to smack the redneck bastard.

Mrs. Paris surged up out of her chair. "You shut your mouth, Ben!" She pointed at the door. "Get out of here. Principal's office. Don't you smirk at me."

1

Ben's smirk evaporated. "I didn't say nothing." He huffed and pouted his way out of the classroom like he was the one who had been insulted.

Mrs. Paris turned to me. "I'm so sorry, Dr. Cassano. I'm sure the rest of my students will behave themselves now."

The anger and embarrassment threw me back to my own high experience thirty years ago. The social classes were clearly separated by clothes, hairstyle, angst, attitude, and income.

Charlie looked like he wanted to sink into the floor. It occurred to me that there was no way this would end well for him. Talking to his class was supposed to score him some extra credit, and I secretly hoped it would make him seem cooler, because of course I was one of the cool parents. But I realized now that it could also backfire terribly for him. What could I do about it now though?

"Were you really on a reality show once?" asked a girl in the front row with pink hair, a pierced nose, and an air of complete indifference.

"Yes, I was on *We Will*." There were a few nods of recognition. It must not be a popular show any more. "It was five years ago; just one episode. They wanted someone from the government to explain the obesity epidemic at a town hall. A lot of people yelled at me."

The girl shrugged and went back to twisting her pink hair.

I cleared my throat. "Let's see how the obesity epidemic started." I showed an animation of each state's obesity rate starting to climb in the 1980s, ending with the 2018 estimates from the CDC, when the rates had reached an all-time high.

"It's not just America; it's happening in many countries. But why? You've probably heard that the rise in obesity is because of greedy food companies, or a lack of personal responsibility, or even because of genetics." I paused. I had the attention of all of them for just a moment. Pauses can be so powerful. "But that is only part of the story, and not a very large part."

And I wasn't going to share the truth with them, as much as it pained me. "It's all the things you've heard before: too many calories eaten, not enough exercise, cancelled gym classes, cable TV, genetics, not enough grocery stores, too many fast food restaurants, etc."

These causes were all actually contributing factors, that was the truth. But it was all half-lies because they implied that the epidemic was an accident, an unintended consequence of a thousand different things. The truth was the

2

epidemic was a well-designed campaign to fatten Americans as much as possible. The goal was to produce enough human fat tissue to feed an army of alien hybrids who we hoped were genius enough to figure out how to stop the environmental collapse that we were barreling toward. Yeah, I wasn't telling them that.

"You didn't mention the food companies," the pink-haired girl said. "That's because they fund you."

Behind me, I heard Mrs. Paris sigh pointedly. But I smiled. I probably would have said something similar when I was a teen. Hell, I would have said something like that in my thirties. "It's true that they fund the lab I work for. It's also true that the food companies bear a lot of responsibility for the epidemic." It felt good to tell at least fragments of the unvarnished truth.

"You probably believe in evolution and global warming," said a tall, preppy guy, like he was calling me out.

"Brian does this to everyone," explained the pink-haired girl, smiling with her chin in her hand. "Don't bother answering, he'll just argue with you."

I couldn't let it go. Global warming, mass extinctions, starvation, peak oil, I believed in it all because, just like with evolution, the supporting scientific evidence was stacked to the rafters. "I believe in the truth. Even when it's hard. Even when it conflicts with my faith. I know not everyone can do that. Or wants to."

"Do you believe in the afterlife?" Brian asked.

As a practicing Catholic, yes, I believed in the resurrection of Christ and a glorious afterlife. Which seemed like small potatoes compared to witnessing undead ghouls, employed by the food industry, who could suck your soul right out of your nose when they weren't yammering on a cell phone. So I simply said, "Yes."

"Brian, let's stay on topic," Mrs. Paris cautioned.

"Fine. I think obesity is a personal failing," Brian scoffed. "We shouldn't pay for people who don't take care of themselves." You could slice the tension between him and the obese girl in front of him with a dull knife.

I put my hands behind my back. "If so, then why haven't we seen a similar drop in personal responsibility, by adults and children, all across the country, for forty years, in areas besides eating?" When Brian didn't respond, I said, "The evidence doesn't support it. What could explain it?"

Charlie covered his eyes. Oops, apparently I shouldn't haven't won a showdown with the class proselytizer. Well damn it, I'm a scientist, not a motivational speaker.

The girl to my left who had been taking notes the whole time raised her hand. "Older people are heavier, and there are more older people. Maybe, obesity isn't getting worse, it's just that a bigger proportion of the population is obese to begin with."

"That's an excellent observation," I replied. "Except that the rates of obesity and overweight have increased in all age groups, especially among children. Your generation has a higher obesity rate than mine at your age, and my generation was worse than the two before it."

The class had no response. Charlie looked around at his classmates. Half were bored but the rest were curious.

I flipped to the next slide. "This will have major effects on your generation's health. The chance of dying increases if you are obese and it's even worse if you are morbidly obese. There's a substantial increase in the chances of heart disease, joint failure, cancer, diabetes, and a number of other diseases."

"And it's worse if you're obese as a kid, right?" Brian asked looking at the obese girl sitting to his left. He was bullying this poor girl, I felt, but he had wrapped it up in an innocent-sounding question.

"Brian, cut it out," said an Indian girl with big glasses from the desk next to Charlie.

"I'm just making a scientific inquiry," Brian retorted with a snooty calm. "Questioning everything, like Mrs. Paris said."

I nodded. "Yes, the sooner someone becomes obese, the sooner the medical problems can start."

"I saw Charlie eating a candy bar in the cafeteria." The pink-haired girl in the front row smiled. Behind her, Charlie froze and turned red. He was mortified, which wasn't like him. He usually laughed off a dig like that. Oh, shit, he had a crush on this girl. The one with the pink dye job, the nose ring, and the attitude? Really, Charlie?

I laughed off her accusation. "Was it Krackel? That's my favorite." The girl nodded, acknowledging that I had sidestepped her little trap and wouldn't come off as holier than thou.

I said to the class, "Mrs. Paris wanted me to give you a sense of what it's like to work in a scientific research lab. What's exciting about science research isn't the how, it's the why."

My next slide showed mug shots of people wearing suits. "I'm going to tell you a true story about science that even Charlie has never heard. It involves yelling, a fist fight, careers ruined, and a bunch of people going to jail."

Everyone perked up, including Charlie.

"The federal government funds a lot of research through grants, in every field. A researcher proposes a project, and if the government thinks it's worthwhile, it gives them a grant. There's a lot of money on the line, so the government convenes experts to pick only the most promising projects.

"I used to be a federal employee who reviewed grants for a federal agency I won't name. This was before I went to the Agriculture Department. The proposals are scored by a panel of subject matter experts who are supposed to be impartial and free of any conflicts of interest."

Brian raised his hand. "A conflict of interest? Like working for the food industry?"

"Good point. Actually, that would not be prohibited in many cases. The reviewer can't be from the same institution or have financial ties to the applicant. So a proposal came from a marginal university that was beating a dead horse, scientifically. But it had a long history of being funded and had Congressional backers. So, politics were involved."

I changed the slide to a stock photo of a red 'Rejected' stamp. "The expert panel rejected the proposal. I backed them up, because they had sound reasons. The only thing I dislike more than wasted research dollars is bad science."

I changed the slide to a picture of my boss, Mark, holding up one of those mugshot cards, looking stricken. "But my boss here, who had not done any science in decades, tried to pick apart the panel's reasoning. He and the other managers questioned the experts' objectivity. They questioned my judgement and experience. They kept pointing out that these researchers had been funded by us on other projects in the past."

"What did you do?" asked the smart girl on my left.

"We have professional review processes for a reason. I stood my ground. Even when Mark here told me that it would cause a political firestorm for us."

I smiled. "The managers were trying to avoid trouble from their bosses. They knew there would be grief if the project wasn't funded. Congress would make calls and upset their bosses; it would get ugly. But the managers ultimately gave up and let the experts' decision stand."

"Please don't take this the wrong way," Brian said. "But this sounds like a morality tale, not science."

I shook my head. "Science is also about deciding which projects are the most promising and where to devote scarce resources. If we're not objective about those decisions, then we undermine the scientific process, just as much as someone messing up their measurements or spilling a beaker."

Brian, chastened, folded his arms.

"My boss was exactly right about what happened next. The applicant brought Congressional staff down on us. They grilled the agency's executives about the process, and conflicts of interest, and subtly threatened my agency's funding."

Charlie listened like his SAT score depended on it. I had never said anything about that job and must have been curious. "The managers pushed me aside and went into full-on twisting the experts' arms. Long story short, the grant was awarded, after one expert was excused for dubious reasons, another quit in protest, and another was taken off the panel by her employer. But as the project officer, it was up to me to sign off on this. I refused."

"Who approved it then?" Mrs. Paris asked.

I looked back at her. "My boss forged my name. And I reported him to the Inspector General. It turns out that there was a lot of shady deals going down with him and the other managers. They were dumb enough to use email to coerce and conspire. Some of the executives and managers went to jail or were fired, like Mark. I had to leave the agency because, well, let's just say a whistleblower is not welcome once they blow the whistle. Even if she is right."

"They punished you for following the rules?" Brian asked. "That's not fair. Does this happen a lot in *the government*?"

"No. Government employees, especially the scientists, are mostly hard-working people who are honest and accept low pay to help the public," I replied. "At least no one stole a Nobel Prize from a female scientist who made the actual discovery, like happened twice in the last century."

Charlie was puzzled. "When did all of this happen to you?"

6

"A couple years before all of you were born. Before I worked at Agriculture. Hopefully, breaking up that corruption helped fund projects that may actually save lives."

Mrs. Paris stood up. "I'm sorry, we're just about out of time. This has been very interesting. Let's thank Dr. Cassano for taking the time to talk with us. For tomorrow, please turn in three ideas on how to reduce obesity in America that I will pass along to her."

The teens gathered up their books and began shuffling out of the room. Mrs. Paris thanked me again and went to the lab to prep experiments for her next class.

Charlie walked up to me with one of his patented long faces. The expression reminded me of his father's look when I took him to meet my mother for the first time. "How come you never told me all that?" he asked, annoyed, but quietly so his classmates wouldn't hear.

I shut down my slides. "It's ancient history, right?"

He looked around, to make sure no one was within earshot, and whispered. "You didn't have to be *that* interesting."

"Why did you invite me to come here and talk to your class then?" I whispered back.

"Extra credit. Which I need in this class. I thought you would bore them and they wouldn't remember you."

Charlie thought biology was hard and did a poor job disguising his dislike for it. Whether his dislike of my subject area was genuine or calculated just to spite me, I couldn't tell. He was fifteen, it could be neither or both reasons, depending on the hour.

I looked at him sternly. He sighed and said, "I don't know what I was expecting. I didn't think about it. I assumed you would speak to some other class, and not mine."

"Do you think I ruined your life in this high school?" I asked, my voice low but panicked. "Should we move again?"

He rolled his eyes. "No. Nothing like that. These kids probably think you're cooler than me now. I, I have to get to my next class."

"Do you want me to walk with you to. No, right, forget it. I'll see you at home, sweetie."

"*MOM.*"

7

[2]

Today was one of the first days where the weather had that crisp autumn feel. The leaves looked less green. Unfortunately, I couldn't enjoy it because I was seeing red. Adrenaline surged through my body as I entered AgSol's suburban office building.

Fiona, our human-alien hybrid receptionist, was sitting at her desk offering the same, completely phony greeting to everyone as they came in. "Good morning!" Her robotic enthusiasm was disconcerting on good days, infuriating on days like this.

I didn't slow down but sent a sober look her way. "Is Dr. Meers in yet?"

Fiona's nodded and her plasticky smile fell away. She saw what was tucked under my arm and wrinkled her brow. "Dr. Cassano?"

"I'll talk to you later," I said. "I have to go."

Donald was at his desk, reading his tablet. I came in and tossed the local community paper on his desk. He looked up at me in surprise.

"Donald, why are you running for the school board?"

He cleared his throat. "We aren't doing enough here in the lab. Progress is too slow. We have to engage in the community, be active in politics to create the kind of change we need."

"And you think someone with your special background can run for elected office?"

8

He shrugged. "I can serve the public like anyone else."

I put my hand over my heart. "Can you drop out of the race?" I kind of blurted it without thinking.

He was shocked. "Why would I do that?"

I paced around his office, realizing distantly how much of an asshole I sounded like. But I went with it anyway. "Jesus, Donald, where do I start? You don't interact well with people. You're not exactly eligible to run for elected office since you're not a citizen."

He scowled. "I have a birth certificate and a Social Security number. I meet all the qualifications. I'm the chief scientist here, a veritable pillar of the community."

"Someone will figure out that you're not quite human. You're supposed to keep a low profile to minimize the chance of discovery. Does running for office sound like low-profile?"

"It sounds like you think I'm a second-class citizen." His tone was subdued but angry.

I held up my hands. "No, no, no. You're just like everybody else. And most of us are not cut out for politics. Politicians are, how do I put it, glad-handing extroverts who are the life of the party. You remember Bill Clinton? Like him."

"Richard Nixon was a successful politician," he replied. "He put the effort together to save the planet. Created the EPA, redirected money from the space race to health and environmental research, subsidized agriculture to finance this lab." Donald thought about it for a second. "He could have been an alien hybrid himself."

Good god, this guy saw Nixon as a political guiding light. Politics to me was just a clash of different perspectives. Uninformed, poorly reasoned, and poorly researched perspectives. "He also had incredibly lousy moral judgement," I pointed out.

"So I'm a first class citizen with poor morals. You are making my case for me!" He clapped his hands triumphantly.

I laughed and flopped into his guest chair. "What do you want to accomplish on the school board?"

"Improve math and science education. Better pedagogy. Higher standards."

"I'm all for that. Not sure most voters will know what pedagogy is. You realize the teachers and the parents will resist. The kids have a curriculum to learn and state tests to pass. Have you studied why they haven't adopted your kind of standards? Especially after Common Core failed?"

"No." He paused to think about that. "Why?"

"Because," I said, twirling my finger in a little circle. "The parents, the kids, and the teachers don't want them. I don't know why, but the educational system has been wrestling with raising standards since we were in school. There are people who think high academic standards ruin kids' childhoods. Or cause anxiety."

"Ah, it's cultural," Donald said.

I tapped my nose. "Yes, bingo. Can't fight the culture."

"I think I'll still do some good though." He looked away. "I can't just fiddle with the beakers and know it's not enough."

I understood. We had a ton of work to do and time was running short. In the early 1970s, a group of concerned scientists called the Club of Rome published a report on the limits of continuous economic growth. The report projected that humanity would exhaust the planet's resources in under a century.

Over time, the report received widespread ridicule from economists as oil supplies rose and food yields jumped. But in 2007, a follow-up report compared the projections to 30 years of historical data and found the predictions for 'business as usual' were pretty accurate. That was a little over a decade ago, years before I became aware of the problem and the conspiracy that had formed to solve it. Time was running out.

The food industry had responded in the 1970s by forming our conspiracy. Our predecessors developed hybrid alien geniuses to science us a way to feeding a growing population and making the earth sustainable. Unfortunately, those hybrids could only eat human adipose, and so the industry created the obesity epidemic. They also wore bell-bottoms, but they were doing the best they could at the time.

Maybe Donald was buckling under the pressure of the planet's ticking time bomb. I could argue that he was taking on too much, but that wouldn't fly. He knew his limits. He had a life outside of work that was none of my damn business. If he thought he could handle the school board in addition to his work, it was because he had planned it out meticulously. His adopted hybrid kids were grown, and he probably had money and time on his hands.

"Your past is a political liability. Your 'skeleton in the closet' is your skeleton."

He gave me a condescending smile. "You're overestimating the risk. They won't test my DNA. I have a birth certificate. And school board races are not that contentious. Candidates don't do opposition research on their opponents. I checked."

That was all fine and good, but when people got a good look at him, they'd probably start digging. I would. I was running out of ways to talk him out of it. "I could forbid you, as your employer," I said, folding my arms and looking as authoritative as possible.

He knew I wasn't serious. "No you can't. I have rights."

"You have rights, but you don't get to exercise them for free. I could fire you."

"In theory. I could also retire and run anyway."

I put my head in my hands. "Do you really have to do this?"

"I feel it that strongly," he said.

I shook out my curls. My last tool to dissuade him was, I hate to admit, fear. "The feds may reopen the Fiesta investigation."

He made a face. "That doesn't make sense. It was closed over five years ago."

You see, the Fiesta scandal, as I called it, had partly been Donald's fault. I was at the Department of Agriculture back then. Obese people went temporarily insane and killed skinny people, all because, as it turned out, of a rage-inducing additive secretly added to Fiesta chips. An additive designed by Donald and his team to encourage social shaming of skinny people to generate more life-sustaining human fat tissue. Donald didn't mean for anyone to die.

I slid my phone across his desk. "*The Hill* says that a new committee chairman wants to investigate how the industry's food products are regulated. He wants the FDA, USDA, and maybe even the FBI to run the investigation."

Before joining AgSol, I would have cheered any government investigator hell-bent on exposing the truth. I had risked my job, my life, and custody of my son to expose the truth behind the Fiesta additive. And the truth was that Donald and his colleagues had designed it to shame skinny people into eating more, but they had blown it. But now that I was committed to helping

11

the industry save the entire damn planet, I found the thought of a government probe annoying, to say the least.

Donald read the story with that intense squint he uses when he's thinking really hard. When he finished he tossed the tablet on a stack of papers. "Do you think the FBI will interfere with local school board races because someone is running who is loosely connected to the food industry?"

Goddamn super-smart aliens were impossible to win an argument against. I wondered what it was like to manage dumb people who simply comply with whatever you tell them. Or at least ask some questions, but ones you can probably answer. It had to be a lot easier than this. I spread my hands on his desk. "It could be an issue if they think you are trying to rig the lunch menu to benefit the food companies."

I got no response.

"That was a joke, Donald." I shook my head. "What the hell? Go run for the school board. Good luck. It needs people like you, despite my concerns. If things blow up, we'll, um, try to fix it. Like we always do. But it will make Stitcher angry."

He ignored that and nodded, happy, and I collected my phone and left. When I returned to my desk I buried my head in my hands. In retrospect, Donald's school board race didn't make the top five of problems I wrestled with that fall.

[3]

The AgSol conference room was silent and dark, with the blinds closing out the daylight so we could see the projector screen better. Every chair was taken, but no one made a sound after I spoke.

Dr. Jeff Ewell pivoted to face me fully. "Elaine, I've been defending you. But I can't keep doing that. We're making progress here. With all due respect, my team is starting to call you the Dragon Lady."

Donald raised his hand. "Jeff, let's not call names."

"I, I wasn't. What I said was, Elaine, you know what I meant."

I smiled. I liked Jeff, he was a full human who could keep up with the hybrids. He was one of the lab's best team leads. I liked his team too, and the work they were doing on immune system responses to toxicity. I excelled at studying an area of inquiry and assessing if the research had fallen into a non-productive rut. I had a nose for the incremental tweaks that could spawn a hundred papers but make no real progress. That's why AgSol hired me. As lab director, I had been kicking my scientists in the ass until they climbed out of those ruts.

"Jeff, there's always a new technique, or a new study to replicate. We need to make much bigger leaps than confirming findings from ten years ago. We have to let go of avenues that aren't promising any more."

This was hard for the scientists here, and they thought I was a short-sighted bitch sometimes. I was disrupting work they planned to pursue for the rest of their careers. "Let me ask you this, if you had to invest your retirement savings and college savings to keep this project going, would you?"

Jeff was a middle-aged guy, balding and wearing wire-rim glasses. He had boys heading to college soon. He looked away and that was all the answer I needed.

"So they call me the Dragon Lady. Big deal. I know this is tough, but we're running out of time. Basic work needs to advance to applied. Applied work needs to move to development. Projects have to meet our standards to be funded. This immune response project barely rose above the line at last year's murder boards. Now, it's below the line."

"Jeff," Donald added "if the hard part for you is telling your team, then blame it on me, the senior scientist. It can help your team bond with you." Oh brother, Donald had been reading more books about leadership and psychology again. Hopefully he wasn't trying to use them on his school board campaign.

Jeff nodded, not buying it. I said, "Your team is excellent. This project is just not worth your time. If we had a B team, I'd have them work on it. But I need my stars chasing bigger payoffs."

Jeff understood and he packed up his presentation and left. After I broke two more hearts, enraged three others, and pleased one with an enthusiastic sign of support, Donald and I took a break from project reviews. The leaves were falling outside on a sunny October morning and I contemplated an afternoon run as I checked the school's website for Charlie's latest grades.

I looked up when my boss, Betty Furman, knocked on my door. She was CEO of AgSol and the widow of a former food industry exec who had connections all over the scientific and industrial worlds. Right now she was as white as a sheet.

"I have some bad news," she said. "I don't know how to say this, but the board of directors wants to pull our funding."

My core muscles locked up and I held my breath as my brain did somersaults. "What? Why?"

She shook her head, her eyes glassy. "Remember last year there was some shuffling in the c-suites at the bigger companies in the industry? There was also those two mergers."

I nodded. The agricultural and food industries were consolidating once again. It seemed like that at some point in the near future, there would just be one giant food conglomerate that ran everything from fertilizer to grocery stores.

"It's those new executives," Betty said. "Stitcher calls them cost-cutting SOBs. They don't care at all about the environmental collapse, or the conspiracy. All that matters to them is the share price."

"How much of our funding are we talking about?" I asked. I would hate to lose the Palo Alto lab we just founded. We had consulted with multi-disciplinary outfits, like the Santa Fe Institute and the Club of Rome, on how to take multi-disciplinary approaches to complex problems. Palo Alto was the result and was doing some amazing computer modeling of the growing environmental problems across the planet.

"Over 80%," was her answer. It smacked my ears, and then my brain, like an open-handed slap. I thought I misheard her for a second.

Forget Palo Alto, losing 80% would mean we couldn't even cover the overhead here in Oak Ridge. The end of AgSol. I shook my head; this didn't make a damn bit of sense. "Betty, we just need to brief these new guys on Project Rogers."

"They *are* briefed in. Can you believe it?"

When I was brought into the conspiracy, I learned the dire extent of the coming environmental apocalypse and how it would destroy civilization. The growing toxicity of water, air, and land would kill off most life in less than a century. It had already started. Not only would that be bad for the food industry, it would wipe out humanity, eventually.

Project Rogers was our best hope to innovate our way out of the mess. The alien hybrids had IQs north of 150 and could help us avoid this disaster. But not if we stopped doing scientific research.

"Then we shouldn't have to make the case to them again," I said in a whiny voice. My throat was dry and I felt lightheaded. What kind of empty suit worried more about next quarter's share price than making sure his company had customers and suppliers in the next couple of decades? I felt like I was taking someone's comedy sketch way too seriously.

"I've been here for decades and I've never heard anything like it. They want to replace the directors on our board too, and reorient the lab to 'more profitable' work."

"What does Stitcher say about all of this?" I asked. John Stitcher was the

15

frantic old bastard who had kept the conspiracy together. I'm surprised these c-suite moves had happened without his approval. He always had an answer and a plan. And he was also the one who promised me that I'd never become a corporate science stooge if I took this job.

"He just swears a lot. Says he's working on it and to leave him the hell alone."

I shook my head. "What do we do in the mean time?"

"Push the rest of the assessments off until next week," Betty replied. "I'm meeting the board Friday to figure out what to do. I need your help making a case that the lab is worth it."

"Basically, we have to justify our existence," I said. That meant resurrecting last year's funding pitches, updating them, and practicing them. It would be a huge amount of time, and at best all it would do would be to preserve the status quo. But what choice did we have? We barely had enough progress to satisfy me as it was.

She nodded. "We can't use the old presentations," she said, reading my mind. "Saying that we're doing God's work by researching how to save the Earth's environment won't cut it with them. And they have passed on word that they don't want to hear about 'sandbox, science-fair projects.' They want actionable work that can lead to new processed food products or improve existing ones. They suggested things like additives to improve 'mouth feel'."

Jesus, I really hated that kind of talk. It was a clear sign of someone who didn't understand how science worked. Someone who thought it was a linear process, like refining a chili recipe to make it spicier. They didn't understand that it was like climbing a jungle gym in the dark; sometimes you had to move laterally, or back up and choose a different direction to go higher. And sometimes you couldn't go anywhere at all and had to climb down and find a new jungle gym. Like I was making Jeff's team do.

"What the hell do they want to hear about from us then?"

Betty started ticking items off on her fingers. "They want to see our results, return on investment, tangible benefits for the industry. They want examples where our work benefitted the industry. They want to see summaries of all of our current and future projects, with each one emphasizing what the business value-add is expected to be. Naturally, they know we'll come up empty-handed in each metric. It's a setup."

I immediately started cataloguing all of our accomplishments in my head.

We usually did this for the lab's annual report to donors, but they didn't expect to kick the tires so thoroughly. Donors were already on board with the basic mission since they chose to support us in the first place.

"This is like trying to land new donors," I remarked. Approaching potential donors was a high volume, low success enterprise from what I had seen in my time there.

Betty shook her head. "It's worse. It's like trying to convince creationists that the Earth isn't flat."

I bit my tongue and didn't explain that creationists accepted that the Earth was a sphere. They just thought it was created as per the Bible's timeline, rather what scientific evidence had found.

I took Betty to Donald's office and we brought him up to speed. He took it better than us. "We have to start prepping now. We have to reschedule the murder boards."

Donald winced. "But the other teams are in holding patterns until we can either greenlight or kill their projects."

"That's not going to matter if there's no lab left to employ them," Betty remarked. As Donald's face fell, I took a deep breath. Here was the first wave of an existential crisis causing it's own existential crises. I saw this happen several times in the government. The threat of a mission change, or reorganization, or even wholesale leadership change, destroyed productivity to the point where the feared change became the solution to the problem its specter had created. Damn it. We couldn't afford to let that happen here.

"We'll get back on track as soon as possible, somehow," I said.

"Don't worry about it," Donald said with a chuckle. The man was hardly ever ruffled. "Most of these guys think these presentations are a waste of time."

I smiled back, but didn't have the heart to tell him that everyone's jobs may depend on Betty being able to give the best presentation she has ever given.

[4]

I had been enjoying a panicked morning, worrying about the upcoming presentation to the Board, when my phone caught a call from Lyle Nunez's number. Seeing his number took me back in time five years. After I joined AgSol Lyle wouldn't return my calls or emails. His silence communicated how he thought I had betrayed him, betrayed the cause. We had discovered the obesity conspiracy together and I'm sure he now thought that I had cashed in to join it.

Eventually I had stopped reaching out to him. There wasn't much of a point staying in touch when I couldn't tell him anything about what Stitcher and I had been conspiring to do.

"Elaine, we need to talk." Lyle spoke in a rapid burst, like we had last spoken yesterday. I pictured him in a phone booth, wearing a trench coat, looking over his shoulder. "In person."

So much for pleasantries and catching up.

"Lyle, it's been a long time," I replied, a little reproachful. He should have understood that I wanted to know where the hell he'd been for the last half decade.

But not Lyle. "I don't want to talk on the phone. You need to come to Cary."

I looked at my desk. There was a ton of work piled up. Betty and I were scrambling on the presentation to the board. "Cary, North Carolina? I'm in Knoxville and super-busy. What are you doing over there anyway?"

"Consulting at SAS Institute headquarters. It's the backup day job."

Our presentation was in two weeks. There was no way I was meeting him sooner than that. And, come to think of it, I wasn't sure I wanted to meet him at all. I'd have to talk to Stitcher first. Decline by calendar, an old favorite dodge of mine. "Ah. I'll be in DC after the holidays, I think."

He grumbled. "This can't wait that long. I feel like I owe you fair warning. The FBI is taking a hard look at your industry. Not just one company, but all of them. Including your lab."

"The FBI?" Fear ran up and down my spine, but it fizzed out into a flat curiosity. "Not the FDA, the USDA, or even the SEC?"

"Rumor has it that someone at the Bureau is looking at the industry's finances. How much money food companies make off junk food and soda, that kind of thing. All these corporate mergers are keeping the industry in the public eye and the epidemic keeps getting worse and worse. Anyway, that initial investigation has some teeth now. The FBI agents are pushing hard, trying to make a career out of it. I thought I should warn you."

"Wouldn't whatever the problem is be an SEC matter?" I asked. I still wasn't seeing why federal cops would care about soda sales or what my lab was researching.

"God, I don't know. Maybe there's a criminal angle. Maybe there's all kinds of odd things that can turn up. You know. Maybe there's a lot of things I'm not saying over the phone. That's why I want to meet."

Was he implying that I should watch out because I was hip-deep in corporate crimes?

"You know they can't tap our phones without a warrant. The NSA scandals made sure of that," I said. If I could just get him to say what was going on, I would have an idea how to respond. And maybe call him when I wasn't buried in this presentation.

Lyle snorted. "You really believe that?"

Well, it was good to see he was still a paranoid conspiracy nut. I couldn't imagine what he would do without his full-time obsession. "None of that concerns me. I'm running a lab," I said. "We do research and write papers. We're financed by the industry, not part of it."

Lyle replied, "Come on. You're wrapped up deep with what is going on.

You expect me to believe that Stitcher set you up with a cushy job out of town and left you alone?"

"Yeah, actually, I do expect you to believe that," I said. "Because it's the truth." Okay, it wasn't the entire truth, but I wasn't admitting anything to him. Stitcher still gave me jobs to do and errands to run. For all I knew, Lyle could be an FBI informant. Great, somehow his paranoia had traveled down the fiber-optic lines and infected me.

"Elaine, you've been on TV five times in the last year, you're a known face of the industry. There's a lot of eyes looking at agriculture, at food processors, all the way to retail. Trouble is coming. I wouldn't assume that you're going to escape attention, especially given the *kind of people you work with*. And the Feds may not be picky about scapegoats for whatever crimes they find."

"I'm the lab director. I review research papers," I said. He was referring to the last time we saw each other, when I was busted for breaking and entering a certain food processor back in 2015. A food processing facility that turned human fat into food for the hybrids. "If the industry takes a beating, our donors may close up the pocketbook some. My boss will figure something out. That's not my job."

"It's a lot worse than that, Elaine," he said, stressing my name. "You know what I'm talking about."

"No, I don't. They can come right in here and see that we're trying to find ways to fight obesity. Help the industry turn out healthier products."

He laughed humorlessly. "I remember when you were overly truthful. Times change, huh?"

"I still am. I'm doing everything to turn this epidemic around as soon as possible."

Lyle let out a long breath. "I was afraid this would be a waste of time. You're in deep, aren't you? God. They really got their hooks into you. Is it the money? The custody? How is Charlie doing?"

"Charlie is just fine. He's in high school now."

"Good, good. Look, I'm trying to help you here, Elaine. There's no such thing as corporate loyalty. You're an expendable pawn with a microscope. If things get too hot, you're fired or in jail. What will Charlie do then?"

I wanted to reply that by the time I was indicted of anything, much less convicted, Charlie would be out of high school. But it didn't seem like something I should even joke about. "I appreciate your concern, I really do, Lyle. But there are squads of accountants and attorneys that work for these companies that I'm sure have their books in shape. And if they don't, how does this implicate me?"

"That lab you work for," he said. "The Feds will be all over that place. All the shady roads of the conspiracy lead back to it. For a scientist, you're not half as smart as you think you are."

What the hell was he talking about? I had done a lot of heavy-lifting to separate my job at AgSol from the conspiracy work I did on the side for Stitcher. I tried to think of what else would draw Lyle's attention to this place. Dr. Meers walked by my office. Had Lyle found out about the hybrids, and that they were alien cannibal nerds?

"What were you thinking, selling out like that? They must have really got to you."

I bit my tongue before I told him off. "They didn't. I have my reasons and my integrity is intact, I can assure you. You don't know the whole story."

He laughed. "You can say that after everything you saw? Everything that I saw? That's rich. You have a nice big house in the suburbs, a nice perch in a lab. God. You're shilling for these guys. For killers. Remember the Fiesta victims? And their families?"

"Yes, of course I remember them, goddamnit. My feelings about that haven't changed. That's part of what I'm trying to prevent from happening again. Why do you think there hasn't been another scandal like Fiesta in five years?"

Lyle chuckled. "Oh, sure. That was all you. Not the FDA crashing the party on those guys. Jesus Christ, your ego has exploded, too. They throw money your way and you think you're worth it. You and Stitcher swaggering around a lot these days, huh?"

Oh, Stitcher. Lyle knew that Stitcher wasn't really alive, in the sense that he was missing things like a normal body temperature and a heartbeat. He was the one who had clued me into that uncomfortable fact. "What about Stitcher?"

"What about him? He's still walking around. Kind of amazing for a dead guy. So are a lot of his buddies. What happens when the FBI takes a closer look at him? The guy who fixes things, does the conspiracy's dirty work, the dark underbelly of the industry, getting hauled to jail. Or locked in some government lab to be dissected."

"Lyle, are you trying to blackmail me?" He was a volatile man and it would not be prudent to push him. Then again, if he ran to the FBI claiming that the food industry had been infiltrated by undead ghouls, odds are the feds would scratch him out as a credible informant.

"Maybe. We need to talk."

I sighed. "You think you know a lot but there's so much more you don't. Things look a lot different when you are fully informed."

"Stitcher is an angel then?"

I was losing my cool. "Have you ever talked to him? Do you even know him? I'm not hiding in the shadows; I'm trying to make things better. Believe it or not, so is Stitcher."

Lyle scoffed. "You're as far from the side of truth and justice as anyone can get. I hoped that you would listen to common sense. Your paycheck is blood money, and you know it. I don't know why I tried to help you again. You got a kid depending on you now, maybe that's why. I don't know what I was thinking."

"Just try to stop helping in general, you're doing more damage than good," I uttered through clenched teeth.

He hung up on me.

I tossed the phone on my desk just to get it away from me. Strange. Lyle was a crazed conspiracy theorist, but he was also very plugged in. Reality was his raw material and he kept tabs on everything. He really thought the FBI might be after the lab, after me. Was that belief coming from his crazed conspiracy side, or something he actually learned?

[5]

The candidate forum for the Oak Ridge School Board was held at the public library. I had promised Donald I would attend to provide moral support, no matter what trepidations I had about him running.

I was also beyond curious about how he would perform in a public forum. I sat next to his wife Amy and her twin hybrid teen boys and watched as people trickled in and filled in seats from the back to the front. A full house; this was the kind of district where people cared about the school board.

I recognized a lot of faces. We could have held a staff meeting, there was so many AgSol employees there.

The questions were asked by two local reporters followed by Q&A with the audience. When it started, I found myself gripping my handbag strap like it was a lifeline and I didn't know why.

After candidate introductions, in which Donald did fine, the candidates were asked how they would address the school system's funding shortfall.

Everyone else gave the usual answers, like finding efficiencies, cutting nonessentials, and so forth.

Not Donald though. "I would look for other revenue sources to fill the gap first," he said. "I would threaten to cut music, art, sports and special education, unless the community, or the state, restored the funding."

"And if that failed?" The reporter asked, eyes bugging out.

Donald smiled. "The bare essentials are math, science and reading, writing, and social studies. Everything else is a nice hobby to offer."

Oh, no.

Half the audience gasped while the other half clapped politely. Were the AgSol folks clapping regardless of what Donald said? I nearly giggled at the thought of a political action committee comprised of clueless extraterrestrial scientists.

The next question was about academic standards and maintaining the school district's stellar reputation. You can imagine the butt-kissing of the residents, the teachers and the school system that followed when the candidates answered.

Except for Donald. "We should consider this school system our contribution to solving the world's problems. How many of our children are prepared to tackle the world's worst problems? Some, but not all. That is why I'm running on a Calculus for All platform. I want not just every high school graduate to pass AP calculus and AP physics tests, I want everyone in the community to do so too."

More clapping from the scientists around the room. I found myself joining in. Maybe he knew what he was doing after all. Of course, this may only play in Oak Ridge, which was loaded to the gills with scientists who worked at Oak Ridge National Laboratory, ORNL.

One of the reporters asked, "What about those students who can't even master algebra?"

Donald smiled. "We don't ask what about students who can't master sentences? Why? Why are math and science held out like an exalted mystical cult that only few are worthy of entry? It's because we, parents, teachers, school board and the public, have made excuses."

My eyes nearly popped out of my skull. He actually looked and sounded like a polished political candidate right there.

"I have to disagree with him," said the former head of the teacher's union. She was the board chair and was running for reelection. "That opinion shows ignorance of the kind of diverse population that attend our schools. We have students with special needs, we have students who really struggle because of factors outside our control. We shouldn't penalize them because they can't become mathematicians."

Donald looked at the woman with a sly grin. "Did you take college-level physics or calculus?"

She didn't look at him. "The reporters are asking the questions. We have to follow the debate rules."

"The teacher contract should require that we only hire teachers who have a degree in their subject," Donald added.

"He's doing pretty good," his wife whispered enthusiastically.

I nodded and smiled. He sounded good, but I don't think he sounded popular.

The reporters didn't return to the question Donald asked and it was time for the audience Q&A. The first question came from an exceedingly well-groomed older man who asked, "Are you all Christians?"

Right down the line, every candidate said yes, except for our intrepid human-alien hybrid. "Good God no," he blurted.

The crowd laughed in shock.

"Oh Donald, you are so out of your element," I muttered to myself.

And then we were off to the silly races. "Do you believe evolution should be taught in science class?" a well-dressed woman asked next.

I recognized the questioner. It was Suzie from Genetics. Behind her in line was Bill from IT, and Sharon from the hybrid incubator lab. Why were Donald's coworkers lining up to ask him controversial questions? Did they realize how much damage they were doing?

Every candidate raised their hands and some in the audience booed.

I put my head in my hands. Next, Bill from IT asked, "If you had to choose between funding high school football or calculus classes, which would you fund?"

The first candidate, the ex-teacher, grinned at the softball question. "High school football brings our communities together. I will never do anything to reduce its funding."

The other candidates nodded vigorously.

"Are you okay, Dr. Cassano?" Amy Meers asked.

I guess I had been whimpering aloud. "Uh, I'm fine."

Donald looked down the line of candidates like they were aliens from outer space. Okay, bad analogy. He leaned toward the microphone. "Even if I could fund both, I would still eliminate football." When the gasps and boos

25

rained down, he held up a hand. "Calculus will bring us jobs. It prepares our children for the future. Football causes brain damage."

"He's not going to win," I whispered to his wife, "but it will be fun to watch him campaign."

She was shocked. "You don't think he can win?"

"No, not in a hundred years. People don't vote for intellectual principles, they vote for people they like, or are similar to them. That's why the rest of the candidates sound so much alike."

She nodded, but it was clear she didn't understand.

"Does Donald expect to win?"

She smiled. "He's certain of it. He's spent all of his free time campaigning." As if that guaranteed victory.

Well, crap. I felt bad for him, because neither of the Meers could read body language and facial expressions very well. He would get a rough introduction to local politics when he got his clock cleaned on election night.

The public asked questions about school boundaries, taxes, teacher pensions, witchcraft in library books and my all-time favorite, sex education. Every candidate but Donald gave carefully hedged answers, or pandered to some constituency. Donald's answers were short, well-prepared, and highly unpopular.

Then a heavy-set white man in his sixties hobbled to the microphone. He pointed at Donald. "I want to see your birth certificate. I want proof of citizenship."

"Candidates for school board are not required to provide one," Donald answered. "We had to prove residency to the Board of Elections to get on the ballot."

"The state says you damn well better have it," the man yelled.

I wanted to slide under my chair. Donald was mainly Asian in appearance. He had an accent that was vaguely from his childhood in Massachusetts. This good old boy probably thought Donald was an illegal immigrant, or worse, an Asian Kennedy.

One of the other candidates, a former home economics teacher, read off of her phone. "According to the state Board of Elections website, the state law passed last year applies only to candidates running for state and federal office." She put her phone away. "But I would be happy to show you my birth certificate, as long as you let me cover up the year."

Half the crowd guffawed, relieved that someone had broken the tension. The older white man sat down and crossed his beefy, hairy forearms.

Amy Meers and I didn't laugh, and neither did any hybrids in the audience. You see, the hybrids did have birth certificates. But they weren't entirely authentic.

Donald was *decanted* in Tennessee, but was 'born' and raised in Massachusetts. The Massachusetts birth certificate had to be a fake, although people around here wouldn't know the difference.

Still my heart pounded away. This was the kind of exposure I feared, and for what? He was going to lose this race badly.

The questions tapered off and the candidates made closing statements. Donald bounded down off the stage and hugged Amy, hugged his sons, and shook my hand.

I leaned in close to whisper, "Are you sure you want to stay in the race after this?"

"Why, you don't think I did well?"

"You did awful, but you're learning. No, I meant the birth certificate problem."

"Oh," he said, frowning at my criticism. Then his eyes went wide. "Ohhhh. *That* problem."

But at that point reporters approached to get a quote from him and I shut the hell up.

[6]

It's not every day that someone comes to my office literally wringing their hands. But today, Dr. Jeff Ewell was standing there sweating, rubbing his hands raw.

"Tia has been arrested. She just called me," he said.

Jeff was a geneticist and fully human. Tia Montoya was a hybrid biology intern with us, daughter of a pair of hybrids who lived in Newton, Massachusetts. She was a junior at Harvard, majoring in biology. Jeff was her boss and human watcher, to help hybrids like her navigate human society.

"Relax, Jeff, sit down. We'll figure this out. Why was she arrested?"

"Drunk driving. She was pulled over."

I scowled. "Wouldn't be the first time that happened to a college student."

Jeff shook his head. "Her family are devout Mormons."

The hybrids joining religions had never occurred to me. They were super-scientists, right, what did they need a human God for? Maybe their human side had the same need for meaning that the rest of us shared, whether we admitted it or not. There were times I thought I was the only believer-scientist.

"Really? Why Mormonism?" I asked.

Jeff shrugged his shoulders. He was a proud atheist and religious belief confused him more than anything. "I think it may be the thing about living on other planets."

"Huh. I get it. Where is Tia now?"

"Tennessee state police barracks. She gave me the number." Jeff fumbled in his pocket and handed me a slip of paper.

"You're going to be a wreck until this is sorted out, aren't you?" I said.

Jeff nodded. "She's just a kid. She probably doesn't really understand what's happening. You know how it is."

Yes, I did. Young adult hybrids were usually like clueless babies in the adult world. They spent so much time on academics, they were aliens, if you will, to the culture and society they were trying to save. Unless they had human parents, in which case they may know their way around a birthday cake and maybe a TV or a soccer ball.

I grabbed my handbag. "Come with me then. And let's take some lab coats. It'll make us look more official."

I drove my minivan to the state police barracks. Jeff rode shotgun like a nervous groom heading to the church. We put the white lab coats on and went inside.

The arresting trooper came to talk to us. She was a burly white woman with black hair in a tight bun. We introduced ourselves and explained that we were Tia's supervisors.

"Lab coats? For real?" The trooper asked in a thick local drawl.

"You're not impressed?" I asked with a smile. I was hoping to build some goodwill.

"No, ma'am. Interstate 40 has science labs all up and down it. I have one speeder from ORNL who I catch twice a month for speeding excessively. Even when he has on a lab coat." She shook her head and folded her arms.

"This is a strange case. Ms. Montoya drove by me and the look on her face just seemed wrong. So I turned around and followed her down the road a piece. She had a taillight out, so I pulled her over.

"After talking to her for about thirty seconds I could tell she was either drunk or strung out. She passed the sobriety test, but something was not right about her. Stoned, probably. Anyway, she's probably an illegal."

"An illegal? Immigrant?" Jeff asked. "She was born in Massachusetts. Her parents are citizens. She's on a scholarship to Harvard."

The trooper gave him a sidelong glance. "That may be, but we have to check it out. This could be a case of stolen identity. The license may be a fake, and even if it is real, she may have obtained it illegally. We're going to check everything out. Run her prints and DNA."

"And in the meantime keep her in jail," I added.

The trooper nodded. "She's not acting like she should be behind the wheel. I can charge her with public intoxication and driving under the influence, but until toxicology gets back it won't stick."

"She's not under the influence," I said. "Tia is a little different."

The trooper raised an eyebrow. "What do you mean? Intellectually disabled? Down's Syndrome?"

Jeff glanced at me in alarm. Yeah, we were screwed if her DNA was analyzed. They would not only not find a match anywhere, but they would realize the DNA wasn't completely human. We needed to get Tia out of there.

"No, more like borderline autistic," Jeff said. "She's not very expressive at times, especially when intimidated. If you let us talk to her, you'll see she's more normal than you saw."

The trooper frowned.

I tried another direction. "Let me see if I have this right. You arrested her because she had a broken taillight. She's not drunk and has a valid license. You're holding her for what?"

"Ma'am I want to see some valid ID for her besides that driver's license. A birth certificate, passport, naturalization papers. We have the power to detain illegal immigrants in the state."

"How many illegal immigrants do you think are scientists?" Jeff asked.

The trooper shuffled her stance. "You'd be surprised. A lot of them let the visa expire, or are waiting on a new one because the feds messed up the paperwork. They think that since they have a job that they don't need to bother with immigration." She shook her head.

I bit my tongue. Forget abortion, this was the front line of the culture wars in the US. Scared white folks in power trying to keep the browner folks from coming in and changing their communities. That was what led to Tennessee passing laws like their deportation-assistance initiative.

And the cops really didn't care if the illegals were migrant farmers, white collar IT workers, or lab scientists. Maybe deporting a scientist was a bonus: they probably thought that would free up a high-paying job for a white, red-blooded citizen who had struggled with trigonometry.

30

"I'd like to work this out amicably, without calling the lab's attorneys," I said. Because Stitcher would ruin this trooper's month if I called him.

The trooper chewed on this for a few seconds. "You want to lawyer up over this?"

"Unlawful detainment, illegal search and seizure sound like pretty good reasons to me," Jeff said.

I put a hand on his arm. "Have you processed her into the system?"

"Not yet," the trooper replied. "I was going to enter the arrest into the system and send off the cheek swab and blood sample when you all came in."

"You have no proof that she's an illegal other than she is Hispanic. All this will do is give her an arrest record over nothing. Which could complicate her getting a security clearance some day and hurt her employability. Because of a broken taillight."

"I want to get that toxicology report," the trooper said, but she was wavering.

"If I thought she was on drugs I wouldn't be here," Jeff pointed out.

"How long will a toxicology report take?" I asked.

The trooper shrugged. "Should be done by tonight. But sometimes the lab gets backed up."

So Tia could be sitting in jail for days. I had heard about minorities being left in jail cells while the system slow-walked their release. I nodded. "I'll let you choose, trooper, you can give her a ticket for the taillight and let her leave now," I suggested gently, "or I call my lawyers."

"I'm just following procedure, ma'am, there's nothing I can do."

Crap. I nodded and stepped away to call Stitcher. The trooper went in the back to process Tia into the system and Jeff returned to wringing his hands. When Stitcher answered I explained the situation.

"Fuckity fuck," he replied. "I'm glad you called. I'll call them on another line and patch you in. Hang on."

Stitcher put me on hold until he got the barracks commander, the trooper's supervisor, on the line. The supervisor called the trooper into his office and put them both on speakerphone.

I muted my phone and smiled at Jeff. "Hang in there, our lawyer is talking to them now."

Stitcher listened to the trooper recite her side of the story.

Then he said, "Here's the problem. In the lovely state of Tennessee, the DMV makes a note of citizenship status on the license. This scientist has a citizen license, and I know you have already verified that it is legit. Right?"

There was a long pause. "Yes, her license checks out."

"So you have a broken taillight, a Hispanic citizen who passed the sobriety test but you think is high because she acted strange. She wasn't driving in a dangerous manner, she just looked odd, is that right?"

"That's correct sir. And that is why I arrested her and we took a blood sample."

Stitcher replied, "She's a scientist, and believe me, they are the strangest damn people you'll ever meet. You have the blood sample, so why are you detaining her?"

"We are going to release her shortly," said the barracks commander. "But if she tests positive for drugs, she will be charged with DUI, is that clear, Councilor?"

"Crystal. Please release her to Dr. Cassano immediately."

The supervisor agreed and the call ended, but Stitcher kept me on the line. "Are we good?"

"Should we worry about that blood sample?" I asked.

"I know what you're thinking. They only test for foreign substances at a certain level. They won't examine her DNA or any of that shit."

Relief poured down from my head to my toes. "Okay, good. I wasn't sure." I smiled at Jeff so he would avoid having a stroke.

Stitcher wasn't done with me. "You were totally fucking unprepared for this, weren't you?"

"I didn't think I'd have to bail my staff out of jail, no," I retorted. "Or that they would be racially profiled."

"Yeah, well guess what, you have a bunch of quasi-autistic extraterres-trials living in ass-fucking Appalachia. Shit's going to happen, Elaine. There's going to be crazier shit than this and you have to be ready for it."

"You bet, I'll just pencil in some planning time while I'm sleeping."

He didn't laugh. "These mother-fucking cops caved pretty quick, so I think you're right about the racial profiling. Which is to say that we got fucking lucky today. Five years ago they'd have figured out a way to throw you and Jeff in the fucking cooler too, just for asking questions."

32

"If I thought that was a possibility I wouldn't have come in here," I said. I just wasn't in the mood for his bombast this morning.

"Yeah, I could tell you stories. But I don't have time. I have to hop, so tell me if everything there is under control."

I could see Tia coming out from the back. She was in her late twenties, my height, and had thick dark hair and small dark eyes.

Jeff ran over to her and she smiled weakly at him, but she had tears running down her face. I hadn't ever seen a hybrid cry before. She must be scared senseless. But scared I could deal with.

"We'll be fine," I said to Stitcher. "I'm sure the drug test will be negative."

"Good. It'd be a real fucking hoot if it wasn't. Make sure you have that arrest cleared off her record. She doesn't want goddamn baggage like that fucking up her life."

"Okay boss."

"And we are going to have a chat about this shit sometime. You can't be unprepared like this," Stitcher said, and hung up before I could respond. I hadn't been scolded like this since I told Ma I was pregnant with Charlie.

I insisted on driving Tia home myself, to make sure she was okay. Jeff drove Tia's car behind us. After Tia snapped her seatbelt, I said, "I want you to know that you're not in any trouble, provided the drug test is negative."

"Thank you, that's a relief."

"Why don't you take the rest of the day off, I'll drive you home."

She grew concerned. "No, you don't have to do that. All I want to do is get to work this morning."

"Are you sure? Because Jeff is so shook up I'm not sure he's going to get anything done today," I laughed.

She shook her head. "Really. I'm fine. Work will be soothing. It will take my mind off of this."

I was worried that she may not want to face her coworkers after something like this. But then again, why not? She didn't do anything wrong. Someone's reaction in this type of situation came down to how he or she copes with emergencies like this, and I didn't know Tia all that well.

"If you change your mind, you can leave early," I said.

She waved off the notion. "Please, we have a paper to present next month on how exogenous circumstances can alter the rate of gene mutation and expression. It builds off work about how the environment may be affecting

33

the prevalence of breast cancer-related genes. We have a very tight schedule."

"You are one driven intern, I'll grant you that."

She gave me one of those almost-genuine smiles I had come to expect from hybrids. I kept her chatting about her work all the way back to the lab. I made a note to myself to not expect any more favors from the state police and to ask Stitcher just what the hell he meant by preparing.

[7]

When Stitcher recruited me to be AgSol's Chief Scientist and director of the Knoxville lab, he insisted I would never have to fundraise. Since we were an industry-funded lab, I didn't think that much about why I was exempt from a chore that consumed the time and energy of every scientist in academia and the non-profit world. It was just another perk of sucking on the corporate teat.

Betty Furman, the lab's CEO and my boss, was the one who had to schlep to Memphis to talk to the lab's board of directors. It was usually to present the lab's annual report, and I never heard much about what happened at the other meetings. I assumed the board did its due diligence and didn't think much of the board members. In retrospect, I should have realized that this situation wouldn't last forever.

Today, as a fog rolled across AgSol's tiny campus, I sat in Betty's spacious office knee-deep in prepping her to brief the lab's new board of directors. The office looked like a law library at a prestigious law school. Almost every surface was covered in intricately-carved mahogany, peppered with green-shaded lights on the tables. Every time I stepped inside it I felt like I had fallen into a time warp to the 1920s.

Betty's husband had been a corporate attorney. He was long dead now but the office was a testament to his legacy. I was pretty sure that the small white woman in her early 70s with the fierce brown eyes and carefully-constructed blond hair wasn't really using the law books that lined the shelves along the wall.

The briefing prep went poorly. There was too much material and Betty didn't have the scientific background to understand it. She lifted her reading glasses and rubbed her eyes. "This isn't what I need."

We had already gone a few rounds on what she needed, but she had been all over the map and back again. I sat back in the leather guest chair. "I'm sorry. I'm flying blind here. I don't even know who you're briefing."

She gave me a look. Since I joined AgSol she had refused to talk about who the directors were and what they wanted. I had long given up on trying to learn anything about them and settled for the occasional passive-aggressive remark.

She never volunteered who the directors were. But I like to scope out the audience I'm presenting to, especially in high-stakes meetings, so I can tailor the presentation to them. It's an old habit I got into when I did public relations at the USDA's obesity truth squad.

"Don't get me wrong, Elaine, this is exactly what I asked for, but it's not what I need." Betty pushed her tablet away. "I think the only way this will work is if you make the presentation." She said it like she was telling me my best friend had died.

I shifted around in the red leather guest chair. "Me?"

"The new board members want to hear technical details. I don't have the expertise you have. You're Chief Scientist, Elaine, don't look so crestfallen. I'm sure you'll do great."

I dropped my shoulders. I'm not the type to hobnob with corporate executives. I didn't speak their language. I didn't play golf or swig scotch or chase secretaries. I imagine they did those things based on what I saw on TV. In college, I was the snarky nerd living in the library while they did jello shots in hot tubs.

She smiled at my dismay. "Okay, it could be rough. They expect us to achieve return on investment metrics, like a business. They call their companies' donations 'investments.'"

"We have to defend our projects and how they'll pay off," I said. "Okay. Does everyone on the Board know about Project Rogers, the hybrids, and our upcoming environmental collapse?"

Betty nodded. "They are fully aware. But they have told me every time I bring it up that we have to find the right balance between competing goals."

I shook my head. "Bullshit. They don't care about our mission."

"I wouldn't go that far, but clearly the environmental situations doesn't make them sweat," Betty replied.

I nodded and gathered up my slides. I had been in sticky situations like this before with bosses who didn't want me, or my function, to stick around for arbitrary reasons. I never thought the same would happen to me in the private sector. I guess any two people could have different 'artistic visions' of the same function or project. Maybe it was just human nature.

Betty and I flew out to Memphis on a rainy fall morning, the kind that sticks wet leaves to everything. After I saw Charlie off to school, we took a short flight that landed at the Memphis airport's charter terminal. A chauffeur service drove us downtown to a massive five-story bank building. A security guard ushered Betty and I into a side door and a pair of guards rode with us up to the top floor. A plush hallway basked in daylight pouring in through huge windows on opposite ends of the building.

The security guard escorting us opened a pair of massive wooden doors to a huge, windowless conference room. The only light came from a single, bright spotlight aimed at our end of the long, narrow table that ran the length of the room. Everything else in the room, from chairs to bookshelves, was shrouded in silhouettes, shadows, and total darkness.

We sat in the bright light, which blinded me to everything in the shadows. As I set up the presentation, I heard the muted scuffling of people sitting down in chairs on the far end of the table. All I could see of the board members were silhouettes of hands in the dim light reflected off the polished tabletop.

"Good morning," Betty said. Paper scuffled on the far end of the table. We had sent our slides ahead of time: there wasn't any projection. That didn't bother me; I had done plenty of presentations from a seat at the table. It definitely took away a chunk of my speaking power though.

"Good to see you again, Betty," said an elderly woman with a quaver to her voice. "We're here today to assess the lab's work. We are so glad that you and Dr. Cassano could join us. Dr. Cassano, welcome, we're excited to hear from you today."

I smiled broadly, feeling like a performer working in front of stage lights. Or the gestapo's latest interrogation suspect.

Betty summarized the history of Project Rogers, which you have heard before, and recounted the lab's early days birthing hybrids and how the lab had grown and evolved over the decades. She reminded them of the growing urgency of stopping the environmental apocalypse and then turned to me.

I described all of the lab's major projects, how closely each was tied to our strategic plan, and the expected benefits from each. If you think I'm going to detail what was in my slide deck, you overestimate by desire to bore you to tears. I described the current portfolio of projects, that covered biology, environmental science, computational models, adipose replication, and of course, food science and human nutrition.

When we finished, the board members continued to scritch away on paper, making notes like gymnastics judges rating our performance. I braced for difficult questions to rain down on my head.

"Does anyone have any questions for Dr. Cassano?" asked the elderly woman.

A gruff voice on my left spoke up. "How much would it cost to shut down all of the lab's projects?"

"What do you need to know that for?" Betty asked sharply.

"We are exploring ways to increase the industries' liquidity," the man said.

"And I want to know," said a voice I recognized as Stitcher's, "how much more progress you could make if the lab's funding were doubled or tripled."

The gruffer voice retorted, "We're just gathering information, nothing has been decided yet."

How comforting.

He continued, "Could you identify which research projects are primarily focused on developing new food products?"

Betty and I looked at each other. Was it possible that he hadn't heard anything we said? "None," I replied. "That's not the purpose of our research or the lab's mission."

He nodded in that slow way people do when they don't understand but don't want to admit it. "I see. I would like to see what you thought about shifting to that kind of work."

"Your companies have their own product development R&D," I said. "Duplicating that isn't a wise investment."

"Maybe. On the surface, maybe. But your labs could do the basic science that our R&D labs could build off of. It would be complementary and coordinated. Not duplicative."

Betty was a rigid rod of flesh and bone next to me. "Why?" she asked without moving a single muscle.

A mellow-voiced man near Stitcher replied. "The C-suites want to increase the industry's ROI from our investments in the lab. Profit margins are tight and times are tough."

Gruff Voice added, "The blue-sky, sandbox science you have done is viewed by some of our executives as a luxury that we can't afford any more."

Blue-sky? Sandbox? We weren't sitting around working on teleporters, alchemy, and immortality potions. "Well," I said, "could you give us some examples of what you're interested in?"

Gruff Voice shuffled his notes. "Your labs helped develop this Fiesta additive that caused short-term changes in brain chemistry. Unfortunately, it caused anger. We think that, if properly developed, such a capability could be very profitable for us."

"By making food more addictive?" I snapped back.

"No need to get defensive, Dr. Cassano. We want to explore the effects of these psychotropic additives and how they could enhance our products. Imagine broccoli that tasted like broccoli and cheese, but without the unhealthy cheese. Or lettuce that had salad dressing flavors grown into it."

"Your companies already have labs that do that work," Betty replied with an icy smile, "We wouldn't want to compete with them on product development. Our mission is to research human and environmental health related to the food industry. As set out by the Project Rogers team decades ago."

"Times change," Gruff Voice stated. "The industry's leaders want us to reevaluate those goals."

Betty fell silent, but I was having none of this bullshit. "Even in light of what the Club of Rome has been warning us about for decades? Resource depletion and environmental damage doesn't concern you? How about your family's health? Or your company's ability to find food to package and sell?"

"There's no need to be overly dramatic," said a younger man's voice on my right. "We are deeply concerned about the environment and people's health. But our job here is improve the lab's profitability. Getting better value for our investment in your lab will make better progress, not less."

It was about the billionth time some asshole had told me to calm myself and stop worrying my pretty little head. "Creating a better-tasting bacon cheeseburger won't slow global warming, or reduce the acidity of the ocean, or flush toxins out of our water and air."

Betty touched my elbow. I shook off her hand.

"I'm a scientist, not a diplomat. I was hired to tell the truth and to tackle the hard challenges this lab has been dedicated to solving since before I was born."

No one moved a muscle, not even the living, breathing people.

The old woman with the quavering voice said, "I think you have made your feelings abundantly clear, Dr. Cassano, and I appreciate your candor. Betty, I would like you to bring Dr. Cassano with you to the next couple of Board meetings."

Gruff Voice muttered, "I hardly see how *that* will be productive."

"We'll discuss it, I'm sure," Stitcher said. He sounded further back, like he was sitting against the far wall. I assumed he would have a seat at the table.

"Thank you for coming and speaking with us," quavering old lady said.

Betty and I gathered up our notes. No one else moved or said a word, and for a moment it felt like we were the only ones in the room.

As we walked to the door in the gloom, someone came up on my left. "Here, let me get the door for you." It was one of the friendlier male voices from among the board members.

Whoever he was, he pulled the big wooden door open, letting the daylight in. He was a good head taller than me, with gray eyes and a fashion catalog, WASP look. He had to be in his fifties. And he was hot. "Hi Betty. I'm awfully sorry about that." He turned to me. "Dr. Cassano, my name is Alex Robie. I'm one of the directors." He shook my hand.

"Uh, good to meet you." I exchanged a look with Betty. She looked twenty years older in the hallway's light. Apparently me meeting the board members face to face wasn't on the agenda.

"Excuse me." Betty said in a strangled voice. She turned and hurried in quick, stilted steps to the women's washroom. If I didn't know better, she was going to hurl.

Alex closed the heavy, soundproof door behind us.

"I'm sorry things went so rough in there. We're under a lot of pressure and well, we're not all nice guys."

I was supposed to sympathize with him, but I couldn't. Corporate executive problems, right?

"Mr. Robie, I appreciate you making sure we're okay. This is all quite a shock. And completely unnecessary. I should go check on Betty."

He smiled grimly and nodded. "Yes, right. I'm sorry. Call me Alex. John Stitcher said I should introduce myself. I was hoping that we could talk more about how to save the lab. Uh, maybe over dinner?"

He was bashful to the point that I expected him to shuffle his feet. I couldn't think of a single business reason he would want to talk to me. And he was cute. Could I say no? Should I say no, for professional reasons? Eh, fuck that, I probably just signed my own termination. "Sure."

We exchanged emails and cell phone numbers and then we looked at one another awkwardly.

"Um, you probably should check on Betty?"

I nodded. "Yes. I better." And I turned and click-clacked my heels down the hall without looking back.

[8]

Betty and I returned to our normal schedule in the following days, but both of us were thoroughly rattled. Like we had been given six months to live. I wanted to fight, to blow the whistle, but it was all I could do to carry on like everything was normal. Stitcher wouldn't return my calls and every time I used the internet I browsed for a new job. On top of that, right before I was going to head home a storm began lashing my office windows with sheets of rain. Thunder cracked in the distance and began to plod closer.

I thought my prayers were answered when Stitcher called me back. He could make sense of this topsy-turvy turn of events, or at least explain it. I grabbed at my cell phone like it was food and I was a starving woman.

"We have a new fucking problem," Stitcher said by way of greeting. He sounded like he was driving somewhere. "The cock-sucking FBI."

I racked my brain for some way that AgSol could have violated federal law. I came up empty, but I didn't know what Stitcher had been up to. Maybe the Fiesta chip investigation, and how the additive made its way onto the market, had somehow led back to us?

"Some dildo told them about our, uh, cheese stick factory in DC that you visited that one time. They have a special agent sniffing around our asshole now."

I closed my eyes. "It wasn't me, I didn't talk to the FBI." That part of the obesity conspiracy was outside my area, other than special errands I did at Stitcher's request. AgSol didn't have anything to do with the production of adipose-based food for the hybrids. But half our staff was hybrids who needed those cheese sticks to stay alive. And we were hip-deep in researching synthetic adipose.

"Of course not. I'm not accusing you, I'm telling you how it happened, if you'd listen. Some sharp-eyed cop in Salt Lake noticed one of our suppliers dumping their shit into a storm drain on a security camera. The story broke before I could contain it. Fucking Mormons don't like me much."

"I can't think of a single reason that could be," I replied dryly.

"Haha. So now the medical waste company is licking the balls of every federal and state badge that shows up. They decided to come clean on everything, including that they sell medical waste to certain customers."

I gasped. "Why would they do that?"

"Because it's profitable and the regional sales manager is proud of it. They thought the state health inspectors would look the other way, like they usually do on industrial waste in the Republican heartland, the dumb shits. But there's an adult in charge somewhere up the chain of command, so this factoid goes over like a mother-fucking Roman candle up the state government's ass. They called in the EPA, FDA, FBI, who of course are super curious about what shithead buys medical waste, and what they do with it. The FBI raided our Rocky Mountain adipose factory and shut it down. The FDA and the local health department are in there nosing around now."

"Oh God," I said. We have such a large population of hybrids that a drop in cheese stick production would make a sizable cut in their food supply. I doubted we had stockpiles of adipose-based food to ride out a drop in production.

Stitcher continued, "Luckily, the plant manager dumped all the fucking evidence before the raid. I'm trying to pass off the appearance of buying medical waste as a database fuck-up, messed-up paperwork. We ordered hairnets and latex gloves and some middle-aged ditty transposed the product codes. It's a thin line of bullshit though, and it may not hold. What would you do?"

I laughed. "You're asking me? Jesus, I don't know. Comply with the investigation; get it over as fast as possible. Limit the damage. Whatever it is that you normally do in these situations. A cover-up is worse than the crime, they say."

Stitcher laughed. "That's the thing of it, there is no normal. Every fuck-up is different. And I could write an entire book about how they're different, believe you me. So, there's no handy checklist based on past experience.

"First thing, there is no such thing as a fucking cover-up. When the cover-up is deemed worse than the crime it's because the response strategy failed fucking spectacularly. One man's cover-up is another's load-swallowing mea culpa; it's in the eye of the beholder.

"Second thing, every crisis is a fucking opportunity. You have to wine and dine that damn opportunity for it to suck your tits, otherwise it'll bite your ass. The response strategy needs to be well thought out. Most fucks faced with a scandal, or a crime, or a crisis, lose their shit and start painting themselves into a fucking corner with a goddamn spray can.

"You've got to fucking plan on brain outages. Practice for them. Have contingency plans and practice them. That way you just choose the contingency plan and goddamn execute. I'm not making this shit up as I go. There's no rabbits in a hat bullshit here, just hard work and planning."

"I thought you just charmed people," I retorted.

"Ha fucking ha. I use anti-charm and back it up. When I say that I'm going to squeeze someone's balls with a rusty garlic press, they know I can do worse. Again, that's due to preparation and strategy."

"Why are you telling me all of this?" Was he setting me up as an accomplice? If it only had turned out to have been so simple as that.

"Because you're herding the worst collection of bumblefuck geniuses in the entire history of our conspiracy. You worry me because you have kept a tight lid on those meteor-babies so far. At some point they are going to dogfuck a situation so bad it will catch you with your panties around your ankles. And then you'll be like all the other assholes who splatter the shit instead of cleaning it up. You need to have more tricks stored in your cootch."

"Watch it, John."

"Consider this more on-the-job training, Elaine."

"I'm always impressed and awed that you are so open over a cellphone," I said. I never saw him sweep a place for bugs or worry about wiretaps. And this was in an age where the authorities treated things like probable cause and warrants as archaic remnants of Victorian times.

"Let's just say that I know no one's listening. If you don't mention the t-word or anything associated with it, you don't have to worry about it. You think those Wall Street ass clowns set up the housing bubble and the Great Recession all with fucking Post-It notes? Hardly. Or all those amateur hour, dick-in-hand corporate scandals like MCI or Volkswagen? Email, phone, none of that stuff is monitored like you think. They got AI fucking software filters combing through that shit. You want to sodomize a bunch of poor people with a balloon mortgage payment - NSA software doesn't give two drippy turds."

"Okay, okay, I get the picture," I said. This was not how I wanted to spend my lunch hour.

"So back to this fucking jack-knifing of medical waste on the highway of skull-fucking retardancy. What do you think we should do? This is a test. Here's your fucking hint - contingency plan."

"Um, you have an alternate supplier chosen who can keep the adipose flowing. Maybe a backup processing facility. And I guess there would be a plan to handle the investigation if it spreads to the other processing facilities."

"Not too shitty, Dr. Cassano, for an ignorant rookie. First of all, you make the other cheese stick factories button up their shit. Make sure they have enough fucking latex glove pallets on hand to match the barrels of fat swill rolling in. And what if the plant manager was such a douchebag he left the creamy barrels of adipose laying around and they're found?"

Well, then it sounds like we would be fucked. God, was I thinking like him now? "I don't know. You can't talk your way out of that. That would be a huge scandal."

"Goddamn right. You cut your losses. Throw the fucking plant manager under the bus. Tie him to the crooked supplier - say he was using the warehouse to store the waste on the side. Make it clear that his shit never got near the food. Have the groundwork already done so the shell company's 'internal investigation' goes to the cops with a lacy ribbon and a blowjob. See, no magic rabbits."

"What if they don't buy it?"

"You pull the isolated incident defense. Have the corporate PACs squeeze the White House's balls. Roll out the PR fucks and fire up the lobbyists to bitch to your politician friends about how this is ruining your business. How it'll cost jobs. At the same time, clean up the facilities, beg the health department to re-inspect and resume production."

"And what about the hybrids who need that food to survive?"

"Fucking rations and diets for them. That's what we had to do back in '92 when a factory burned down. Took six months to get production back to normal."

There must have been thousands of hybrids slowly starving back then. Producing human adipose-based food form them was so sensitive, so risky, and yet the consequences of failure were so much greater than a 100,000 dead alien-human hybrids.

Stitcher chuckled. "Luckily, I had the plant manager properly prepped. He was rebuilding before the ruins stopped smoking. But we did have a lot fewer alien bird brains back then."

"Having contingency plans ahead of time is critical, huh?"

"You bet your sweet tits. Plans. Goddamn plural. Which brings me back to the FBI and the FDA. The FDA is nothing to worry about, on their bravest day they're cowering in their own piss puddle, thanks to our dick-swaggering Capitol Hill friends."

I replied, "Oh, I know all about the pressure your friends can exert on regulatory agencies."

"Used to be, used to be. But now the *federal bureau of irritation* is all over the food industry because some cheeseball shrimp industry bribed that snatch-warbling Louisiana congressman. Who doesn't mind some crude oil in their fucking scampi, right? They're sniffing around every Congress-hole for racketeering, bribery, and campaign finance fuckery. So of course, food-processing, distribution, agriculture, they're all getting a steak knife colonoscopy. You've got to keep your earlobe pressed to the ground so you don't get caught at back to school night fucking the PTA president in the mouth."

I rolled my eyes. "So what's the plan?"

"The PTA president? My brother had to procure a pricey divorce for not knowing that the Jehovah's Witnesses had rented the band room."

"No, I meant the feds," I said.

"You have to leave something for the badges to find easily, to misdirect

46

them. In this case, it's a fuck-up in the supplier's database info. You hand them one or two easy explanations. Right under the fucking streetlight. Nine times out of ten they'll never go searching in the dark and they'll leave you alone. They want to close the case fast and don't want to look dumb for ignoring the obvious."

"What if they don't go for a misdirection?"

Stitcher laughed. "Ignore a good lead? They are too fucking tight on resources to ignore it. This is why I always vote for those Republican assholes who pillage the budget. The feds have to grab at every juicy low-hanging fruit. You can run a freight train of shit past them because they don't have the resources to catch a tenth of it. Exhibit A is the war on drugs."

I shook my head. "You give them a good lead? I'm not sure I follow."

"You create a fake little conspiracy for them to chase. Lead them down a trail they suspected was there all along, but don't give them enough to prosecute. It's a game of attrition. You just need to pick the right farce: corporate scandal, illegal aliens, gangsters, drug-running, bribery, insider trading, you name it."

"And how do you do that?"

"Fucking easier than you will ever believe. False informants, fake records, misdirection, planted confidential informants, ever-deepening mysteries. How fucking hard is it to write a fake memo?"

"Don't they figure out that it's all a setup?"

"Rarely. Every FBI agent sees himself as Eliot Ness, Fox Mulder, or Clint Eastwood. But eventually, they have a pile of cold shit in their hand. Not enough to prosecute but they've spent too much time and money to walk away. Their boss pulls the plug and chews them out for wasting resources and having a low closure rate. It's a beautiful fucking game I've run about five times now."

"And the few times it doesn't work?" I felt like I had him cornered, for once.

"It's an opportunity, not a problem. Sometimes there's an annoying douchebag interfering with my plans. So if the fake stuff doesn't work, I throw the lawmen a real catch. I point the fake conspiracy at the douchebag and let the cops take him off the board for me."

"And your sacrificial lamb is actually guilty of something?"

Stitcher laughed. "Of course. I have files on all the corporate shit stains. Preparation. Contingency plans."

"Okay, hotshot," I said. "Why the hell are you telling me this? You need to misdirect the government so they leave the cheese stick factories alone and you can keep the hybrids fed."

"No, Elaine, not me. You."

"Me? I have a job already that's turning into a three-alarm fire. And I have a teenage son. Why can't you do this?"

"Tsk, tsk," Stitcher said. "I have to see to this problem with your lab's funders. I can't do that and handle the FBI at the same time. So you get the easier chore, boo hoo. It's the least you can do while I save your ass, right?"

I groaned. This would make a great prison yard story, if I was lucky enough to avoid solitary confinement or a permanent bunk in a mental hospital.

[9]

An FBI agent did indeed come sniffing around, as Stitcher put it. His name was Vernon Pierce and a New York City area code popped up when he called Betty. He wanted to eyeball our lab, he told her, a pro forma visit just to make sure we exist and did legitimate work. The government suspected that anything connected to the food industry was phony. He wouldn't be satisfied by checking out our website and talking over the phone.

Betty, Stitcher and I all agreed that we wanted to keep Agent Pierce at arm's length. So Betty told him to visit our West Coast office, where I would meet him. The West Coast was as far from his home turf, and Knoxville, as we could get domestically.

Our West Coast office was in Palo Alto, the heart of Silicon Valley, because it was easier to recruit genius, non-hybrid computer scientists. The food and agriculture industries had a quiet presence in the computing world going back decades. Early in the computing revolution a lot of computer models were created to increase crop yields as part of the Green Revolution.

These days, we scooped up computer scientists and mathematicians that flocked to the area. Plus, there were plenty of billionaire-funded do-gooder projects that laid the groundwork for us to recruit cutting-edge geeks who understood strict NDAs and wanted to save the world.

We were betting that Agent Pierce wouldn't be allowed to visit, since the government considered sending a fed to the Bay area almost as bad as paying for an ethics conference at Hooters. We expected the Bureau to send an agent from the local office and simply file a minimal report.

But it didn't work out that way. Agent Pierce got the okay for the trip and so I grabbed a flight out west to meet him.

It had been six months since my last visit to Palo Alto, and I was due to check in anyway. While the Palo Alto office had its own director, Ben Gavde, as Chief Scientist I had to visit a couple of times a year. The emerging field of scientific computing was making every field pay attention to neural networks, Big Data mining, and high-powered computational models. And as the conspiracy's person in AgSol, it was on me to handle any FBI interest in our lab.

Ben Gavde always sets me up in the conference room when I visit, and then tries to fill my tablet with more research papers, briefings, and lab reports than I could ever read. With a degree in systems biology, I was conversant in computational biology but it was still tough rowing for me.

Another cross-country flight, another day lost to domestic airline travel hell. It was a foggy afternoon in San Francisco when I caught a cab out to the lab. Like so many other businesses, our offices were in a nondescript building near where the 101 and San Antonio Road meet. Science labville, and it had the ridiculous rent to prove it.

Two hours later, Ben brought Agent Pierce to the conference room. I was deep into a benchmark report on modeling ocean acidity. It was so depressing I was eager to meet our federal threat instead.

Vernon Pierce could have been a black action star who moonlighted as a personal fitness trainer. Traps, biceps, lack of a gut, despite being well into his forties. He was bald and clean shaven with a quiet intensity to his face. His eyes swept the room and took everything in.

He shook my hand. "Dr. Cassano? Special Agent Vernon Pierce."

"Call me Elaine," I said with an eyelash bash.

He didn't smile. "Call me Agent Pierce." He took a seat. "You don't work at this office. Are you out here because of me?"

I shook my head, "I do site visits twice a year. We operate satellite locations around the world. As Chief Scientist, I keep tabs on all the projects, and provide guidance where necessary."

"So how are you fighting obesity out here in Silicon Valley?" He waved at some machine learning mumbo jumbo someone had left on the white board behind me.

"That's proprietary information, Agent Pierce." I softened my tone. "Computer modeling of metabolism, gene therapy, and food digestion, and sophisticated software development to support research applications. Nothing the FBI should be worried about."

He looked disappointed. "Why do I get the sense that if I push, you'll just call in your attorney?"

"Because you're perceptive. And because I don't know why you are interested in our lab. Some context would help me figure out how I can best help you."

He made a hand motion to indicate that my point was well taken. "The food industry kind of threw you under the bus. They told us that you guys are their do-gooders, trying to save overweight America from itself with health research. I've been sent here to see if this is like when the beer companies throw pennies at alcoholism research to make themselves look good, or if it is legit."

He didn't frown or smile, but had that same expressionless look Bob's lawyers did when they didn't like my answers during the custody depositions. They were hoping I would get nervous and fill the silence. Pierce seemed to be playing the same card.

I didn't break and he gave up and glanced around. "And yet here you are not being all that helpful. Which is really making it hard for me to believe that your lab is entirely above board."

"Out here we tap into Stanford and Berkeley and the private sector for hardcore math, computer science work on health and medical issues. Cancer protein research, calorie-burn estimates, biological modeling, that sort of thing." I pointed at the reports on the table between us. "Check them out."

Which was true, to a certain extent. We did most of our heavy duty modeling out here, but most of it was of climate change, environmental pollution, and population dynamics. The computational expertise living out here, plus the philanthropical groups hanging off of the dot-com billionaires, meant that we had a rich area to work with those interested in fixing the 'big' problems, like ocean acidification, sustainable farming, and clean energy.

Agent Pierce bought it wholesale. Without a science background or many specifics, this all sounded perfectly reasonable. Stitcher was right.

"Can you show me around?" he asked.

A tour could lead to more questions and him wanting to talk to the staff. But if I stopped him from doing that, he would get suspicious.

I smiled. "Sure. It's all people tapping at keyboards and server rooms. You'd get more out of tours with some of our collaborators and partners. NASA Ames, the universities, a couple of biotech startups or angel investors. They would make it clear to you why we need to tap the resources we have out here."

Only his mouth moved when he replied, "I came all this way to see this lab in operation, Dr. Cassano."

"Yes," I replied quickly, "and if you were to tell me what the Bureau's interest is, maybe I could figure out what to show you."

He looked away, debating how to respond. I expected to get threatened with a warrant, or an oblique mention of suspicion of criminal wrong-doing. Stitcher told me not to be too cooperative. Pierce looked back at me. "The food industry made certain statements to Congress about it's anti-obesity work. When Congress pressed, smelling possible perjury, they pointed us at your lab. So this is due diligence. To put our eyeballs on your work."

"Ah, then I could have solved this much easier for you. I can email you the work. We have published dozens of peer-reviewed studies."

"A bunch of scientific articles won't help me," he said. "Can you give me a list of your ongoing projects and the costs of each? It would help if I could verify that you are not simply doing product development rather than trying to combat obesity."

He was lying. He didn't care about due diligence. He was just fishing for information. I shook my head. "I'm sorry, you're asking for proprietary information. I can give you a written summary of the relevant work we do. But not internal budget documents."

He tilted his head as if a thought just occurred to him. "You used to be a fed. What caused you to leave the government?"

I smiled. The less I said, the better. "AgSol has more resources, better equipment."

"The industry doesn't breath down your neck if your research makes them look bad? Oh, wait, you wouldn't admit that to me, right? But I hear that you have a reputation for spewing the unvarnished truth."

I folded my arms. "When it comes to the obesity epidemic, the industry and I are on the same page. They let me set the lab's research agenda. There is much less interference than I faced from Congress or the White House when I was a fed."

He smiled, knowing what I was talking about. "So you really don't think you're a false front to provide cover for your corporate masters?"

I laughed. "The unvarnished truth is that I would quit in a second if this was a sham. We're doing legitimate scientific research here, and making good progress too."

"Pays better too?"

"Yes, and Knoxville is cheaper to live in than DC, so it feels like a bigger pay raise."

"Your critics say that your lab is just a boutique PR stunt to draw attention away from the industry profiting off of the obesity epidemic. What do you say about that?"

"I would say that was ironic, because we keep a low profile. The industry hasn't trotted us out as an example of their altruism, now have they? Plus, I have four times more researchers than the USDA human nutrition group."

He actually looked disappointed to hear that. I wonder what made him so skeptical about the lab. Was it just our corporate nature or did he know something else?

"Are you sure I can't get the two cent tour?" he asked.

I stared at him like I was considering it. Could I make an FBI special agent sweat? He met my gaze. Nah, probably not. Vernon Pierce probably had his sweat glands removed.

"Okay. But I'm doing this mainly to show how cooperative we are. I don't want to spook the staff by letting them know that you're FBI. So no questioning anyone, taking any pictures or anything like that."

He agreed and I led him out of the conference room. The lab was just another office building. Researchers sat in offices or cubes and there weren't any beakers or microscopes. I walked him through a cube farm infested with IT hipsters.

"Not much to see, other than the computing cluster," I explained.

He nodded and peeked at offices as we walked by. Typical San Fran geeks, they had bikes in the hall and a couple of them either stood at their desk or were walking on a treadmill as they worked.

The server room was in the far back. Inside, amidst the howl of high-powered air conditioning, were racks of the latest server tech along the right wall. Each one barfed cables and winked and blinked at us. The left side wall had four dozen of the latest video gaming consoles wired together, their outer shells missing.

"We use one cluster for internal modeling jobs." I pointed at the server rack filled with utilitarian black rectangles. And then I pointed to shiny boxes wired together with thin white cables, like a series of interconnected digital brains. "We use the homemade cluster of video game consoles as a super-computer on the cheap. We also buy cycles off various cloud computing companies, and participate in crowd-sourced charity operations where people donate processing power to us. An idea we got from the Air Force a few years back."

"What are you doing with all of this number-crunching?" Agent Pierce asked.

"Modeling. There's only so much we can do in a lab. We can narrow down promising possibilities faster this way and then go test the best options in the lab. We also run larger metabolic and systemic models to capture thousands of interactions with body chemistry. So we can avoid unintended consequences and get FDA clearance for obesity treatments and medicines faster." He made some notes.

I didn't mention the simulations of the environment, or modeling the effects of pollution on human physiology, or the projections of the effect of resource shortages on global food supply. Those projects were all proprietary business, after all.

He made some more notes.

"Is there anything else you wanted to see?" I asked over the sound of the server fans.

He smiled and shook his head. "I have enough to make a report. Can I follow up with questions I may have?"

"Absolutely." I handed him my card. I would wait until I returned home to make my own report to Stitcher about this chat.

I escorted him to the lobby and watched him walk to his car and drive away. I slumped against the receptionist desk. "I'm glad that's over," I said to the secretary, an Asian kid tapping away furiously at a terminal.

"Feds don't scare me," he said with a chuckle.

I looked at his screen, but none of the text on it made sense. It was all brackets and multi-colored text. "There's a lot of guys like you sitting in federal prison who thought the same thing." I gathered my things and left for the hotel in one of those driverless taxis. The West Coast was weird, even for someone who was used to dealing with ghouls, aliens, and scientists. My phone rang just as the taxi pulled away from the curb. It was Alex Robie.

"Elaine, hi. Your office said that you were in San Francisco until tomorrow. I'm landing there in two hours for a conference. Can you have dinner tonight?"

A giant smile broke out on my face. "Yes, I would love that."

[10]

I had a couple of hours to mull whether to have a relationship with Alex, my boss's boss. At this point, it could be written off as just dinner with a work acquaintance. Little more than networking, right? But in reality, I was thinking that it was a date.

I stopped at my hotel to freshen up. I turned the question over a few times in my head as I got ready. Alex and I had a professional association. His being on the Board could affect my relationship with them, but Betty was my boss, and she reported to the Board, including him. It could be uncomfortable for Betty if he and I became a thing. Office romances were always doomed. But, the Board was killing the lab anyway, so screw the rules, right?

I was wearing my business suit and didn't have anything fancier or more casual except the too-casual clothes I wore on the airplane. I let down my hair and redid my makeup. I aimed for something between professional and hot.

I took a streetcar ride to the small Italian restaurant off Columbus Ave in North Beach. I kept asking myself if this relationship, if there was a relationship, would be worth the trouble. But the answer came back the same and it made me want to giggle as I stepped off the streetcar.

The place smelled like my Italian grandmother's kitchen on Christmas Eve, only if she had cooked a lot of seafood. We sat at a table in the back. He had a microbrew and I had a rum and coke. I did my best to stop smiling and in general acting like a girl on her first date with the football captain. But that's how I felt.

"So you're not married and have no attachments?" I asked, hoping adult talk would wipe the fool grin off of my face.

He shrugged. "Being a CEO doesn't allow for any of that. I may have only one or two nights free a week. Can't swing a family or a relationship with that kind of time. Everyone I have seen try that arrangement has failed. Who wants that mess? What about you? Ever been married?"

"No, but I have a teenage son," I said, violating all kinds of first-date rules, I'm sure. "Being away from home even one night is hard. It was quite the effort to get custody of him and I don't want to spend another day away from him."

"Oh, once in a while is okay," he soothed. "I'm sure you're a great mom, letting him throw wild parties while you're away and being the cool kid in high school."

"Questioning my parenting decisions will get you nowhere, mister," I said with a grin.

He fired up the twinkle in those blue eyes of his. "I'm pretty happy right here, actually."

I think I blushed.

The food arrived and it was delicious. I had smoked potato gnocchi with prosciutto and grilled salmon with brussels sprouts. He had angel hair pasta and clams in a white wine sauce.

When we finished eating, he paid the bill with his corporate card and we walked out into a chilly evening. He took my hand loosely and hailed a cab. "Where to?"

I stepped in the cab that drove up. "I have an early morning flight. So let's go back to my hotel."

What the hell, don't judge me, I needed this. I may even deserve it. On the ride across town, we didn't speak much. He lightly rubbed the back of my hand and wrist with his fingers. The lights of the city flashed by like we were soaring down the steep streets in a plane. Did I mention I had a glass of wine or two with dinner?

I'm the type to toss the handbag on the floor as soon as I close the door, ready to get it on. Once I'm in the mood, I don't like playing footsie.

That's just what I did. Under the room's feeble entry light I threw my arms around him and licked his molars. He smelled like the ocean, salty and husky. He put his arms around me and I could feel his cock stiffen against my abdomen.

"Slow down, you minx." Alex pulled away. He was the type, apparently, who needed to get comfortable first.

I walked over to the bed and took off my shoes while making my best come-hither look.

He smiled, hung his suit jacket up in the closet and stepped into the bathroom.

I started unbuttoning my blouse but stopped on the second pearly white button. He should do it. Besides, him going into the bathroom took the steam out of the situation. Were we going to fold our clothes neatly?

I settled on standing with my hands on my hips, acting impatient when he came out. But he was completely nude and fully erect. He smiled sheepishly.

"Mr. Robie, oh, my, gosh, like there must totally be some kind of misunderstanding," I said in a dumb Valley Girl voice.

His face turned bright red and became uncertain until I laughed.

"Oh, damn you, you're toying with me," he said.

I giggled all the way over to him.

I ran my hand over his hairy chest. He leaned in to kiss me. Our tongues swirled and his hand grazed my cheek. I could feel things developing between my thighs.

We pulled apart. "Aren't you worried about your clothes?" he asked. Ah, so he was a clothes guy. Interesting.

I shook my head no. I guess I'm a jeans in the lab kinda chick.

We kissed again and he pulled my blouse up, massaging my side right above the hip. He knew what he was doing.

He deftly pulled off my blouse and then the skirt.

I pushed him down on the bed, slipped off my underwear and sat across his hips. The hair on his waist tickled me. His tip pressed against the top of my bare ass, which was anything but unpleasant.

I unhooked my bra and let my breasts fall free.

He cupped them and I pinched my knees tightly against his waist. I pushed his hands hard against my chest, mashing my breasts against my rib cage. A warm, wet, delicious feeling spread down from my nipples to between my legs.

His hands dropped to my thighs and his fingertips brushed my clit, but he didn't linger there. Good boy, don't go for the gold before you earn the bronze.

A short squeal came out of my mouth as his fingers slipped inside me. I ground my hips against him, closing my eyes and enjoying the ride.

His neatly parted hair had fallen against his forehead and that made him look even sexier. I bent over him, letting our nipples graze one another and kissed his parted lips and the stubble on his chin.

His fingers were rubbing my wetness and then they fell on my clit. He knew how to move slow and easy, and I could feel myself climbing a hill of pleasure. I didn't want to summit yet. I ran my hand across his hairy chest and backed away from him, kneeling between his legs with him throbbing in my hand. He got my best sultry smile and then I engulfed him.

He was hot in my mouth but his thighs were cool, tense and rigid. He let out a ragged breath and watched me with intense seriousness. Yeah, he'd be whacking off to this memory later on.

I was still hot, but it had started to ebb. I pulled him from my mouth, a hint of saltiness on my tongue. "Please fuck me."

He rolled me over on to my back on top of a pillow and towered above me, his hand massaging my clit. I closed my eyes for a while until the blood started to boil in my face, chest, and groin.

He slid into me easily. I hate having to help with that part. It's just something a guy should figure out on his own. Somewhere along the way he had put on a condom, thank God.

We began to move together, then apart, then together again. I pulled him into a long kiss as we fucked.

I wasn't sure what he was doing, but he was banging my g-spot. I clamped down hard on every part of him, with every muscle I could. I squeezed the life out of his torso, legs, and cock. That took him to the edge and he bucked wildly in my arms.

After our groans subsided, I found myself still holding him tight. I didn't have any particular desire to let him go. I loved his smell. Well, this part was unusual, nice, but unusual. Most guys I wanted to shove away immediately after I climaxed. All the old repulsions usually kicked in.

He snuggled into my embrace, and our bodies relaxed. Finally he pulled away.

"Huh," he said looking down at me and then himself. I was waiting for him to mumble an excuse and leave in under two minutes. He slid off the bed without a word and lurched toward the bathroom, working the condom off.

He came back and climbed into bed next to me. "This doesn't feel like a one-night stand, does it?"

I shook my head and we exchanged a long look. We kissed for a while. Yeah, yeah, I was feeling all that new-relationship, puppy-love, but neither of us were kids. Something had connected beyond just the physical.

"I don't even feel like leaving," he declared, like the idea surprised him.

"Good." I pulled him to me and we held each other until I dozed off with my arms for the first time in years.

[11]

After working closely with human-alien hybrids for over four years, I had figured out how to tell they were upset. They went more deadpan than normal, like they forgot to work the muscles of their face or they were having a stroke.

Donald Meers hurried into my office as soon as I got in from the airport. He was completely expressionless. He knocked on my door after he stepped in. He was wearing his lab coat and his hands were encased in blue latex gloves, the other one clutching his tablet.

"Elaine, I have an important finding. One of my side projects is working on *The Meteor*," he said. He closed the door but remained standing.

A lab funded by the agricultural and food industries to conduct top-secret research does not normally study meteors. But Donald didn't mean any meteor. He meant *The Meteor* - the one that dropped his species' DNA into a corporate farm field in the 1960s. Luckily it fell in the hands of the industry rather than the government. AgSol scientists had extracted the alien DNA and used it to birth ultra-smart human-alien hybrids, starting with Donald.

You could say that the existence of extraterrestrial biological material was the core secret of the conspiracy I was entrusted with protecting.

"What made you study the meteor itself?" I asked. Donald and the other hybrids had an odd kind of intuition that ranged from ingenious to completely misguided. They could advance knowledge by a full decade with a stray thought or have the poor judgment to create murderous food additives. I had to keep a constant watch, especially these days with the FBI sniffing around.

Donald shrugged. "I've always wanted to know more about where I came from. Was *The Meteor* an accident? If not, who sent it and why? Was it thrown off the Earth from some other epoch with different DNA? Are we from outside the solar system? These are age-old questions, yes?"

"Yes, the meaning of life," I responded.

Granted, Donald and the other hybrids had a more interesting mystery to unravel about their origins. At least Superman knew why his parents sent him to Earth. Donald didn't know if his DNA was sent here by accident or on purpose.

"Meaning of life, exactly," Donald said and smiled. "I hoped that we would learn where *The Meteor* came from."

He looked at the tablet like it was a teleprompter. "No one had analyzed the non-organic material that makes up the meteor itself. When they discovered the alien DNA, they focused on its biological possibilities. Created hybrids like me. But there's a lot more there. A lot more."

He held up his pad. "We've analyzed a number of samples. The crystalline structure is strange. The dislocations in some areas aren't naturally-occurring. It looks like a manufactured substance."

I didn't want to think about the implications of that right now. "How can you tell?"

"We borrowed time on a TEM and SEM at the university - they have the latest equipment. Oh, sorry, transmission electron microscope and scanning electron microscope."

"Donald, are you serious? How much do the university people know about this?"

He paused. "Oh, they think we're working on an industrial product under development, a ruined crystal growth. I told them it was one of those swallowable cameras. They were happy to take the money, do the work and move on, as the saying goes."

I nodded, but wasn't really satisfied with that answer. That was the kind of seeming-loose end that the FBI could find and tug on, unraveling all of our work. Maybe Stitcher's paranoia was contagious. Maybe I should be concocting contingency plans for the inevitable scandal.

"The university people analyzed the structure and found that there was a non-random repetition to the dislocations. They labelled it a manmade structure, part of the crystal.

"Plus they found trace amounts of multiple rare earth metals. Beryllium, gallium, gold, platinum, uranium. They shouldn't be there, and not all together in such low concentrations. I've secretly suspected that *The Meteor* is a landing craft. Now I have proof."

I shook my head. "A landing craft? You mean a vehicle built on purpose? Are you thinking that it ferried the DNA to Earth?"

He paused to consider that. "A deliberate vehicle, yes. I don't know if the builders were trying to send the DNA elsewhere. Or if they targeted Earth. It's possible, but the researchers who found it found the DNA by accident. It wasn't in a vial safely tucked into the center or anything obvious like that. I can't speculate that they meant for the DNA to be there or to be discovered."

"Did the meteor have any rocket on it, or any sign it was meant for space travel?"

Donald shook his head. "No, it appears to just be a rock from outer space. But the question I have been trying to figure out is the purpose of this crystal structure that runs all through it. The structure doesn't provide any additional feature or capability. It's just buried inside. But I finally figured it out: it's a coded message."

I tilted my head. "Donald, you sure you're not seeing patterns where there are none?" He may be part alien, but he was also part human, and his desire to have some meaning emerge from this burnt interstellar rock could color his perceptions.

He shook his head. "I've been studying language structures and decryption. The structure of the crystal's dislocations, and the distribution of the rare earth metals is non-random and repeats like a code."

He brought up a picture on his tablet. The structure of the crystal looked like a close-up shot of denim: parallel and perpendicular gray lines close together. There were dark blotches and lighter smears that looked like a pattern to me.

But I was expecting to see a pattern, wasn't I? And the human brain, trained for its entire existence to decipher nonrandom repeating signals, like predators moving through the brush, can always spot a pattern even when there is none.

"Have you deciphered it?" I asked. The real test, I didn't want to say, was when he found utter gibberish in the crystalline pattern. A nonrandom-seeming pattern may yield a few words, like bird poop on a stop sign could change the spelling, but only in a small number of instances. The rest would be useless.

"Only a little."

Uh huh. "You need to get an outside opinion on this," I said. "Just to make sure your desire to find something doesn't cloud your judgment."

Donald nodded. "I agree. I wanted to talk to some encryption experts. But, given the past incidents, I wanted to run that by you first."

"I'm glad you did. Is there any other hybrids you could reach out to?" Donald's fellow hybrids were scattered all over the world across high-tech, high-skilled industries. Each one was doing their part to make enough progress to stop the environmental apocalypse. They were all in the loop on their own genetic heritage and were eager to lend a hand on any research related to their origins, rearing, feeding, and care.

Donald thought about it. "Felicia Wittenberg has a top secret clearance and works as a NSA contractor. Degrees in mathematics and linguistics. She would be my first choice. Class of '83." Meaning, a human-alien hybrid born in 1983. Working for NSA meant she knew how to keep secrets, she knew about our lab, and she would be discreet.

I wagged a finger at him. "Okay, but don't tell her the context. Can you convert the structure into a facsimile that she can decode?"

He nodded.

"And I get first dibs on your report, right?"

Donald looked down at his pad. "Um."

I rapped my knuckles on the desk. "I don't want you sharing this with your kin before I see it first, okay? I don't want you guys getting carried away again."

Donald gave me his phony, overly big goofy-sized smile. "I understand, Elaine. Thank you."

If there really was an embedded message, what the hell were Donald's long-lost ancestors trying to tell us? I had no way to put myself in the heads of the aliens who launched or otherwise sent the meteor to our solar system. Hopefully it was how to grow food their people could eat that wasn't human fat tissue. But I would settle for the secret to stopping a global civilization from poisoning the physical world that sustained them.

[12]

There comes a time in a mother's life when it becomes crystal clear that she should stop washing her teenage son's laundry. That moment just happened to me. I was gathering up clothes to make a laundry run. With only two of us in the house, sometimes I had to scrounge enough for a full load. But now I'm standing in Charlie's room holding a semen-encrusted t-shirt.

I stared at the shirt in horror. I'm not disgusted by semen; the mention of it usually creates a flicker of arousal. I just was not expecting to come across any that had come from my little boy. Except he wasn't little any more. Time, it does fly by.

I looked around his room and realized that he was in a state of transition. When we moved into this house five years ago, he had all kinds of boy things - superhero bedsheets, Pokemon card decks, toys, the random bits of plastic that seem to accumulate near kids between ages three and twelve.

Now, layered on top of all that were role-playing game manuals, high school textbooks, a tablet, some manga, and Rachel Carson's *Silent Spring*. The Carson book made me happy; Charlie had taken an interest in environmental issues lately.

And there was a semen-spattered t-shirt. He had crossed a hormonal Rubicon. He wasn't really a boy any more, was he?

I wasn't comfortable with the thought of a sexually-awakened male in the house. Is this why mothers never really come to grips with their sons growing up? Fathers and daughters were different. A girl gets her period, hey, it's not her doing, and dealing with it is a hygiene thing most fathers shy away from. Hell, mine certainly did.

But with a teenage boy, the beast was within. And the boy's mother belonged to the same species as the targets of that supposedly insatiable lust, assuming he was straight. I didn't really understand what happened to male hormones during these years, I have to admit. Clinically, but not viscerally. If a teen saw his mom dressed in a sexy way, what went through his head? It added all kinds of extra ick to an already icky situation.

My eyes came back to the tablet. Used to be when there was a family PC, you could be assured that if anyone was around in the house that a horny teenager wouldn't be porn-surfing. Now they could put a tablet in their pocket, take it to their room and masturbate.

What do I do about all of this? Have Bob deal with it? No, if Bob said anything, Charlie would know that I knew something and made his dad address it. Charlie would think I was embarrassed, or upset, or grossed out. He would think I was dodging my responsibility, and he'd be right. Not a good starting point to address sex education in a mature and responsible way.

I went into the bathroom and sprayed the shirt with stain remover. I could just keep cleaning his jerkoff clothes and never say a word about it. A small price to pay to avoid an awkward discussion neither of us would want to have and neither of us would probably ever forget. What was the upside anyway? What did I want him to do different? Be more discreet?

I could try the vague approach and chide him to not let dirty clothes lay around. If he figured it out and wanted to talk about why his clothes were stained, it would be on him.

That was cowardly, something my mother would do. I could ask her for advice but, ew, no. Not about this. Not after the talk she had with me when I was twelve and caught me rubbing one out. I couldn't relive that.

What was wrong with me? I could face the end of the world, and the undead, and alien cannibal nerds, and every kind of asshole, but I couldn't tell my son to use Kleenex? Somehow we had stumbled into his teen years without having discussed sex. We squeaked through his voice cracking a year ago and talked vaguely about cleaning up hair in the shower.

I had assumed that he just wasn't into girls yet, given his focus on Pokemon, and now role playing games. But I realized now that he just wasn't going to brief me up on this aspect of his life. Was it because I am Catholic and Catholics frowned on any kind of premarital sex?

Not talking to him, I realized, just meant that I was letting him twist in the wind, probably afraid, uncertain, unsure. The t-shirt could be a subconscious signal for help. Why else would he leave it laying around where I would find it?

I had to talk to him, I decided. I had to be a grown up about it. He was outside playing touch football with the other guys on the street.

He came in when it was time to make dinner, shed his jacket, washed his hands, and drank a whole glass of water.

I started on safe ground. "How was school?"

Charlie rolled his eyes as he put the frozen enchiladas in the microwave while I made salad. I could see his face in the microwave oven reflection.

"Not worth mentioning. Highlight: a girl was drawing all over her leg and sent to the office. How was work?"

I kept my head down and chopped kale. "I read five papers today. Hopefully I'll get in a lab later this week before I have to worry about performance reviews."

Charlie chuckled. "I'm glad I'm not the only one you're the boss of."

"Ha, no one makes me rate you. And I don't do their laundry and feed them." Well, okay, in some way, I did make sure half of the scientists had something to eat, but the kid didn't know that.

I searched his face for a reaction with a sidelong glance.

"I'm a lot more fun," he retorted. "Those guys wouldn't hang out with you when you watch those terrible reality TV shows."

"Speaking of laundry," I continued, "I came across some stained clothes in your room." God help me, I paused to let him take that big gulp of apple juice. I'm such a bitch. "Next time you're wanking off, I suggest you use Kleenex for the catcher's mitt."

He sprayed apple juice across three cabinets. While he choked, I laughed my ass off as apple juice ran down the cupboards.

He tried to bolt from the kitchen, trying not to look at me. I gripped his arm. "You can't just keep spraying all over the house and leaving it for me to clean up!" I managed to say and dissolved into more laughter. I kept a firm grip on his arm.

The poor kid was mortified.

"I'm sorry, Charles, I am, that was out of line, really," I gasped. "At least I didn't walk in on you like my mother did to me."

"Dear God," Charlie said, staring away from me. "I don't want to know. *Please* stop talking."

"My mother caught me in the act when I was twelve. She said I should feel ashamed and repent. I'm not saying anything like that at all. You do what you have to do, and you don't have to be ashamed about it at all. But please don't catch any diseases, electronic or biological, and keep it discreet, okay? Discreet means not leaving a mess for your poor mother to clean up."

He looked at me, blushing from his ears to the neckline of his Star Wars Episode VIII t-shirt. "Okay. Grandma really said those things to you?"

I nodded. "I paid her back. When someone at Thanksgiving asked if I wanted a car for my sweet sixteen birthday, I said I'd rather have a vibrator. My mother nearly died right there at the table. My dad yelled at me and made me leave the room."

"Oh, Mom."

I laughed, remembering how awkward the ride home from that Thanksgiving was. "I had actually argued that batteries were cheaper than gas."

Charlie laughed again, thank God. Crisis averted, I handed him a dishrag and pointed at yellow juice stains on the cabinets.

[13]

I had just finished a department head meeting and was walking back to my office when a voice behind me said, "Holy fucking Christ, you don't have these assholes well under control, do you, Doc? Fucking drunk driving now?"

I turned around and saw his grin. "Mr. Stitcher, always a pleasure."

John Stitcher gave me a hug. Have you ever hugged a re-animated corpse? Your brain can't decide if it's a human because it moves like one, or a corpse because it's room temperature. Except you don't feel a corpse's muscles move under the skin. But an undead ghoul's muscles do that.

I tried not to act grossed out but shivered involuntarily. Stitcher noticed and I couldn't believe it, but it seemed to make him sad for a second.

I chucked him on the shoulder. "What brings you by? Did we cause a plague? Ruin the drinking water of a municipality?"

"Everyone always accuses me of breaking their balls all the time," he said, grinning again.

"It's not an accusation, more of an observation based on recent history," I joked.

"I'm here to see one of your scientists about something. Nothing for you to worry about. You're not in trouble yet, Cassano."

Was John Stitcher being more gentle than usual? He almost sounded like a normal person.

Donald came around the corner. "Ah, John. Here for your treatment," he said. "Sandy will take care of you in Exam Room Three."

Treatment? What kind of treatment does a ghoul need? Using medical science on an undead creature struck me as just wrong. Sandy was one of our chemists. John had told me he had been brought back to kind-of-life in some way that he never bothered to learn about. There was probably no magic involved, asserted the scientist in me.

John's face fell. "Thanks a fucking bunch, you dumb shit." He looked at me. "I'll, uh, talk to you later." He passed Donald and speed-walked down the hall.

Donald searched my face. "Is something wrong?"

I shrugged and went back to my office. Donald and I never had discussed John Stitcher's unique status. I couldn't be sure that he knew about the ghoul thing. And he had never mentioned that Stitcher used the lab as his personal clinic.

Half an hour later, Stitcher leaned on my doorway. "It feels good to be alive." He buttoned up his shirt sleeve and then put his jacket back on.

"Is that irony?" I asked.

"Um, I guess." He closed the door and flopped into my guest chair. "I was kidding about the DUI. Ever since you got this job, I haven't had to clean up a single fuck-up caused by your hybrids."

I folded my arms. "Are we going to talk about this treatment you're getting?"

He waved a hand. "Oh, that. It turns out being dead is a chronic health condition. I need injections every couple of months."

"Are they allergy shots?"

He glared at me. "I don't like talking about this. I have rights under some health care law, don't I?"

I shook my head. "Those only apply to living people. You're kind of in a fuzzy area, legally. And as lab director, it sounds like my facility has a way of keeping dead people alive."

"Alright, alright, fuck me," Stitcher said. "It slows the tissue decomposition. Even when you're undead, you can't escape death."

"You told me you could live for decades more, though," I said.

71

"Maybe," he replied wistfully. "Life expectancy estimates for the undead are not as accurate as for the living, I'm finding out. I'm falling apart faster than I expected."

Who wasn't, I almost retorted. I wanted to ask him what we could do to slow it. And how much time he had left. But I sensed I had pushed him beyond his comfort zone. And what business was it of mine, anyway?

"On to cheerier subjects," he announced. "You said there was good news on the genetic link to obesity? Congress is whining to our funders again about hearings on saturated fat or calorie counts or some shit. Any news that diverts their attention from all that would be great right now."

"The work isn't done yet, but we're fairly confident that there is a genetic component," I replied. "We're looking at genetic differences between the obese and the non-obese." I never would have thought there was a link, but the interactions of genes with illnesses, disorders, and plain old body chemistry was not the one-way street the scientific community had once assumed.

He nodded. "I'm not exerting a fucking iota of pressure here, but if you could announce something in the next two months, that would help us quiet talk about investigating the industry."

"If the science holds up, sure," I said guardedly.

He leaned forward. "Absolutely. It's misdirection for us in the public debate on the epidemic, so if it doesn't hold up, no big goddamn deal. We'll find some other shiny shit to distract them. Keep my bosses off my back." He folded his hands together under his chin and looked at me.

I tilted my head in mock surprise. "You have bosses? Aren't you on the Board?"

He grinned. "No, I'm a back bencher, a hired consultant. The Board runs the lab, the conspiracy, the whole show. They don't intervene much in what you or I do, but when they do intervene, I fucking sit up and start taking notes."

"Got it," I said. Now that I was well-entrenched in the conspiracy as Stitcher's part-time assistant, I knew I had to ignore my curiosity about the conspiracy's actual leadership. Information needed to be compartmentalized lest someone expose some portion of the conspiracy. I whispered, "So are we going to lose the lab?"

Stitcher nodded and my stomach dropped. "Things are changing, these new corporate motherfuckers don't listen to old guys like me. I'll do what I can, but I don't have a good feeling about this one, Elaine."

I could feel adrenaline and cortisol flooding my body. "What do we do? We lose the lab, we lose everything."

Stitcher wouldn't look at me. He covered his mouth. "I don't know. We'll figure something out. It's just a bigger than usual shitstorm to clean up." He patted my arm, still didn't look at me, and left.

When he was out of earshot, I muttered, "Good pep talk, boss."

[14]

It wasn't long after Stitcher's medical visit that my phone rang with an internal ringtone while I slayed emails during my lunch break. Yes, I'm one of those get-things-done people who empties their inbox every day.

"I have a Mr. Lyle Nunez here to see you," Fiona said at the receptionist desk.

"Excuse me?" I said. Lyle didn't live or work within hundreds of miles of here. And we weren't on speaking terms.

My heart pounded. How he had found this place? Had he been tailing me from home to work? He could probably find my address in the state real estate database. Or he just bought my file from some data warehouse operation. It was amazing how quickly my mind slid right into Lyle mode - the overreacting paranoid conspiracy theorist.

"He doesn't have an appointment," the receptionist added.

"I'll be right out." Halfway to my office door, I looked frantically around, trying to spot anything incriminating or revealing. I shoved some journals on ocean acidification in a drawer. Of course, I didn't leave the Project Rogers secret papers on my desk, but Lyle was highly observant. He would see the books about environmental damage and papers on energy grid hardening. His mind would shoot him in a thousand directions and one of them may actually land close to the truth.

74

Forget it, I thought as I hurried up to the lobby. We would talk in the conference room. There was just too much fodder in my office for his overactive imagination. And I had to keep him as far away as possible from the alien cannibal nerds.

"Lyle?" I said when I entered the lobby.

He was standing at our video display, intently studying the digital crawl of the lab's latest announcements. He looked a lot older than the five years since I had seen him. He had a gray goatee and crow's feet flanking his eyes with dark circles underneath.

"Dr. Cassano," he said stiffly and without a smile, "we need to talk."

"Fiona, we'll be in the conference room." She nodded absently while she filed her fingernails. For a hybrid, she was oddly full of attitude and not aptitude. A small percentage of hybrids failed to have the intelligence the others did.

"What brought you all the way out here?" I said as I closed the door to the conference room.

Lyle took a seat and kept his back rigidly straight. "You and Stitcher had to fuck me over, didn't you? Couldn't leave me alone."

I acted confused. "What are you talking about?"

"What, Stitcher didn't tell you? Or are you playing dumb now? The old Elaine was an unrepentant truth teller."

"I still am. What happened?"

Lyle spread his hands on the table. "First thing is my contract with SAS wasn't renewed. They admitted that a third party had leaned on them to let me go. It was a business decision, they said."

"And you think Stitcher did that?" I said. Maybe Lyle had gone off the deep end. People lose contracts all the time.

He nodded. "My consulting business is also dead. Every client dropped me in a two week span. Why? Because unnamed 'colleagues' created a whisper campaign telling them they shouldn't work with me. These were clients I've done great work for over a decade."

I stared at him, uncertain what to say.

He flung his arms out. "What do you people want from me now? I have no job, I'll run out of money soon. What the fuck?"

"Wait, wait, Lyle. Did you ever talk to the FBI? They've been dogging us."

"I'm not answering that," he said with the hint of a smirk.

"If you did, it's possible that someone found out about that and decided to keep their distance from you. Also, your reputation as a conspiracy theorist precedes you. Your clients may have dropped you for any number of reasons."

"You're denying that it was you guys?"

I shook my head because I really didn't know. "I'm just saying there could be other reasons. But it wouldn't be the first time a large industry gets back at the people bothering it."

Lyle huffed. "What gives you and your zombie boyfriend the right to wreck my entire life?"

"Hold on," I said. I called Stitcher.

Stitcher answered on the second ring. "Yeah, what do you want?"

"Hi John, I have one pissed-off Lyle Nunez sitting in my conference room here in Oak Ridge. He says that you ruined his life. I'm putting you on speaker."

Stitcher laughed as his voice echoed around the conference room. "Fuck him. He became an FBI informant. He can live off of that from now on."

Lyle started turning red.

"Um, you're on speakerphone, John," I said cautiously.

Stitcher chuckled. "Okay. Lyle, fuck you in your discolored asshole."

"You piece of dead dogshit. I don't care what happens to me any more," Lyle yelled. "I don't! I'm going to blow the top off this entire place. You'll have the FBI grabbing all your equipment here, Stitcher, shutting you down."

"Thinks he knows something, but he doesn't know fucking shit," Stitcher retorted. I could tell he was scared though.

"Hey, the both of you, I didn't put you on speakerphone so you could scream directly at each other," I stated in a thunderous tone.

They both shut up for a second.

"I am not here to get bought off by the deep pockets of your corporate blood money," Lyle declared.

"Shut it," I said quietly, in the voice I used when Charlie was way out of line. "Now, we can go on taking shots at each other and make things worse. Lyle, you're going to lose everything if you keep going. But in exchange for what? Giving us a hard time? It won't amount to much more than an inconvenience. Is that about right, John?"

"Damn straight," Stitcher said.

Lyle shook his head. "I'm already talking to the FBI. You can't touch me or they'll come after you. In a few hours they'll know exactly who to suspect if I disappear."

I stared up at him from under furrowed eyebrows and said slowly, "No one is going to hurt you or disappear you, Lyle. Jesus."

"Really? I know too much. I know about the factories, I know about Stitcher being a walking corpse. I know you sold out to get custody of your kid."

"If you weren't such a fucking asshole, we'd have bought you out too," Stitcher said.

"Why, don't like the competition?" Lyle shot back.

I slapped the conference table with my open hand. Although it stung like a mother, it usually nipped dick-measuring contests in the bud. "I'm telling the honest truth here, old-time my big mouth getting-me-in-trouble truth. We're the good guys."

"Elaine," Stitcher warned.

Lyle snorted. "Good guys? Corporate errand boys and crooked scientists? I guess the world really does look different when your paycheck depends on it."

"Upton Sinclair was an ass," Stitcher grumbled.

Now I was irritated. "And you, John, why the hell did you ruin his work and his reputation?"

"Well, I deprived the fucker of resources he used to spy on us. Also, hoped it would discredit him with the FBI. The more desperate and pathetic a conspiracy theorist is, the less credible. How does that sound?"

Unfortunately, it sounded evil but very shrewd.

"Is there some way that you could undo the damage you did to Lyle, in exchange for Lyle breaking up with the FBI?" I asked.

Lyle laughed. "Are you kidding? I'm ruined, and you want me to accept charity now in exchange for my silence?"

"I was about to say yes, myself," Stitcher said.

I noticed that a staffer who had walked by the conference room was doing another slow pass. She must have heard the yelling.

"Okay, boys, we need to wrap this up, because people here are noticing. Are we going to agree to disagree but get along?"

Lyle rolled his eyes. "Can I get a tour of the lab?"

"Hell no," Stitcher said, unnecessarily.

I shook my head. Lyle threw his hands up in the air.

I said, "How about Stitcher sets you up with a neat job somewhere doing what is it, SAS, yeah, SAS?"

Lyle's cheek muscle twitched. "I'd rather live in a trailer and wear a tin foil hat than take money from you people."

"Jesus fucking Christ, this guy," Stitcher moaned.

"Screw you, you undead freak," Lyle yelled. "Go fucking rot in a corner!"

Stitcher laughed in such a way that I think his respect for Lyle tripled, if you can believe that.

"You don't look like Mother Theresa to me either, Elaine," Lyle said. "The FBI is already coming after you. All of you. They know that there is an industry-wide conspiracy to make the population obese."

"Funny, that's not an actual crime," Stitcher added.

Lyle looked around the room. "And there's something not right about these labs. You all do a lot of odd research for a public relations front for the industry. Carbon dioxide levels in the atmosphere, crowd control prediction modeling, analyses of oil futures price variations. I've kept tabs on your publications."

"Hey shit head, also, research is not a crime," Stitcher commented.

I kept quiet to see if Lyle could put this all together himself. He was astute, technically knowledgeable, and had great analytical skills. It was his paranoia and over-thinking that sent his trains of thought off the rails and turned him into a conspiracy theorist.

Lyle looked at me. "I know you, Elaine, you hone and focus lines of inquiry. That's your talent. None of these projects are related to the food industry. Or obesity. They can't be tangential to your actual research interests. You have marching orders to do something bigger for the food and agriculture sectors."

I locked my diaphragm in place, afraid to take a breath. Until now, I hadn't realized we were so obvious. Lyle had pointed out what anyone would notice if they had looked closely at our research and knew how I operated. We didn't look like your typical food science shop.

"And what the hell, exactly, do you think that nefarious goal is, smart ass?" Stitcher asked, amusement dripping from his voice.

Lyle paused. "This industry, like all the other ones, wants a leg up as the world changes. How do you fatten up starving North Koreans and malnourished African kids? Market expansion, resource exploitation, profit maximization. It has to be."

Stitcher guffawed. "Was the FBI stupid enough to buy that bullshit?"

I just felt bad for Lyle getting so close and missing. I pictured a bullet train derailing at high speed and exploding into the side of a mountain.

"Well then tell me, Dr. Cassano, why are you doing all this research?" Lyle asked.

I replied, "I can give you the obvious, pat answers to that question. For example, agriculture uses a lot of petroleum for fertilizers and food processing uses it for packaging and transportation. Our interests are greater than propping up next quarter's earnings. But you will never find out the truth, so long as you keep the FBI after us."

I could see a kernel of panic flit across Lyle's eyes. Panic that his curiosity would never be sated, that the truth would remain hidden from him forever. This awful thought would either sprout inside his head and drive him mad or wither away. Only time would tell.

I stood up to signal the meeting was over. Stitcher hung up without saying goodbye. Then I escorted Lyle to the front door.

He turned to me with his hand on the glass. "I'm going to figure it out, whether you and your room temperature partner in crime help me or not."

I had little doubt that he would try, and that made me a mite jumpy. But to not let on, I smiled grimly. "Have a safe trip home, Lyle. Take care of yourself. Really."

79

[15]

One of the perks of working for the private sector is the parties. In government, you can't use tax dollars to buy donuts for a staff meeting. In the private sector, however, it was all a tax write-off. So catered breakfast arrived every morning in some firms, and they were gourmet donuts.

Our lab's tradition was to hold a big, lavish Halloween party every year. No Christmas party or summer picnic. Maybe Christmas just wasn't a big enough draw when a decent proportion of the staff were heathen alien-human hybrids. Maybe they liked the idea of wearing disguises. Halloween was our thing.

That year we rented out an Italian restaurant for the night, bought a grand worth of booze and food, and left work early. Charlie hung back at the house to handle trick-or-treaters, having declared himself too old for going out and too cool for his mother's work party.

Being the lab director, and a woman, choosing a costume was no easy task. Slutty was out, unfortunately, because it would kill my professional image, especially since most of the lab was men. Witches or other bitchy costumes wouldn't reflect well on a female boss either. Neither would anything that could be considered insensitive or offensive. In this case, that meant no Frankenstein monster, and mad scientist was a lame choice. The first year I went, it was without a costume and I was heavily scolded. Last year, I came as an Erlenmeyer flask.

This year, I went old school: Strawberry Shortcake. I was curious to see how many of these guys who stumbled through the 1980s with their noses in books would even know who she was.

Fiona spotted me first and waved from the bar. "Great little Red Riding Hood costume." Uh huh. She was the alien from *Alien*, with her head in a rubber mask of the monster.

The alien hybrids always dressed as monsters. Not the typical Halloween ones, but monster monsters. The Wampa creature from Star Wars, an Ent, Cthulhu, Godzilla, they were all represented, plus whatever showed up in the latest fantasy movies.

The human scientists usually went with the nerdiest, inside-joke costumes they could. Higgs-Boson particles, a greenhouse, three different stick-and-ball molecules, and a white lab mouse.

"What the hell are you supposed to be? A Care Bear?" someone asked from behind me.

I turned around to face Stitcher. "I didn't know you were in town."

I expected to see Stitcher in his typical bespoke suit. But he was wearing an old suit covered in burn marks, rips, and blood stains. Immediately, I assumed he had been in a car accident, but I noticed his grinning face was more grayish-white than usual. There was a patch of skin hanging off his cheek, exposing bone beneath. Cheap, plasticky flesh and bone. "John, are you really dressed as a zombie?"

"Why not? These freaks are all dressed as freaks and the geeks are all dressed as geeks. We're all letting our true natures show. As have you, apparently."

I looked down at the red skirt with the white apron over it. "I'm Strawberry Shortcake."

He shook his head. "No shit. Wait, are you breaking my balls here, Cassano? No? You're dressed as a character named after a goddamn dessert, who bakes fattening treats for her friends. You're a fucking walking obesity billboard."

I felt myself blush as red as my oversized hat. Was everyone's costumes a subconscious statement? "It's a good thing the FBI isn't here or they'd figure us out real fast."

"Or not. Those assholes don't get subtle irony. What in God's zoo of fuck-tards is he dressed as?" Stitcher pointed at a guy dressed in an orange muscle suit.

I knew this one. He had blue pants, his skin was made of fake orange rocks. I snapped my fingers, trying to remember.

"Don't tell me he's dressed as a fucking golem," Stitcher said. "I will rip that shit right off him in front of everybody."

I raised an eyebrow. "Golem? No, he's that guy from the superhero group. The other heroes don't look like him. Um. *Fantastic Four*! He's dressed as the Thing."

Stitcher shivered and turned around so he didn't have to see The Thing. "Okay, never mind. It just freaks me out. Old childhood trauma, I think."

"There's a Hulk, Iron Man, and Solomon Grundy here too," I said, nodding in the direction of the oversized superhero fans, who were clustered around the cannoli dish.

"Great fucking party," Stitcher said to change the subject, "if this were a 3rd grade class. Jesus, no music, no dancing, no prostitutes, no drugs. What the ever-loving fuck?"

I laughed. "This is pretty wild compared to the parties at USDA. There, everyone had to bring a dish, and the strongest drink was spiking the Diet Coke with Sprite."

"Meh, what should I expect from a bunch of autistic science shits. Now lawyers, we know how to party. Fucking bankers too. Anyway, let's talk business since this place is fucking dead."

I touched his arm. "Now wait, see there's someone dancing. Right over there." I pointed at a guy in a complicated dragon-octopus costume waving his arms around.

Stitcher just shook his head. "How's the home life? How's Charlie?"

"He made the mistake of asking me to speak at his school," I replied, walking over to the food spread.

"No chance he'll ever get laid now," Stitcher said wistfully.

I paused with a cauliflower halfway to my mouth. "Hey, I'm his mother here, remember?"

Stitcher's eyes sparkled with mischief. But after reading my face, he held up a hand. "How are things going in the lab?"

I shrugged. "Same as always. No one else here knows about what the Board wants to do to us."

Stitcher winced. "What about hybrid production?"

"Production is solid. The problem is the food chain; we're going to be short in a few years. We need an alternative to human adipose."

Stitcher said, "Yeah, I know. FBI not crawling too far up your ass?"

"Agent Pierce?" I shook my head. "Not really. Just a couple of conversations, in passing."

Stitcher nodded slowly. He picked up a carrot, dipped it in hummus and bit it. He chewed for a second and flung the remainder in the trash. "He's poking around. A real fucking crusader; I've read his file. Sees corporate conspiracies to ripoff hard-working folks left and right. At some point we'll have his superiors reel him in."

I folded my arms. "You're worried."

"About this guy? Damn right. Every time someone starts groping an elephant in the dark, they can easily grab his balls by accident. In this case, the balls would be the lab."

"Yeah, I got it. How much is my son's custody hanging on my success here? What if the FBI busts this place wide open, or I fail to stop one of my scientists' boneheaded ideas from causing havoc, or the Board shuts us down?"

Stitcher stared at his shoes before looking directly in my eyes. "If the worst happened, Elaine, I would do whatever I could to help you get another job. Hell, a better job."

I held up my hands. "And, my custody of Charlie? Is my work here all that keeps Bob from getting custody?"

Stitcher visibly relaxed. "Hell if I know. I can't guarantee he wouldn't try." If the lab closed, I had a feeling we would find out in a hurry. "Don't get worked up about this, Doc," he said in a gentle voice. "In a couple of years, Charlie will be of age anyway. All of this gloom and doom shit may not hit the fan before then."

I could tell he was lying. I nodded and tried to not get teary. If the lab closed it would be sooner than that.

Stitcher saw that and indicated the crowd. "Anyway, before I hit the road I need to give Donald shit over dressing up as Cthulhu. Fucking again."

My custody of Charlie probably was wrapped up in my success here, regardless of what Stitcher said. He couldn't control everything.

And just like that, the importance of keeping my position, of saving the lab hit me like a brick wall. If the Board defunded the lab quickly, it would probably be a matter of months before I was out of a job and Bob was filing a custody motion. And other than Stitcher's generosity, the conspiracy wouldn't have any reason to intervene against Bob like they did five years ago.

I couldn't let that happen.

[16]

Stitcher called me out of the blue in the first week of November, sounding positively forlorn. "Goddamn industry is drinking its own KoolAid. Now these fuckwads really are trying to jack up the obesity rate. They don't want an epidemic, they want a motherfucking global pandemic."

"Hello John. Do you realize it's almost eleven on a weeknight?"

"So? I need to talk."

I always imagined that Stitcher had a team of operatives to do his bidding, an industrial Dirty Dozen of undead tough guys and lawyers. But in the years since I had signed on to the conspiracy I had never encountered such a team. He alone sent me on errands. He never mentioned anyone else. Being his henchwoman wasn't exactly what I had in mind when I joined the private sector science community. And I never expected to be his confessor. "Okay, what are you talking about?"

"I've seen their plans. They are going to sodomize the local food culture. How? I'll fucking tell you how. They'll undermine a local government's food safety to destroy confidence in the local food supply. Then they'll force the poor assholes in those countries to buy good old, highly-processed, imported American food made in China. It's beautiful in a fucking horrible way."

"Is this because of the recent mergers?" I asked. The industry had been on a consolidation binge lately. The sun never set on the corporate empires in the food industry.

"Absolutely right. Word is that the junior execs want new worlds to conquer. The American and European markets are saturated: stagnant populations of aging fat people who are dieting. These Millennial executive fucks see the success of fast food in the developing world and they're jealous."

"What's the point if there's no way to harvest the adipose?" Would we somehow convince Doctors Without Borders to add liposuction to their commonly-performed procedures?

Stitcher cackled. "Well, the fucking profits, what else? A Hot Pocket in every fucking hut. The point is that our cabal doesn't have much sway with these assholes. We created an obesity-based business model but they don't give a shit about why we did that. They just want to maximize the money."

Soothing John Stitcher like a profane, colicky baby was not something I knew how to do. Especially not this late at night. He always told me what the score was, but added how things could get arm-twisted to be right. How was I supposed to do when even he didn't have the answers? "I thought you were in, connected," I said.

Stitcher clucked his tongue. "I was, with the old guard, but they're moving on, dying off. Their understudies are getting kicked to the curb by the new gang, who grew up jerking off to Ken Lay and Bernie Madoff. They're cooking the books all the way to the top."

"Hold on, do these new executives know about Project Rogers? About the environmental crisis?" I had no idea if or when Stitcher briefed in new corporate execs. After all, most corporate executives seemed to last only about two years. But if he showed these new executives the truth, they had to get with the program, right? Or get their souls sucked out of their noses, I thought.

Stitcher hissed, "They know everything. They know the planet's becoming a cesspool. They shrugged their fucking pin-striped shoulders," Stitcher yelled. "And I can't twist them on this point. These younger shits believe the world is already cluster-fucked. They think every company, even their own, is a ticking Enron time bomb and they just hope to extract as much cash as possible from the corporate husk before the end times. They are in it only for their own compensation. Fucking mercenary motherfuckers."

When he got on a rant like this, I usually lost all sense of what he was going on about. "That makes no sense to me."

"You're not in business. These younger shits are scared of Chinese and Brazilian motherfuckers who would coat food in cyanide if it saved fifty fucking cents. They think the only way they win is to get leaner and meaner while the stock options get richer and richer. Fucking ironic, isn't it? And that means killing Project Rogers, killing the lab, pillaging the companies' pensions and anything else they can lay their sweaty hands on."

"Can't you just fix it? Regain control?" I had no idea what I was asking, but he had me worried now. I winced as I asked a "can't you just" question. The answer to those was almost always depressing.

Stitcher replied, "I'm maxed out just to keep the cockshitting-conspiracy going. We have whistleblowers popping up like goddamn mushrooms after a monsoon because their bosses have decided to take a big steaming shit on food safety laws, foreign and domestic. And in my free time, I'm getting rammed up the ass by these executives about the cost of supporting the conspiracy. All they see are useless charity donations to cut. Your lab is just part of that shitshow."

"This is enormously dispiriting," I said, trying to get a word in. I shifted my legs around under the covers, feeling a cramp beginning in my calf.

"Abso-shitly. So I'm wearing my ass down running around trying to justify every dime we're spending. It'd be nice if we didn't have to keep fucking burning money to make human cheese whiz for the alien geniuses, by the fucking way."

I sighed. "I'm working on it. We co-authored the reports on vat-made meat. We're hoping that we can grow more adipose in a vat. But it will take years, if we're lucky."

"Well that just won't help me a damn bit then," Stitcher said wearily.

I shook my head. "Sounds like you need a vacation."

"Ha, this fucking job didn't come with fringe benefits. A minimum expense account and a clothing allowance. It's a good thing I don't need to eat anymore or I'd have died of starvation during the Bush Senior Administration."

I rolled my eyes at that. Haven't met a lawyer yet, alive or dead, who didn't complain about their inadequate compensation to everyone who earned a fraction of what they made.

"So is this your colorful way of telling me that you failed to get the Board off our backs?" I asked, rubbing my forehead. A stress headache was lurking inside my skull. I didn't need this before I tried to sleep.

"Hell yes. It's worse than you think. I'm calling to get your help, Elaine."

"What do you have in mind," I asked trepidatiously. I wasn't primed to think clearly, half asleep in my flannel pajamas.

"This is fucking brilliant, trust me," he gushed. "We fuck all these assholes at once: the whistleblowers, the corporate frat boys, and the FBI cocksuckers. We use the whistleblowers to leak the execs' new obesity pandemic, and it sends the FBI down after them and away from the actual conspiracy."

This was one of those misdirection, take out an enemy, plays that Stitcher had mentioned before. But several seconds passed as I pictured Agent Pierce as Wiley E. Coyote and tried not to giggle. And then I tittered, snickered, and snorted.

"What is so fucking funny, doc?"

I busted out laughing. But he was serious, I realized. Was he out of his mind? It only made me laugh harder. "I have no idea what the hell any of that meant."

"Jesus H. Fucktard with a soft helmet on, Elaine. This is *so simple*. We leak this obesity pandemic plan to the whistleblowers. The whistleblowers go to the FBI, meaning Pierce, and he goes running off after these new asshole execs. A huge misdirection. It should knock the corporate execs down a few pegs, maybe give us some breathing room. Also, if Pierce buys it, he'll lose credibility in the Bureau when it turns out to be a dead end. Maybe we can regain control of this shitshow."

Oh. Everything became a lot less funnier. "What are the chances that this scheme backfires and brings the FBI down on the actual conspiracy instead? It's a huge risk. This is crazy."

"You're an ignorant shit," he retorted gleefully. "It's not your fault. You know how many executives ever undermined their own company or their entire industry just to gain power? Get fucking real. The answer is all of them, they just hide their fingerprints real well."

"How does this not blow up in our faces?" I asked. Also, why was this all 'we' and 'our'? I'm just a scientist who runs a lab, after all.

"We just have to manage it properly," he said. "We expose the planned obesity pandemic that these fucking suits are dreaming up. They want every favela to be filled with fatties, we pass that on to the whistleblowers, who lead the FBI after them and away from our cheese stick facilities."

"But all the attention could expose the actual conspiracy, John. Or at least limit our, I mean your, ability to execute it," I pointed out. I flashed back to tearful obese people begging for help, feeling powerless to save their children and themselves from the battery of obesity-related diseases facing them.

Stitcher kept talking. "Yeah. The press, the government, the public all goes wild when they find out the food industry has been trying to stuff them for decades. There could be some short-term damage to the conspiracy. The scandal will suck in the FBI to look for criminal activity across the industry. The FBI finger the new execs, or they resign first, and our guys are waiting in the wings to take over."

"It could take the FBI years to nail these guys on criminal charges." I couldn't remember the last time I had heard of any corporate executive going to jail for crimes committed on the job though. "And what happens when one of these executives you're targeting sell you out and tell the FBI about Project Rogers and the *actual* conspiracy?"

Stitcher cleared his throat; it sounded like a tank starting its engine. "Non-disclosure agreements. There's a lot of fates worse than federal prison, or death."

I groaned. "How come those NDAs don't stop these executives from shutting us down?"

"Tsk, tsk, Elaine. Executives dreamed them up, so they made sure not to cramp their own freedom too much."

"Fine. You're the lawyer. But while all this plays out, how will the lab last? And Project Rogers?"

"That's why we need to move goddamn fast. To have our guys take over. The first thing I need you to do is funnel the whistleblowers to either your pal Lyle or straight to Pierce. You will be the missing link."

Where's his Dirty Dozen? "Why me?"

"Because Elaine, you're about to go on a grand tour of academic conferences on obesity, nutrition, and health. And you'll just happen to meet with some industry folks at these conferences who will be eager to talk to you."

I have a house, a mortgage, and a minivan. I'm not a cloak and dagger operative with nothing to lose. Was he desperate, crazy, or both? "How am I going to do that, John? Lyle doesn't trust me. And Pierce already suspects me and the lab of something. He wouldn't buy that I had suddenly turned on the industry. I can't approach either one of them."

"You have a solid reputation for exposing wrong-doing in the food industry," he pointed out. "You'll figure out the right way to get the information to the right people."

Leading the FBI on a wild goose chase didn't sound like part of my vague plan to stay out of jail. The legal ramifications were staggering. "I'd really rather not go to jail and endanger Charlie's wellbeing. Thanks."

"You won't. You're just relaying actual information to whistleblowers, and you'll have a phalanx of lawyers to protect you.

I groaned. "Okay, that was the first thing. What else?"

"You have to get Agent Pierce off the industry's back. We need to have a scandal at AgSol. Out you guys as shills for the industry as part of the obesity conspiracy."

"What the hell will that achieve?" I asked loudly. It felt like he asked me to cut one of my own arteries with a tomato knife.

"Like you said, when the obesity pandemic blows open, the real conspiracy will be in danger of exposure. We need to deflect attention. I want you to string along Special Agent Pierce on a wild goose chase that leads to the new executives."

"Jesus Christ, don't you have a team of bad dudes who do these things for you?" I asked. "You're like the Shadow, but with more swearing."

"Funny. I don't. One man operation, more or less. I call in favors when I really need them. Like now."

The silence stretched out as he waited for a yes while I stuck with no.

"What's the problem?" he asked.

I slapped my knee. "Besides the legal consequences? Oh, I don't know, this could jeopardize my custody of Charlie. And my reputation. And ruin my career."

I expected him to argue, but instead he said, "Yes. Your reputation will almost certainly be shredded. And Charlie could be fucked for a while, especially if things turn shit-like and you go to prison."

I whispered harshly into the phone, in case Charlie was still awake. "That is one gigantic fucking favor you're asking, Stitcher!"

"We need to do this to still have a chance at averting the environmental crisis, or we accept that we're fucked. It's a big enough thing that everyone is making big sacrifices like this, Elaine."

I wanted to ask him what fucking sacrifice he was making, because, despite his hopeless tone, he sounded to me like he was enjoying this.

"I don't know how to do any of this," I whined.

"You just need to plant certain shiny fucking objects in the good agent's path and let him pursue and investigate. The more he discovers on his own, the easier he'll believe that each shiny object is legit. If things get kinky, legally, you call me and I get corporate counsel involved A-fucking-SAP, okay? Do not play too many games with this cocksucker. He is relentless, has a badge, a gun, and the federal government behind him."

"You don't have to tell me," I said. My brain wheels were really spinning now. I wanted to tell Stitcher to piss off. But I could see that he had already thought this through and I was a key part of this idiotic plan. "How long do I have to prepare?"

Big sigh. Stitcher sounded tired. Do the undead sleep? Wasn't every night a sleepless night? "Just stay alert, I think shit will douse the fan in rapid fucking fashion." He hung up, leaving me with a powerful case of anxiety-induced insomnia.

"I better not go to jail," I growled at the phone, and hung up.

[17]

"I ain't voting for no pointy-headed Mongol who hasn't been saved by Jesus Christ," the man on the phone yelled at me. And then he hung up.

I checked the phone number again. I'm sure I dialed it correctly. I looked at the call list in front of me. Something wasn't right.

"Who came up with these call lists?" I said, putting the cheap plastic receiver in the cradle.

Charlie looked at me from across the line of phones between us and shrugged. Everyone else at our phone bank continued new calls.

I caught Fiona's attention and asked. "Who are these people we're calling?"

Fiona had a blank look on her face for a second. "They are highly-educated registered voters. A lot of doctors. Donald got these names from the Republican Party."

That was it. The names seemed very WASPy to me. Didn't Donald know that not all highly-educated people liked the public schools? Especially in the South, where there was a tradition of wealthier people sending their kids to private school?

I made another seven calls. The verbal abuse I caught on some of them made me drop the black, plastic receiver down into the cradle like it was covered with swamp scum. "I have the strong feeling that no one on my list wants to vote for Dr. Meers."

Charlie held his phone away from his ear. An old woman with a thick Tennessee drawl chewed him out for being the kind of hippy who was helping the terrorists.

"What do you mean, Mom? This is kind of fun." He dialed his next number with a mischievous grin. "Yes, can I talk to Dr. Carlyle? Yes, I'm a supporter of Dr. Donald Meers for school board. I just know that someone like yourself is ready to support high-caliber schools that can prepare kids like me to be the next surgeons and scientists."

Charlie listened for a moment and grinned. "I don't know his position on income taxes or immigration."

I bit my tongue, thinking about what Donald's position on immigration probably was.

"No, I don't think he is a socialist. Yes, he supports charter schools, if they can raise test scores. He supports the new state standards... okay, thank you." Charlie hung up the phone. "He was nice about it, at least."

I didn't want Donald to win; it would increase the chances of exposing the hybrids, the lab's actual work, and maybe the conspiracy. On the other hand, I didn't want some asshat to win who would cut school spending or water down science education. And I didn't want to see my friend hurt by defeat.

I pulled Fiona into a back room. "Who is Donald's campaign manager?"

She smiled. "Me."

The spaciest hybrid. Great. And not a political junkie, from what I could tell. I tried to be diplomatic. "We're not getting a lot of success with these phone lists."

"People don't like to be called at home," she replied.

I shook my head. "No, I mean this subset of voters may not be the ones who are likely to vote for Donald. You said this list came from the Republican party?"

"Yes, but this race is non-partisan," she said. "These are all registered voters who are higher-income and who are doctors or went to college. Our strategy was to target these people because they are more likely to support him."

What could I do? Run around, looking for a list of Democrats? Donald had not come close to winning the teachers' union endorsement.

"There's other factors that affect voting preferences," I said. "Culture, tradition, other issues."

"Yes, but after he didn't win the teachers' union endorsement, we figured we had to focus on those who wouldn't vote only for the endorsed candidates. And studies show that income and Republican party membership are correlated."

I wasn't getting anywhere. "Well, Donald is Asian. Did you get any lists of Asians in the county?"

Fiona shook her head. "How would we do that?"

I shrugged. "I don't know anything about running a campaign." I guess I thought that the elections board handed out voter lists or something.

I looked at the clock. The polls would close in two hours. What were the chances that revamping his campaign strategy at this point would make a difference anyway?

"I thought you were opposed to Dr. Meers running for the school board," Fiona said.

"I am. I was." I looked around for the right words. "I... just want him to do well. Right now, I want him to win."

Fiona looked as confused as I felt.

Yeah, why did I care? Because I felt that sinking feeling of disappointment. It was like I wanted him to win. And it was more than just because he was my friend. Where was that coming from?

I looked at the main room where Charlie and the others were still working the phones. There were fifteen of us huddled around three tables of ancient phones. The campaign was housed in the storefront of an old gas station off a heavily-forested rural road.

Jeff Ewell walked back to join us with his hands jammed in his pockets. "Are you asking her about the heat?"

"Are you cold?" Fiona asked. She wandered off to look for the thermostat.

I looked at Jeff. "Has anyone at your table had a single positive call?"

He grinned helplessly. "You know how it is, calling people on election night. I wasn't expecting to convince anyone, it just seems like one of those fun things you do to participate."

"We're calling Republicans to ask them to vote for Donald," I noted. "It's not going well."

"Oh." Jeff made another face.

I nodded toward the window. "Fiona, God love her, is the campaign manager."

He facepalmed. "Ohhhh."

And then Fiona, thinking she had found the thermostat, opened the circuit breaker box and shut off the electrical power.

[18]

Donald came by the campaign headquarters when the polls closed. He and his wife had been out shaking hands near polling places all day. They both looked windburned but happy.

"We won't know the final results until tomorrow morning," Donald said to us. "But I wanted to thank you all for your hard work on this campaign. I know you are all committed to improving our schools and you all know how important that is to the world we live in."

Our small band cheered.

"Me and the other candidates for the school board have been invited to the Democratic campaign headquarters for their party. I want to pass that invitation on to all of you." He waved a handful of passes over his head. "Free food and drinks."

Politicians and free food. I just wanted to go home and curl up with a glass of wine and a journal or three. I didn't want to see the look on Donald's face when he realized how badly he lost.

Charlie looked at me with a hopeful, happy expression. I rolled my eyes. "Ugh, Mom. Please? The Meers kids are going."

I nodded. He was in high school and election night was like a civics thing, right? What kind of parent would I be if I said no? But I suspected he had his heart set on the free food. After all my hard work to slim him down.

We joined a small caravan of vehicles that left the abandoned strip plaza and headed into Oak Ridge's commercial district. The Democrats were partying at the Holiday Inn ballroom.

I'm not into politics but it was heartening to see so many fully committed, enthusiastic people hoping for the best, despite certain defeat. Donald's intrepid campaigners fit right in. There were the liberals with the slightly unkempt hairstyles, the older teacher union folks, and proud social justice activists. I guess we constituted the science wing of the party. Both parties, really.

Charlie made a beeline for the buffet table with Donald's son, who had come home from college to help his dad. They both returned with a plate of chicken wings drowning in barbecue sauce.

I held up a finger and mouthed 'enough.' Charlie grinned devilishly and proceeded to smear his cheeks with ruby sauce as he mowed through the wings.

I drifted into the crowd, looking for familiar faces. After I circled the room, I realized that I had gone to the wrong party if I wanted to network with other scientists. I recognized a few local celebrities in schools, business or politics, but no one I knew.

Bob could work this room like a hooker on a prison bus. Especially if he had his corporate checkbook handy. He would come in knowing most of the elected officials and leave knowing their staffers and the up-and-comers.

The election returns streamed by on a huge TV. The crowd took turns groaning and cheering as they saw which races their party was losing or losing badly.

The school board results flashed by, with 15% of the vote in, Donald was trailing four other candidates by at least ten percentage points.

All of Donald's volunteers congregated at the back of the ballroom. We exchanged knowing looks. Donald would be lucky to crack the top three, much less the top spot.

"Why is everyone looking so glum?" Fiona asked. She had changed into a stunning black cocktail dress. "It's too early. They probably received results from our worst districts."

Everyone nodded and mumbled agreement. I couldn't bite my tongue so I went to the bar. There weren't many happy Democrats there. I got a club soda and hung around, waiting for the concession speeches to begin.

I spied Charlie for a second through the crowd. He was talking to a trio of other teens and eating cake. He was having a great time, which lifted my mood.

"Come on Donald," I said, feeling like I was rooting for a horse in a race I couldn't see. The school board results updated, finally, and Donald had slipped from 21 to 17% of the vote. I knew he would lose. The top two candidates would be elected, and he wouldn't come close. Jeff Ewell came over, putting on his coat, and shook his head. "Politics is stupid."

I nodded. "I wish I could say politics didn't matter to us."

Jeff grunted and said good night.

I saw Charlie passing through the crowd, headed back to the buffet table. Teenagers. They'll lie right to your face and go do whatever they want. I was about to chase him down when Donald appeared at my elbow.

"Elaine. You were right. I'm not going to win," he said sheepishly.

I hugged him. "I'm so sorry. I know you wanted this a lot. Believe it or not, I wanted it to for you. I think you're right, that we have to do more than publishing research. We can't be on the sidelines any more."

"Yes. Politics may not be the right way though. What can one school board member do anyway?"

"You would have done great," I said, rubbing his arm. "What's the next step?"

He looked up at the ceiling. "I should take some time, try to figure it out. When we started working on the meteor's crystalline code, it got me thinking about how I fit into what my ancestors have tried to do. Plus with the kids going out on their own, it's a sign that time is passing. I'm not going to live forever either. Maybe I'll dive further into my work."

"If you stay engaged, you could still have the same kind of influence. There's textbook-writing, test-production, plenty of other ways to influence education."

He nodded. "I wonder if it's not education but culture that needs to change. We don't need 300 million scientists working on the same problems. It's the society, how it ignores problems or solutions. That seems to be the biggest obstacle. Anyway, sorry for the digression, Elaine. I have a lot to think about."

I watched Donald go off and talk with more well-wishers. He had that plastic, pleasant smile on his face. Underneath that, he was unreadable.

My phone rang, just barely audible over the din of the party. It was Stitcher and I moved out to the hallway where I could actually hear. "How's Donald taking it?" he asked.

"I don't know. He's philosophical."

"He used to be a stone-cold sociopath, but I think some actual fucking humanity has shone through over the years. I'm kind of proud of the dumb bastard."

"How heart-warming," I said, but with a smile. My smile vanished. "You didn't have a hand in him losing, did you?"

"Me? Hell no. I don't mess with school board races. Jesus, Elaine. I wouldn't do that to the poor guy anyway - we're on the same team."

I winced. "Sorry, sometimes it's hard to know where you draw the line."

"It's just as well," Stitcher said. "Can you imagine the shit-ton of trouble he would cause with a public-speaking role?"

"He's not that bad," I said. "And the school board is not a high-profile position."

"He reminds me of a curious space cadet," Stitcher said. "Brilliant, but he gets into the weirdest kind of shit. He's better than he used to be, but Christ with a beaker up his ass."

"What do you have against people advocating for our position in the public arena?" I thought of what Donald said about the real obstacles, like culture.

"It's people's reactions to it," Stitcher replied. "They ignore you even harder or freak out and kill you. The direct approach doesn't work; people can't handle the truth." He paused. "Eh, you're too young for that joke. Anyway, they'd rather set the messenger on fire than think about the message. The only way we get the fucktards to play ball is to trick them into it. This electoral debacle is a case in point. Gotta jump."

I shoved my phone back in my purse. What I didn't say to the mouthy ghoul was what if the sneaky approach wasn't enough? What if we needed the good people of the planet on our side, openly committed to stop an environmental collapse? Did that mean we were doomed if we stayed hidden?

Charlie walked up to me. "Can we go?"

I studied his face and body language. "You have to go to the bathroom, don't you?"

"Not here, Mom. What I need to do isn't fit for public restrooms." He winced.

"You ate too much." I had to say it. Maybe sometime the message would penetrate his thick skull.

"Ohhh. Mom. Can we just go?"

Depending on who won or lost tonight, I figured that the hotel maintenance staff would have a lot worse to clean up in the bathrooms nearest the ballroom. But the boy looked like he was hurting. Jesus, he'd been like this since he was little. What is it about boys avoiding going to the bathroom?

We grabbed our coats and fled the ballroom, just as the crowd booed some new results. The Democrats would have a lot more to boo about tonight in the state of Tennessee, I bet. Nationally, the Republicans were poised to run the table from the White House to dogcatcher.

Charlie groaned and hurried to the bathroom, unable to endure the ride home. I stood a respectful distance away from the bathroom and checked my messages. The lab was quiet because many staff had taken the day off to help Donald.

"Dr. Cassano?" asked a semi-familiar voice. Special Agent Vernon Pierce was carrying his coat and was dressed in casual clothes.

"Vernon," I replied somewhat coldly. "What brings you out here? Not work, I bet."

He shook his head. "No, of course not. I'm here for something else."

Something about the way he said it sounded like he was hiding something. Was he spying on me, or Donald, or the others? Had he overheard my call with Stitcher?

I was about to indulge in some full-on paranoia when Charlie emerged from the bathroom with a spring in his step. From the opposite direction, a teenage African-American girl with braces walked up to Special Agent Pierce.

Pierce and I realized that we had children that needed to be introduced. He went first. "This is my niece, Aisha, who dragged me here because she is a political junkie and a hardcore Democrat."

I put my hand on Charlie's shoulder. "This is my son Charlie. We helped out a friend's campaign. Charlie, this is Mr. Pierce; he works for the FBI."

"I have consulted with Dr. Cassano in the past," Pierce explained. Charlie didn't suspect anything, but Aisha looked at me skeptically. I wonder if she had been with him when he accidentally bumped into other suspects when he was supposedly off the clock.

"So you are Democrats too?" she asked Charlie.

I was about to mutter no, but Charlie grinned and said, "We're here for someone who lost a school board race."

"Oh, who was it?" the girl asked, like she may know the person.

"Donald Meers," Charlie said. "He works with my Mom."

She thought about that for a second. "Yes, I remember him. Didn't get the teachers' union endorsement. He had some interesting ideas though. Maybe next time." She added, matter-of-factly, "Sometimes it takes multiple tries, to build up name recognition and to learn how to campaign better."

Agent Pierce pointed at the jacket folded on my arm and said, "You look like you were on your way out."

"Yeah," Charlie said. "I'm not feeling well - ate too much at the buffet."

"It's just as well; this party isn't going to get better, is it?" Pierce said to his niece. "Another clean sweep against your side, Aisha."

Aisha twisted her lip. "It's progress. Well, it was very nice to meet you both." She shook our hands firmly.

When we got in the minivan, Charlie asked, "You know FBI agents?"

"Yes," I replied guardedly. I scrambled to think of a plausible explanation of how Agent Pierce and I had crossed paths. I wanted to tell him that if he ever saw Pierce again to let me know. But there was no way that would come out without sounding very strange. "Are you feeling better?"

"Yeah."

So I said, "I worked with the FBI on some of those food industry scandals a couple of years back."

He looked out the window. "Oh. Dad isn't in any trouble, is he?"

I laughed. "No. Why would you assume that? Because if I have talked to law enforcement, he must have broken the law?"

Charlie kept looking out the window. "No, no," he said quickly.

How nice it must be to be a teenager and think the world revolves around you and your parents. But Charlie wasn't daft like that. He was acting like he knew something. That was interesting.

I kept my eyes glued to the dark road and tried to to make my next question sound innocent. "Is there some reason you think the FBI would be after your father?"

Charlie rubbed his stomach. "I'm never eating like that again."

I waited for a thirty count. "Charles."

"No, no. I was thinking that because he's a lawyer, and a lobbyist, that maybe something was going on. You know, DC intrigue, illegal campaign contributions, spies, secrets."

"Your Dad bugs Congressmen to do favors for big corporations. It may be slimy, but it's perfectly legal."

"What about bribery? Or what if he found classified files?"

I shook my head. "You have quite the imagination, kid. Being a lawyer is doing a lot of studying and listening to other people talk for hours."

"Says the woman who likes to hide in her lab," my son huffed with fake outrage.

"I was on a reality TV show once, you know," I retorted. "I was a *star*."

His eyes searched the roof of the minivan, like he was looking for an escape hatch. "Oh, not this again."

I chucked him on the shoulder, he laughed, and hopefully forgot all about FBI agents.

[19]

This was the first academic conference I had attended in over a decade without any of my own publications to present. I wasn't here for the talks, or the poster sessions, or even the networking. I was here to smuggle secret documents out of the industry. I felt like an imposter.

Stitcher had given me the dossier on my contact, a Gavin Bottrell, junior corporate executive in the biggest food processor corporation at the moment. He had a thumb drive full of documents that would incriminate the new CEOs who wanted to introduce the children of the developing world to Type II diabetes.

Gavin and I had arranged to meet during the evening poster session on the conference's first night. Until then, I busied myself with attending the most relevant talks I could find, if for no other reason than to mask my real reason for being there.

I dreaded meeting him face-to-face. Maybe it was because I knew whistle-blowers paid a heavy price for doing the right thing. The whistleblower from the Fiesta additive scandal probably lost his life for blowing the whistle. And in my own case, I was bounced from a federal agency I won't name because I followed my own pangs of conscience about illegalities in external research funding. I ended up losing my job, my house, and custody of Charlie.

According to the dossier Stitcher had given me, Gavin was a young, tall,

Nordic-looking executive in his early thirties, with straight dirty-blond hair expertly cut and styled. He was in charge of purchasing for an overseas distributor who wanted to fatten up billions of foreigners. If you know anything about how lousy multinational companies treat their agricultural sources, it wasn't a stretch to imagine why a purchaser may develop a guilty conscience. Food companies usually squeeze their suppliers so bad on price that they drive family farms out of business.

Gavin figured he had killed a dozen such farms in his twenty years in the business, according to Stitcher's dossier. And now Gavin was part of the group that would undermine confidence in local food supplies in southeast Asia to make way for packaged American crap.

I spotted Gavin on the far end of the concourse outside the main ball-room. The poster session had taken over the space, along with new snack products from vendor-sponsors. We met near a poster on possible interactions between ADHD medications and diet soda by an eager graduate student who talked in a high-pitched squeal.

I shook Gavin's hand and came away with the thumb drive, which I slipped in my purse. "Can I ask you why you are doing this? I have a bet with my boss."

Gavin scowled. "It's wrong, what we're supposed to do. I was a missionary in Zimbabwe before I joined the company. Being tough on price during negotiations is one thing. The people in these countries don't need to get addicted to chocolate-covered pretzels on top of being poor."

"This is a risky way to get a promotion," I replied.

He made a pouty face. He probably didn't have blunt honesty aimed his way all that often. Too bad. He'd need some blunt honesty if he wanted to be an executive who dealt with John Stitcher. "I have young kids," he said. "I'd like them to have a planet to live on whether that hurts my paycheck or not."

I thanked him and we went our separate ways. It felt weird walking around with these files in my handbag, so I went back to my hotel room and read them.

Stitcher hadn't been kidding. There were memos and strategic plans to vacuum up profits from fattening up the developing world. The key was to equate American junk food to prosperity to capture market share and instill a food culture which would guarantee a stream of perpetual profits.

There was a twenty-year timetable to addict a population to a high-fat, sugar-heavy and salt-heavy diet. It involved using soda and fruit juices, flavoring popular foods with coconut oil, butter and salt. Dangle money to the government to allow vending machines in schools, public buildings, and in local businesses.

A white paper discussed how to undermine the local food supply. The genius who wrote it used the car companies' dismantling of American street cars and trolleys in the '50s and '60s as a model. Lobby for 'better' food safety regulations that local food companies couldn't comply with. Then buy those local companies quietly. Ruin the local brands with targeted bad press events like food poisoning and deliberately ruining the taste. Offer free pre-packaged breakfast and lunch to kids in schools, and give the schools complete curriculums on health and nutrition based on a 2,500 calorie 'American' diet.

Until that moment, I had suspected that Stitcher was exaggerating his claims about plans to make the epidemic a global pandemic. He had sounded angry enough to have stretched the truth. But having a thumb drive full of incriminating documents made it more real to me. These new corporate executives really were on a crusade to fatten everyone on the planet.

In a way, I suppose there was some cosmic justice in having an altruistic national obesity epidemic descend into a profit-generating global pandemic. The machinery Stitcher and his generation had built was too effective for evil minds to not use to squeeze it for more profit. That was a price we all had to pay for juggling double-edged swords in a capitalist circus.

The next morning I caught a flight to Kansas City. The other half of my conduit role was to transfer these files to conspiracy theorists who would put them in circulation. This way I could insure anonymity for the whistleblowers. One of Lyle's fellow travelers lived on a compound outside the city.

The poor gullible conspiracy nuts were ready and willing to believe anything they heard or saw if it was minimally plausible and came from an inside source. Like Lyle, we couldn't bring them inside the actual conspiracy, but there was little risk to using them as pawns to stop the new conspiracy.

Yeah, I felt like we were using them. Stitcher made them expendable pawns in an evil game of chess. It's one thing to reject a research paper, or defund someone's dream project, but it was another to manipulate conspiracy nuts, praying on their psychological problems and their sense of morality just to fuel a cynical corporate coup.

The conspiracy nut I was visiting today, Ty Anderson, lived in a modest split-level in the rural outskirts of Kansas City. According to my phone's map app, there was a worn blue pickup in the driveway and a homemade swing hanging from the tree.

I rented a car and drove out to Ty's house on a sunny day. He worked out of his home teaching piano lessons to home-schooled kids when he wasn't tossing outlandish claims around on the internet. Everyone needed to pay the bills, right?

I parked by his red barn-shaped mailbox and put the mailbox's flag up. Then I honked once and drove away. I made my way to a specific cineplex near I-70.

Stitcher had intel that Ty had been in touch with Agent Pierce already. While the documents I had were revealing, I wasn't sure if they were incriminating. If Pierce didn't bite on them, Ty regularly bothered the FDA as well as conspiracy bloggers who were in touch with the media. They would find a home one way or the other.

Lyle would probably snark that corporate plans to subvert the health of foreign populations would probably be rewarded by the government rather than prosecuted. But I wasn't Lyle, and the FBI didn't do corporate America any favors.

This was just the first faked leak of actual insider documents; Stitcher was setting up several more. He wanted publicity about the first leak to appear to help spring the others. I don't know what he planned to do if the government sat on these documents to study them for a few years, but I imagine that he had a contingency plan. Either way, the PR wings of multiple companies would be pulling a lot of late nights trying to react.

Stitcher had set up Ty and I on a dummy email account we both had access to. I wasn't comfortable with a face-to-face. Instead, I told him to go see a particular showing of the latest superhero movie and sit in the third row from the bottom, in the middle. I also told him not to try to spot me, for his own protection as well as mine. I wore a baseball cap and my hair was pulled back, just in case he did look my way.

I had seen this particular movie with Charlie a week earlier. When I walked in the darkened theater, the hero Cyborg walked down a dark street that made the theater nearly pitch black.

Just like when Charlie and I saw it, the theater was two-thirds empty. After the last couple of years of mega superhero movies, the studios were cashing in on their second-tier heroes. It seemed like every hero had the same story arc.

I sat a row behind Ty and watched the movie for a few minutes. I waited for the right scene to tap him on the shoulder with the thumb drive. He took it without taking his eyes off the screen. He was good to his word.

I settled back in my seat and watched the action for another five minutes. Then I threw out the hat in the theater bathroom and drove a different route to the airport for the flight home.

[20]

A week later, word leaked to the press that the feds had opened an investigation into crooked practices in the food industry. The press reported unconfirmed stories about the industry planning to make people fat on purpose, rather than doing so accidentally, as had been the case up to now.

I had the cable news on as I prepared dinner. Charlie was in the living room, bent over his laptop, supposedly doing school work. I had told the kid a million times to do his work somewhere without distraction but he didn't listen. Teenagers.

"If true," some talking head opined from the TV, "this could be a bigger scandal than Big Tobacco hiding the fact that it knew nicotine was addictive. This could be absolutely huge, no pun intended."

Charlie looked over the back of the couch at me. "This sounds like that thing you were involved with a few years ago."

"Yeah, you'd think these guys would learn," I said sardonically and shook my head.

Charlie watched me for a moment. He had become proficient in reading me like an open book. Teenagers. "Is this going to affect your job?"

I kept chopping carrots and didn't look up. "Maybe, but not badly. I mean, we're the happy face these companies use to show the world how much they care about health issues. If they were doing something under-handed, it shouldn't reflect on AgSol."

Charlie shrugged and went back to his schoolwork.

It sounded like the leak came from the feds themselves, which was inter-esting. Was Agent Pierce the type to apply external pressure to support his investigation by leaking details to the press? Or was this Stitcher's doing? It probably was Stitcher, I decided. Pierce was such a straight shooter.

I turned the salmon over on the broiler and returned to the salad. Charlie and I had an agreement that he would dutifully eat what I made for dinner each night if he got a dessert. Well, actually if we both got a dessert. Why should I miss out?

Real estate agents say that location is most important when buying a home. But my realtor was surprised when I wanted to know the proximity to a farmer's market or an organic food store, in addition to good schools. I didn't care so much what was visible in my backyard.

Oak Ridge turned out to be the right place, because of the national lab and University of Tennessee nearby. Find where the other scientists live and you'll also find the organic food, good schools, decent wine selection, and the best internet service provider.

The carrots dinged in the microwave. Charlie adores cooked carrots in a small amount of brown sugar and butter. I put dinner on the table and was just about to call Charlie to eat when my cell phone rang. It was the ring tone I assigned Stitcher - a Jonathon Coulton song about zombies. I figured since he would never hear it ring, he'd never find out.

You'd think I'd answer his call in a hot second, but I just frowned and declined the call. Then I called Charlie over and we sat down to dinner. I texted Stitcher: I was eating, give me a half an hour. The phone chimed back with my sound effect for a Stitcher text: the sound of a screechy old door closing.

Charlie looked at me through his bangs. His hair was getting really long. What was it with teenage boys and trying to look like the early Beatles? "Isn't that your boss?" he asked.

"No, it's John Stitcher."

"Yeah, your real boss," Charlie said around a mouthful of carrots and a lopsided grin.

I looked at the text, which read: "More sharing is goddamn caring. Need you to meet an agricultural corp 'contact' in Tampa two days from now and take his samples to an 'analyst' in Atlanta." The text included a link to a series of airline tickets.

I looked up at Charlie. "I have another overnight trip coming up in a few days. Can you arrange to stay over at a friend's house again?"

"Okay," he said in an odd tone.

"What's wrong?"

"I can stay here by myself," Charlie said. "I don't think Aidan's mom wants me over. He says she doesn't like other people staying in her house."

I tried not to groan. This was the real friction in my life. Without another parent nearby, I couldn't leave Charlie by himself. At least, I didn't think I could just yet. I couldn't imagine him getting himself up in the morning in time to catch the bus. Or remembering to lock the front door. Or going to bed on time. Or brushing his teeth. If you think that sounds like the worries of a parent of a 9 year old, rather than the parent of a 14 year old, then you have never parented a 14 year old.

"Mom, I'm not twelve."

I checked the text. Stitcher already bought airline tickets and said he had a carefully-timed schedule worked out. And I seemed to be his only option to be a document mule. At least for the southeastern states and the Midwest.

"I don't know, kiddo."

"Then take me with you. I'll do my homework on the way there and back. I can get new assignments off the web."

A mom and son conspiracy team? I tried to envision that. Would I leave him on the jet doing homework while I played cloak and dagger? No way. How would I explain any of this to him in any coherent way? I couldn't. And I wanted him as far away as possible from all of this. I shook my head.

Charlie was looking at me, waiting for an answer. I realized that he wanted me to say no. He didn't want to go on a boring business trip. The little punk was trying to psych me into letting him stay at home by himself.

Was this the time where I threw it back at him and suggested that he figure this one out himself? One of those 'try to make an adult decision' exercises? Eh, that seemed like dodging my responsibility completely.

I threw up my hands. "I would have to be confident that you would go to bed on time and get up in time for school. And remember to lock the house when you leave. And brush your teeth."

He was nodding eagerly. Too eagerly.

"I'll call you at night, and in the morning, and when you're supposed to be home from school."

Charlie spread his hands. "I can do this, Mom. It's not a big deal. I'll be driving in less than two years. I can operate a door knob."

I pursed my lips and gave him a hard look. If he giggled even a little, it was not happening.

"Okay," I said.

"So, uh what flights are you taking?" he asked, trying to sound innocent.

I grinned. "None of your business. I could be coming and going at any time that day. *Any time.*"

"Uh-huh." He bounced up and down in his seat, pleased with himself. God help me.

[21]

I flew out to Tampa only after leaving Charlie a dozen voice mails on his cell phone about ordering pizza, going to bed on time, and taking the trash out.

This week's target was the new CEO of the largest snack and beverage company in North America. Stitcher arranged for a whistleblower in the company's headquarters to meet me inside a mausoleum at the cemetery of the historic Centro Asturiano de Tampa.

While a downpour roared outside, the woman, Vera Velasquez approached me and we pretended to mourn at a grave together. She passed me a thumb drive tucked inside a flower bouquet.

I never asked any of the whistleblowers why they did what they did. I tried not to face them but Vera insisted on meeting like this. And I could tell when she handed the flowers to me that she felt compelled to explain herself.

"I love my job, I am loyal to the company," she blurted.

I held up a hand. "It's okay. You don't have to explain."

That didn't stop her. She needed to empty her conscience. "But what they're doing is suicidal and immoral. I had to do something."

I nodded, patted her arm and walked away. I had two hours to kill before going to the airport and had a taxi take me to the nearest mall. It was never too early for a single mom to go Christmas shopping. With my carry-on bag filled with Pokemon paraphernalia, I boarded the flight to my 'analyst' meeting in Atlanta.

To kill time on the flight, and my own curiosity, I plugged the thumb drive into my laptop. There were hundreds of company emails from the COO discussing their false labeling of diet foods to mask their high calorie and saturated fat content. They went on at length about how to circumvent FDA rules and inspections.

The plan was to deliberately spike the fat, calorie, and sodium levels of their popular brands over time while taking a much more 'casual' approach to the accuracy of the food labeling. Sugar would be hidden in the ingredient list and numerous oversights and mistakes may happen in calculating calories and sodium levels.

Even more reprehensible was that they would boost the sugar, fat, and sodium the most on diet foods. Low calorie sodas and single-serving snack packs would have a calorie count right in the name, but a higher, unreported one in reality. They had run estimates on how much this would increase the profits as customers failed to lose weight. They figured that about half of customers would consume more and more overloaded 'diet' food, while the other half would give up and return to the even worse 'regular' food.

It's a good thing I didn't bring Charlie along. He would have wanted to know why I quietly bawled my eyes out on the descent into Atlanta.

It occurred to me that Stitcher could be setting up the new guys for continuing crimes that had been committed all along by his cronies. Every piece of damning evidence I had seen was forward-looking, which implied that none of these companies were doing these things *now*. None of it mentioned continuing a tradition of playing the public for ravenous fools. Maybe by exposing the conspiracy, we were all seeking absolution. Even Stitcher.

I fixed my makeup in the jet's bathroom and deplaned to a car waiting on the tarmac. Atlanta didn't have the swarming humidity of Florida, but it was still noticeably warmer than Knoxville.

I actually had a legitimate business meeting with some colleagues from the CDC. I was consulting on a joint NIH/CDC project to study the social networking aspects of obesity prevalence. It was being funded out of the Healthy Communities Study as part of NCCOR, or the National Collaborative on Childhood Obesity Research.

This particular dropoff I wanted to make myself. I needed to win back some respect from folks in the government who thought I now played a corporate shill on TV. And Stitcher let me choose who to hand it off to. The less he knew, the better, he said.

My old friend Jim Knox was down here for the same meeting, representing my old shop, the USDA's Agricultural Research Service. Originally, I was just going to call in, but I saw a way to kill two birds with one stone by showing up in person.

The meeting was at Emory University's conference center, pretty much right across the street from the CDC complex. I cleared security at the CDC's main complex and was directed to a conference center on their campus. I picked up my name tag and spotted Jim in the hallway.

He greeted me with his usual hearty handshake, but I could tell he felt uncomfortable. He did this thing where he looked at your shoes when he couldn't stand you. His bald spot on the back of his head was getting worse, I noticed.

"Jim, I need to talk to you after this is over," I said.

He raised a bushy eyebrow, but didn't have time to reply because the meeting started. The project involved a behavioral psychologist from UCSD had split up the most overweight kids in a grade to see if breaking up the fat clot, as they inartfully called it, would provide enough social pressure for each overweight kid to lose weight to fit in with their peers.

Part of the problem, it shouldn't surprise you, was that all the kids were becoming larger anyway, so it was hard to tease out whether the social engineering worked or not. The study showed a barely significant drop in BMI for the largest kids.

When the meeting broke up, Jim and I went to a coffee shop on the Emory campus. It was a student-run cooperative that used fair trade beans and the place smelled as delicious as warm apple pie feels on your tongue. When we sat down with our coffees, I focused on the small, black coffee that I cupped with both hands. "I know you think I have gone over to the dark side," I said. "I keep telling you that's not true, and now I'm going to prove it."

Jim leaned back like he thought I was capable of doing something crazy. "Okay."

"Remember the old days, when I was bent on getting the word on the streets about obesity? That anti-obesity task force in communications?"

"Yes, you were miserable then," Jim said with a grimace.

"That was for other reasons," I replied. "I broke open that Fiesta scandal, right?"

Jim nodded sadly. He was on the verge of comparing my former yearning for justice with my current occupation.

I slid the flash drive over to him. "This is a thousand times bigger."

"What's on this?"

I told him about the revelations, the scandal, the proof contained in the drive's files. I concluded by saying, "It makes the Fiesta scandal seem like small potatoes." Pun intended.

"I'll say. Aren't you biting the hands that feed you?" Jim asked.

Suddenly, I wished there were a bowl of peanuts or crackers so I could munch on them nervously. I hadn't expected that question.

I swallowed. "This is so much worse than Fiesta. The industry has become much worse. These new company execs only care about share price gains and beating quarterly earnings expectations. That's it. They kind of bought into the conspiracy theories floating around."

Jim sighed and looked out the window. "This will cause a big damn firestorm," he said, shaking the drive like it was a sharp knife. "They'll want to know how I got it. And from whom."

"Don't tell them the truth or they really won't believe you," I retorted, followed by a snicker.

"I'm serious. It doesn't take a lot of dots to connect me to you, you know," Jim said. "And quiet handoffs like this is how we got the FDA the evidence in the Fiesta scandal, remember?"

I nodded. "And that evidence was legit. So is this." Stitcher had to know that. What Jim didn't know was that this was all a setup. We were betting that the Fiesta evidence appearing in Jim's hands five years ago would make it easier for the government to believe the validity of this new stuff.

Jim looked at the flash drive skeptically. "I don't suppose I could talk to the whistleblower? Just to verify things?"

I shook my head. "Whistleblower wants to keep a low profile."

"And you are just sticking a knife in your funders' backs?"

I folded my arms. "Jim, I've always been committed to beating the obesity epidemic. If some frat boy asshats in a C-suite want to do the opposite to such an extreme that the company's *own employees* are blowing the whistle, I'm doing the right thing."

Jim slipped the flash drive into his pocket. "Fair enough."

"I've got a flight back home I have to catch. Charlie is holding down the fort, but I don't like letting it go on too long."

Jim cracked a grin as we stood up and hugged. "You're a braver parent than most."

"Or stupider." I grabbed my handbag and left.

[22]

Alex Robie buttoned his shirt, standing at the hotel room window, watching the Knoxville rush hour start to build. The sun kissed the horizon and the city was bathed in an orange light. I liked watching his back muscles ripple under his shirt as he put his tie on.

Is it wrong to sleep with someone who is kind of your boss' bosses? I'm a scientist, he's a corporate CEO. It just didn't seem wrong to me.

"When are you headed back?" I asked. I did this thing where I lounged around naked while he got dressed. I knew it made him happy and teased him all at once.

"Tonight," he said. "I have a small crisis I'm dealing with."

Screw the nudity, I was cold. I slid off the bed and pulled my panties on. I had spent most of the day working in the lab, and so wore jeans and a turtleneck.

Alex frowned when he saw I was getting dressed.

"Rough days to be a CEO in the industry, huh?" I said as I pulled my socks on.

Alex walked over to the mirror to adjust his tie. "Other companies have whistleblowers and disgruntled people making all kinds of claims. We're trying to lock things down before we're hit next."

The royal we. It's how CEOs talked about their companies. Something I wasn't used to yet. And then what he said hit me and I dropped my cross trainer. I could end up framing Alex. Was he on Stitcher's list? Did Stitcher have incriminating evidence on him? But for that to happen, Alex would need to have done something really obnoxious, like the others.

Of course he hadn't, I told myself. He couldn't be like the other CEOs. He was nice and giving and not skeazy and he slept with me so he would not hide things from me.

Ugh, that was loaded with personal bias and wishful thinking. For Alex to be one of the good guys, he would have to know about Project Rogers and be willing to do without the cash flow from exploiting it. He would have opposed closing down the lab.

"You look worried," Alex said.

I picked up my shoe. All of the sudden, I had to know if he was a good guy or not. But I couldn't just straight out ask him. "Yeah, I can't help worrying about how these industry scandals will affect Project Rogers."

He frowned.

I brushed my hair and watched in the mirror as he put his pants on. "Sorry. But I've seen this before, in the government. People get burned once and they crouch in a corner and let things go from bad to worse."

Alex didn't say anything for a moment. "Priorities change, Elaine. I'm getting a lot of pressure to cut expenses, like charitable giving and research and development. And Project Rogers, and the lab, well, they are more charity than R&D, aren't they?"

I put my brush down and looked at him. He was cringing. "You know what we're trying to stop."

He brushed his hair back with his fingers and of course it fell right into place. Men. "Yes I do. But the odds that AgSol will singlehandedly stop environmental damage is slim. It's been years since your scientists have produced something that the industry could profit from. That's hard to swallow when I have to lay off workers who are turning a profit."

"So you're going to vote to close the lab, aren't you?"

He nodded. "I don't want to, but it's the right decision."

Alex wasn't one of the good guys. There was a bunch of nasty words rolling around my mouth, but I kept my jaws clamped shut and settled for crossing my arms.

"Hey, what can I do to make this easier? We can reduce the funding gradually, and I'll help you replace it from other sources. I know how important the work is, I just can't justify investing shareholder dollars in it."

"The problems are getting worse, Alex, and *now* you pull our funding?"

"It's not that simple. I have a board of directors, a CFO and COO all watching every decision I make. I can't make special exceptions because of this," he waved at the tousled bed sheets.

"I am not asking you to," I said. "I want you to keep doing what your company has been doing for decades before we met, because your company's strategic plan assumes that there will be a habitable planet for it to operate on for the next century."

He shook his head. "I can do the right thing, lose my job, and not have it stick. Or keep my job and do what I can for Project Rogers. And I have an idea on how to do that. Something that would let you carry on the work without the lab."

Did that make him a good guy?

As we finished dressing, he explained his idea. At first I didn't want to hear it, but the more he said, the more sense it made. By the time he said goodbye I was intrigued.

He gave me a peck on the cheek as he left. The kiss felt awkward, like one you would give your grandmother. Were we a couple now? Romantically involved? Caring for one another? Helping each other professionally? Or was this just his way of apologizing? Or breaking up?

Could I let myself develop feelings for him when I may have to help ruin him? Or he might ruin me? And could I stop those feelings if I wanted to? Hell no. I think I was falling in love with him. Sometimes it sucks to be honest with yourself.

[23]

Despite the darkness outside, everyone was still at the lab to get a grant application ready to send out first thing tomorrow. We were out of practice in scrambling for money, and Betty and I had resolved to keep the lab going after outside funding until Stitcher could work his magic on our reluctant corporate funders.

Stitcher gave me a text heads-up about what he was about to call me about. I had no trouble talking about Project Rogers or the conspiracy in my office, but this particular topic wasn't suited to it. I left the building, stepping into the quiet parking lot like one of those furtive smokers who pretends to want to admire the great outdoors.

"You are not going to leave AgSol." Stitcher's voice sounded distant and weak. "No motherfucking way."

I strode the length of a parking spot and turned around. "I may have a soft landing that may be too good to pass up."

"And what the flying fucking hell would that soft landing be?"

I had to be evasive here. Alex had suggested that I land an assistant professorship at a university, endowed by his company, combined with science consulting for the government, industry, and academia. He had put me in touch with his favorite headhunting firm already. "A position that would let me continue the Project Rogers work. It's not as good as the lab,

120

but it's better than going back to the government or working for a truly corporate lab."

"The goddamn lab is not going anywhere."

"You don't have a backup plan in case the lab bites the big one, do you John? And I need to get Charlie through college." For some reason, I felt more confident talking on my feet. I reached the end of the white parking lot and did an about face.

"As a matter of fact, no, I fucking don't," Stitcher replied with a tinge of sadness.

I stepped on the grass and watched fog roll down the forested hill. "We can't do this without money, John. If we don't find it and word gets out, there will be a stampede among the staff."

"Fuckity fuck a duck's ass," Stitcher rattled off. "Okay, another goddamn problem to throw on my heap. Thanks." He stopped for a full two seconds. "Are you boning Alex Robie, CEO and member of our fucking board? Sweet cock-sucking Christ, Elaine."

I didn't say anything. What was I going to say? That it was none of his business that I was having a fling with one of his bosses? Lying about it didn't make sense. "How do you know?" An old fear made the hairs on my neck stand up. Was Alex bragging about banging me like an immature high school jock?

"I'm very perceptive. Fucking Robie, I should have known. I hope you're using protection because that asshole's cock has seen the inside of more labia than a speculum in use since the motherfucking Civil War."

I rolled my eyes. "Not that this is any of your business, but who's to say I haven't had as many partners?"

"Ha. Because I know C-suite types. They celebrate every bank holiday by having a go with three hookers in Miami. And despite you two making moon eyes, Robie is still not on our side!"

"He's under pressure from shareholders to cut off the lab's funding," I replied.

"Yeah, yeah, I know. Everyone is. We've got to take down these CEOs and punks just to take off that pressure. Crap on a corndog, he's try to give you a soft landing because he's decided to pull the funding and he doesn't want to hurt you. Fuck me. I don't know what to do about this one."

"Are you going to take him down?" The idea sounded nuts to me. Isn't

121

this what always happens to conspiracies and secret organizations? The infighting does them in eventually. I should have thought about that before leaving USDA.

"Would that bother you? He is your boyfriend, after all."

I closed my eyes and lied. "It's, it's not like that."

"Thank the fucking Lord." Stitcher breathed a sigh of relief. "Because you're going to be the one to take him down."

"I'm what?" My voice echoed in the woods.

"I thought you said this wasn't emotional," Stitcher teased. When I didn't say anything he continued, "You not only have to take him down, but you have to figure out how. No one else is better positioned to get dirt on him. We don't have a whistleblower in his case. His company hasn't signed up for the 'squeeze dollars from fat' trick."

Stitcher wanted me to be the femme fatale. A middle-aged honey pot. It was salacious and powerful but it also made me nauseous. "Listen to yourself. Now you've decided to take down members of the Board? Who are you to do that?" From everything I had seen, Stitcher answered to the Board, not the other way around.

"I'm the lucky fuck who is trying to keep the world from ending in some environmental meltdown, while the rest of you are busy goddamn boinking each other or slurping down all the single malt Scotch in North America."

I wanted to ask who the big Scotch drinker was but he was on a roll and the moment passed. Besides, my bare ankles felt cold with the fog creeping across the ground. I wanted this call over with and to get back in to my warm office.

"Elaine, are you with me or with your cabana boy toy? Adventure or romance? I can't offer both; I don't have enough spare fluid in me for an erection."

"Well, when you put it like that..."

"Stop thinking with your ditch, Dr. Cassano. I need you with me. I can't do this by myself. I don't have time to cultivate a whistleblower in his company who is close enough to him to have a shot at finding a smoking gun."

"What do you want me to do, slip him a sleeping pill and rifle through his briefcase?" I asked.

"I could think of a whole fuck-ton worse."

I sighed. "This isn't 1985. He has a laptop that is password protected. I also don't know how to do email phishing or social engineering. I am not a hacker."

"Well, I'm shit out of options. All I can think of is pillow talk then. Old fashioned Pussy Galore shit."

"Look, would you at least take a second to see if Alex really is a problem? If he pulls the funding but tries to make it up to us, that's not the same thing as these guys trying to shut us down. Go talk to him. He doesn't want the lab to fail," I said.

"Goddamn it, you're sweet on this guy, aren't you? Take it from me, better dead than wed."

I headed back to the lab's front door. Something was creeping me out about being in a dark parking lot. "Yes, I was trying to not wreck every facet of my life all in the same month. Thanks a lot for not letting me, John."

"Any time. Gotta jump." He hung up.

[24]

It was parent teacher conference time, and being a single parent, I always make time to talk with all of Charlie's teachers whether it's needed or not. So when his gym teacher emailed asking me to meet with her, I was surprised. Since when do gym teachers hold parent-teacher conferences? In high school? Maybe southern schools were more into sports than I thought.

Even stranger was that this parent teacher conference was she wanted to meet me in the school psychologist's office. Had Charlie been throwing the dodgeball too violently? I mean, this is Tennessee, where football is sacrosanct. Maybe gym class had become a little too aggressive? Was there an incident in the locker room? Why hadn't Charlie said anything to me?

After making the usual rounds of his academic teachers I found the psychologist's office with five minutes to spare. There were a dozen parents milling around outside the door. Most of them were locals, judging by the accent. Not one of us knew why they were meeting with the psychologist and the gym teacher. The psychologist called my name eventually and I passed an unhappy-looking father on his way out of the office.

Inside were three women of varying ages. The one in the track suit was the gym teacher, the one in the pantsuit was the psychologist, and the woman in the lab coat was the school district's dietician.

We all took seats around a small circular coffee table.

"Charlie has been identified as being at-risk for becoming obese," the gym teacher said. She stopped because I made a face.

Okay, Charlie had chubbed out a bunch initially when we moved down here. He loved the local barbecue and now that he had hit puberty, his body was doing any number of odd things. Had he become overweight since his last physical? I didn't know, but he could have been. He was gearing up for a growth spurt, I had told myself for, well, since last spring. Shit.

I cocked my head. "What's his BMI?"

Tina, the perky gym teacher, looked inside a folder. "23. For a 14 year old boy, technically, that makes him overweight."

I wanted to retort that it was just by a hair. And going from a little overweight to obese was no mean trick. I folded my hands in my lap. "Okay."

"The state wants us to intervene early to deal with childhood obesity. The purpose of this meeting is to inform you and to work out how we can address this together." The psychologist slid a notice across the table. It was from the state.

Together. As in, you are failing as a parent so we need to step in and help out.

The notice mentioned all the downsides of early onset obesity. Lifelong weight problems, Type II diabetes, kidney problems, higher risk of heart disease, cancer, dementia, joint problems.

I could have written this. Oh, the irony. "I can assure you that the last thing in the world I want for Charlie is for him to be obese," I said. "He and I have fought about food and activity since he was a little kid."

The gym teacher asked, "Does Charlie play sports, or do anything physically active?"

Other than shuffling a Pokemon deck, no. I shook my head. "I tried to get him interested in swimming, soccer, and running. He's just not into sports."

"Is his father around?" asked the gym teacher. Perky little minx in a track suit rocking a purity ring. Probably a virgin.

Do I mention that his dad is a morbidly obese lobbyist for the food industry? That Charlie was the product of a one-night stand and I had nothing in common with the guy other than being at the same conference once?

I gave her a dead-eye stare. "He lives in Washington, DC. And if he was here, Charlie would be more than just at-risk for obesity. His father was careless about food and nutrition."

The dietician smiled and nodded. "Oh, I understand. And now that Charlie is a teenager, there's only so much you can do, right? You should see the fights I have with my girls about food, and being a dietician doesn't help me one bit."

I smiled. She understood me more than she realized.

"Is there anything that you think may be contributing to Charlie's weight problem that we need to address in the school environment?" The psychologist asked.

"Look, he has stress, but nothing above average. He doesn't eat for comfort. No mental illnesses or stresses like bullying that could trigger overeating. I don't think he's sneaking food or has a food fixation."

The psychologist nodded slowly, not believing a single word I said.

"I'm pretty strict on nutrition. I shop at organic food stores, we have home-cooked dinners almost every night. Heavy on fruits and vegetables, limit the sugar and grains, no sugary beverages or junk food in the house." I looked at the gym teacher. "But as far as things in the school environment, he does buy lunch every day, and probably hits those vending machines you have in the hallway. Are there calorie counts posted for all the food items here at school so kids can see them before they buy?"

The school had three national fast food chains in the food court. The vending machines were loaded with candy, cookies, and soda.

I let the pause hang there. "But there's not much any of us can do about that, is there?"

The psychologist fidgeted in her chair. "We can certainly work on those things on our end. Our annual assembly on healthy living is in two weeks. Today we want to kick things off by talking to parents first. With parents like you, as soon as they hear about their child's weight they take action. But let us know if we can help you any further." She handed me a page of contact information and I got the clear signal my time was up.

I left the office feeling like I was picking up my kid after he was suspended for some heinous infraction, like pantsing the principal.

The other parents out there looked at me expectantly, hoping for a clue about what awaited them, but I simply hurried by with my head down. Obesity expert gets chewed out at school for having fat kid, news at eleven.

I hurried through the parking lot as dark clouds dropped fat drops on the pavement. By the time I reached my minivan, it was pouring. I shut the door and then the storm pounded on the hood.

I took one deep breath, and then two, and looked for people nearby. The coast was clear. So I sat back and let the tears and snuffling take over for the next ten minutes.

[25]

In the movies, congressional hearings always happen in grand hearing rooms that are Gilded Age-ornate, with tall windows that poured daylight on richly dark, wooden tables. The walls were always cream-colored, or covered in expensive wood or curtains. Reality is much different, I found, when I walked into the hearing room I was set to testify in.

The House Energy and Commerce Committee hearing room had giant, green walls that reminded me of the felt on a pool table. The dais was made of dark, rich wood that stretched upward almost two stories. It felt like the library of an upscale hunting lodge more than the Palace of Versailles.

I was on the third panel of a Health subcommittee hearing on the obesity epidemic. The FDA Commissioner testified on the first panel, by herself as is done for Administration witnesses. She had been very measured and balanced about the extent of the epidemic and the Administration's efforts to combat it. She had refused to comment about ongoing investigations into the food industry deliberately fattening up the population for profits.

That was left to the second panel to address. That panel consisted entirely of corporate CEOs from the food industry. You may have seen this part of the hearing on TV, so I won't recount very much of it. I was sitting in the audience, next to Ma, waiting for my turn on the third witness panel.

Honestly, I didn't hear much of what went on during the second panel. I was reviewing my notes, skimming my statement, and flipping through index cards that had my practice questions and answers. I noticed that the FDA Commissioner had left with a giant binder under her arm, and I wished I had thought of that. All I had was Ma dropping my papers all over. She was more nervous than I was.

The second panel involved a billion flashes lighting up the room from dozens of cameras as each CEO raised his hand and promised to tell the truth. There were incensed statements sputtered by the chairman and other Congressmen.

Needless to say, some of the witnesses' voices were the same voices in the dark I recognized from my first meeting with the lab's board. Alex was among their number, and every time he spoke, I put my notes down and paid close attention.

An overweight Congresswoman with a puffy cloud of white hair read her questions from a piece of paper. "Mr. Robie, your industry has perpetrated one of the most damaging attacks against the American public. Your products are specifically geared to cause people to gain weight and avoid healthy food, in addition to releasing occasional murderous rages. I would love to hear you convince me that I'm wrong."

Alex gave them his megawatt smile. "Congresswoman, I want to thank you for having me here today. It's easy to demonize an industry, or a corporation. I could tell you about all the good work my company and its competition does to improve the well-being of all Americans. But I won't. I could tell you that cracking down on my industry will only hurt the people you are trying to help by raising food prices and causing countless family farms to close. But the other witnesses have done that already.

He leaned into the microphone. "I'll tell you something original, the truth. The food industry fell into fueling the obesity epidemic accidentally. My predecessors were enticed by the promise of a slightly bigger profit if we added a little more sugar. Or salt. Or fat. Or a bigger portion size than last year. Over time, the food we sell has become enormously appealing. We're trying to undo that now, and we're asking for your help."

"Our help?" the Congresswoman looked up from her notes. "Did I hear you correctly?"

Alex nodded. "Yes ma'am. We lose money if our customers die before their time. Our biggest area of sales growth is organic foods. We realize we went too far. That is why we work with FDA and NIH to combat the obesity epidemic. We have been investing in health and obesity research. Not just because we care about people's health, but also because it's a good business decision."

"That sounds all well and good, Mr. Robie. But this Committee has a hard time believing that you and your fellow CEOs accidentally fell into making food more unhealthy as a way to increase your profits. Tell us please, how this all happened accidentally, and how it wasn't a cold, calculated decision."

Alex replied, "It's simple, really. We keep close tabs on consumer preferences for price, taste, color, texture, preparation time and yes, portion size. We react to what people want, not the other way around."

He was good. The chairwoman looked annoyed, probably because Alex's company had no whistleblower problems. She shuffled some papers and thanked him for his answer. The grilling moved on tot the next CEO and continued for over an hour. The Committee had the internal memos and other documents that Stitcher's whistleblowers had passed along to the FBI through me.

Every CEO made solemn promises to look into these disturbing matters which, in some cases, the documents noted they were in charge of. There was a lot of failure to recall and claims of innocence.

For the third panel, I was testifying alongside a pediatrician and health advocate, Dr. Darien Farrior, who kept giving me dirty looks as we settled in at the witness table. When the CEOs hurried out of the room, they drew away most of the reporters, cameras, and circus atmosphere. Only the subcommittee chair and a member of the minority stuck around for us.

The chairwoman gaveled the hearing back to order, leaned toward her microphone and said, "The third panel of this hearing will address what science and health experts can tell us about the obesity epidemic." She introduced me as a biologist and Dr. Darien Farrior as a pediatrician who worked with a non-profit that dispensed free care to inner city children.

After each of us summarized our statements, the real fun began: questioning. The chairwoman thanked us for being there and made a rambling statement about the importance of the scientific research we did and how we helped save lives. She consumed her time with her statement, and then it was the ranking member's turn.

The ranking member, a white-haired man with a walrus mustache, made a similar statement and then dove into questions. "Dr. Cassano, you are the Chief Scientist at Agriculture Solutions," he stated. "It is a private research lab that has been doing health and diet research for a long time. Could you explain to the committee who funds your lab's work?"

"Gladly," I replied. Here is where I had to step into the trap. "We are funded mainly by the food processing and agricultural industries. We work closely with experts in the industry, health advocates, and government experts on improving food safety, studying the obesity epidemic, as well as a range of research into environmental areas that they are interested in."

The ranking member looked me straight in the eye. "Now you heard what happened in the last panel. Some of your funders have all but admitted that they have been deliberately planning to make people as obese as possible. So tell me, Dr. Cassano, why do you think that they fund you to do the opposite? Aren't you a public relations stunt to make the industry look good?"

I shook my head. "No sir. I think they fund me because they are genuinely concerned with the health of their families and communities. My lab had nothing to do with making the public more obese to boost profits." Which was entirely true from a technical standpoint. But it was hard to spit out Stitcher's lame-ass statement verbatim.

"Dr. Farrior, what do you think about these industry-backed labs such as this one?"

Dr. Farrior pursed her lips and bent the microphone closer. "Agriculture Solutions is an industry front, a showpiece. With all due respect to Dr. Cassano, her lab's backers undermine the credibility of any research her lab produces. The truth is, these companies poison our food with dangerous additives. And then they toss a fig leaf over it all by throwing pennies at phony labs that do good works."

The ranking member nodded at me. "Dr. Cassano, your response?"

I sat up taller. "I have a reputation for being too honest, to the point of hurting my career. I have been a whistleblower in my own career. If anyone in the industry ever tried to have us twist our work to make a corporate talking point, I would resign and make a loud exit."

131

The ranking member squinted at me over his walrus mustache. "Has the industry ever tried to change your lab's results, edited publications, or otherwise influenced you?"

I shook my head vigorously. "The industry has never interfered with us."

"But your lab was involved in the development of the additive that poisoned those Fiesta chips, which lead to several deaths a few years back. I know you weren't there then, but I want you to address what that means for the role your lab has played in making America obese."

"I was working for the Agriculture Department at the time. I can't speak for what the lab's involvement was with the Fiesta chips. But I can tell you that I delivered the initial Fiesta samples to the government for testing. I have made several career-limiting moves because I blew the whistle on illegal or immoral practices. I helped bring those behind the additive to justice. I wouldn't have joined the lab shortly after if I thought they had an ongoing role in the kind of things that you have accused the industry of today. In fact, when I was hired, I was told that I could pursue quality research into stopping the obesity epidemic. And we have."

"Would you be opposed then to talking with government investigators about your lab's work with the food industry?"

There was the trap for Agent Pierce, neatly laid out. Last week, the minority subcommittee staff who had invited me to testify let me know that because of records they possessed, they were requesting that the FBI take a closer look at my lab. This was Stitcher's misdirection plot unfolding, but it made my insides turn to liquid.

I smiled. "Of course not. We would welcome the opportunity to clear our name. I was brought in to make sure nothing like the Fiesta scandal ever happened again. Our scientists did conduct the initial work on how to manipulate brain chemistry. Our lab no longer engages in food development research. We have refocused on basic and applied research. We publish our work in peer-reviewed journals and conferences without interference from our financial backers. Our research is in the public arena and I would be happy for you or anyone else to scrutinize it."

The clock in the hearing room began to chime and flashed an orange light. All the congressmen looked at it and then looked at one another. They had a vote on the House floor across Independence Avenue.

The ranking member nodded and turned to the chair. "That's all the questions I have. Thank you, Madam Chairman, for having this hearing today. Thank you to all of the witnesses. I have found this discussion very productive and useful."

The chairwoman began gathering up her papers. "Thank you both for coming to talk to us today about this very important issue. Let's move to closing statements."

I'll spare you the slow torrent of meaningless words that followed.

[26]

With the hearing over, and it being long past lunch time, Ma and I went off to eat and decompress at a noisy Tex-Mex place behind the House office buildings. For the first congressional hearing either of us had ever seen, it was both exciting and boring. But more importantly, it was over. I felt like I had just passed my dissertation defense all over again.

We munched silently through our refritas and chimichangas. I felt talked out and Ma always gets quiet when she's really proud of me. She just sneaks stares at me.

"Ma, you're doing it again."

Ma dabbed her chin. "What?"

"Looking at me like a puppy dog."

She waved me off. "Oh shut up and let me enjoy the moment. It wasn't that long ago that you were stuck in a cubicle, thinking your career was over. Remember? And now, you had Congress hanging on your every word."

Ironically, everything turned around for me when I stopped blurting the truth, as I saw it, to the wrong people at the wrong time. And Ma was right, people did want to hear me. Whether it was because of anything I said or just because I was part of some chess game I didn't fully understand was another story.

I shoveled refritas into a grin and started feeling good. Really good.

Ma caught my grin and beamed back at me. "Why don't we take the rest of the day off? We'll go see a museum or something."

I frowned. "I have to prepare for a reception tonight. Hob-nob with politicians and watch our lobbyists shower them with money. I didn't get to choose my schedule for this trip."

"Are you trying to make it sound like you're not ditching your poor old mother?"

"The next time I'm up here in DC. This is a boring work trip from beginning to end. I had to duck out of a lunch with the other witnesses from the industry." Which may have cost me some networking points, but Ma took off work in Silver Spring to come down to see me, and that was at least worth having lunch with her.

I walked her to the Capital South Metro station. She turned to hug me, her SmarTrip card in her hand. "I wish your father was here to see this. He should have been. He would tell you that this is a resume moment. Enjoy it, because it may not come again."

She had never gotten over my father's illness and early death. She held it against the universe, and possibly even God. I hugged her hard. "I wish I pulled Charlie out of school for this. Life's that way though." I looked at her. "I'm just happy you could come see it. It meant a lot to me."

She ran her hand through my curls, something she had done since I was a preschooler who absolutely hated her frizzy hair. "I love you, daughter."

"I love you, Ma." I watched her walk to the escalator and then texted my driver. I went back to the hotel and changed into the hotel bathrobe. I needed some time out of the monkey suit, especially since I would be back in it later today.

I reviewed the talking points that Betty and Stitcher gave me for this political fundraiser. I was the substance person to showcase all the good efforts the food industry was making on health issues. This fundraiser would be as much a performance as testifying to Congress. But this was to rebuild some Congressional goodwill towards our besieged industry. And at this moment, anything I could do for the industry, within reason, of course, could help keep the lab alive. If I impressed any congressmen or lobbyists along the way, I got extra credit or something.

I practiced my talking points aloud, a trick I had learned in graduate school. You could read notes over in your head a thousand times and still

135

have your tongue knot up when you spoke them the first ten times. Best to get those ten times out of the way through practice. Then it was back in the monkey suit and downstairs to the car.

The fundraiser was in a classy old restaurant of brass fixtures and wood paneling a few blocks from the White House. DC is one of those cities that I never have a sense of where I am when I step out of a car or come up from the Metro. I always need to see a street sign to place myself on the map in my head.

They actually checked names at the door and it was equal parts thrilling and depressing to have them find my name right away. I swept into the ballroom where the reception was just getting started and had that brief disturbing sensation that I didn't know anyone in the room.

First things first: I obtained a glass of white wine. Open bar. It must make the money flow faster.

A U.S. senator on the short list for a cabinet position was behind me telling a story about a hunting trip. His attentive audience was a half-dozen blond lobbyists half his age. They looked like they were formerly of the cheerleader persuasion, most likely at southern colleges where not a single hair was left out of place or a facial blemish tolerated. I looked like an ogre near them.

The Chairman and the ranking member of the health subcommittee were there too. They were talking amiably together, which was ironic since they were on opposites of the aisle and everyone supposedly hated everyone in the other party. They were both here to scare up checks for their respective campaigns and parties, shouldn't they be undercutting each other? But since it was the lobbyists throwing the reception, maybe they set aside party in a desperate scramble for corporate cash.

I shook their hands. "Elaine Cassano, I testified on the third panel at the hearing today."

"Of course, Doctor, it is good to see you," the Chairwoman shook my hand. Off the dais, she looked more like a blue collar grandmother than a sharp-tongued legislator. "Thank you for speaking today."

The ranking member, who had treated me like a hostile witness, smiled just as warmly. "You did a great job."

"I don't have any money to donate," I said. "So you can tell me how bad I was."

"Nonsense sweetie, you did fine." The Chairwoman elbowed her colleague. "No money here, Ira, let's go."

"Haha, no, I really meant it." The ranking member's walrus mustache twitched into a smile. "My staff learned a lot preparing for this hearing. We pushed you hard, but it's because we can't mess around."

I nodded appreciatively and remembered my talking points. "I was hoping that the hearing could take some of the FBI pressure off of the food companies. Some of those CEOs didn't sound like they were deliberately fattening up the public."

"I'll see what I can do." The Chairwoman held up a hand. "We can't interfere with a real criminal investigation, of course, but if there is a fishing expedition underway, a few phone calls may curtail it."

Translation: I'll see how much hot water you're in before deciding to stick my neck out. Which actually was fine, apparently, because Stitcher could probably pull the strings so the Chairwoman didn't have any neck exposed if she did do something.

"That would be great," I said. "As you know, I've been on the other side when the industry misbehaves. But there's a clear difference between gathering evidence of a crime that's happened and looking for a crime long past the point where it's clear nothing has happened."

"In this town, we call that playing politics or we call it transparency, depending on who's investigating." The Ranking Member chuckled. "Now I have to be off, but you let me know if you find that cure for obesity, okay?"

I raised my glass. "I will see what I can do."

He smiled in a way that looked like he was gritting his teeth and moved off.

The Chairwoman asked me where I was from, about spouses, children, and where my mother lived, who I had given a shout-out to when she introduced me. I rattled it all off and she paid close attention, like she was studying for a test. I couldn't help feeling flattered. She was a real pro.

I didn't know what she was angling at. She was a genial grandmotherly type. Maybe she was just a politician working the room?

"It was great to see you outside the hearing, Elaine. I have some people I need to go beg for money so I can keep my chairmanship," she said with a gentle smile. "You give your mother my best and tell Charlie to give his poor mother a break or I'll have to call him."

137

Ah, she was the type who had a mental contact list filled with personal details of the people she met. She probably knew the ages of every kid of every parent in her district. Politicians.

I turned around and saw Alex. He raised a glass and walked over. "Elaine, you look stunning."

"I wore this to the hearing earlier," I said.

"You looked stunning then too." He didn't miss a beat. "Oh, I don't want that to sound wrong. You're too cerebral for me. I like dumber women."

"You're intimidated by smart women who speak up?"

"Terrified. Can't have them in my company. If you ever see a company fall apart, there's usually some smart woman there who saw all the trouble. She tried to warn everyone but no one listened. So *annoying*."

"Dumb women wouldn't pick up on your finely-honed sarcasm."

"That just makes it funnier," he plucked a bacon-wrapped scallop off a tray as a waiter passed by. His lack of a gut and jowls for a man his age suggested that he didn't eat bacon very often.

He sipped the amber liquid in his glass. "I'm surprised to see you here tonight. The usual suspects are the only ones who come to these things."

I looked around. It looked like a hard-working crowd of bankers and lawyers were gathering for happy hour. But a good chunk of the crowd was probably billing by the hour to drink free booze and eat fancy finger food.

"So this is where it all happens, huh?" I said, smiling at him. "The lobbying, the deal-making, the connections, the influence, and the access."

Alex laughed, flashing his perfectly veneered-teeth. "No, no. That all happens on the golf course and smoke-filled back rooms." He winked at me. "I already agreed to give a summer internship to the daughter of a Senator's chief of staff."

"In return for what?"

"I get a discount on renting one of the Navy's aircraft carriers for company retreats."

I laughed.

"If you'll take my arm, I'll introduce to some of the high rollers you should meet since you're here."

I accepted his arm. "Is this just a thin excuse for you to steal more time with me?"

"Would I do that?" He grew serious. "No, I want you to meet some people. And yes, it is a thin excuse."

He guided me to a group of eight elderly and middle-aged people talking in a group. A series of faces and names blurred by in rapid fire introductions. Some had European accents, some were American, but nearly all were old men. All of them dripped wealth and corporate power from their power pantsuits and tailored suits. CEO of this, CFO of that, sitting on boards of directors here there and everywhere.

Was he trying to impress me with all of his rich and powerful friends? Or was he simply trying to juice more money out of these folks for my lab?

I didn't figure it out until I was shaking the small, bony hand of a woman named Alice who had to be in her late 70s. Alex rattled off a number of corporate boards that Alice sat on, including his own company.

Alice smiled graciously, but her ragged, quavering voice jarred me. "Nice to meet you, Dr. I have heard a lot about you." She sounded like she had smoked seven packs a day her entire life.

And I knew that voice. I had heard it in the darkened conference room of a bank in Memphis. "Um, have we met before?" I regretted blurting that the second I said it.

"Oh, I don't think we have." She smiled. "We may have rubbed elbows at some function or another."

"Ah, yes, that must be it."

Then I looked around realized that I was standing there chit-chatting with the lab's board of directors.

Alex shrugged helplessly. "I thought it was time for Elaine to see who funds her petri dishes and microscopes."

"It's about time," said Christian, the executive with the French accent.

"You did really well today," said the gruff voice, which belonged to Luke Mars, a man with big puffy silver hair. "C-SPAN broadcast the hearing online. You will get some press attention from this."

"Our friend John will be pleased." I looked around. "I'm surprised he doesn't come to these things."

"Ah," Christian waved his hand, "he hates these events very much. He avoids K Street as much as possible."

"We look forward to working with you, Dr. Cassano." Every time Alice

139

spoke I felt like she was giving me orders, even with a polite smile attached. And now she was dismissing me.

I dipped my head. "My pleasure. It was good to see you." I moved on and mingled with people for a good half an hour. I actually got to see a lobbyist in a pin-striped suit hand a check to a congressman. The congressman acted like he just received a life-saving blood transfusion.

"You don't want to see this," Alex said from behind me. "Let's get out of here."

"I'm staying at the Westin," I said. "Let's get a drink at the bar there."

He grinned like a kid who was surprised to learn it was his birthday.

[27]

When I saw the number on my phone, I hurried out of the lab before answering. A cold rain pelted me.

"Motherfucker dove in," Stitcher announced. Caller ID had wrecked certain rules of etiquette, I guess, because you already knew who the caller was.

"What are you talking about?"

"Vernon Pierce, FBI pain in the ass. He raided our fucking West Coast cheese factory."

Shit, shit, shit. That factory supplied the special food that thousands of hybrids needed to survive: cheese sticks, yogurt, and cheese slices, all fortified with human fat. We didn't have alternatives or even a stockpile to tide us over. Production could barely keep up with demand before this happened. "Is it offline now?"

"For now. They had to fucking toss their ingredients when they saw Pierce coming. May take them a week to get back up to full production. A couple thousand hybrids will be fucking dieting for the next year."

"But you goaded him into doing this."

"I sure as shit didn't lead him in this direction. I was pumping a financial conspiracy up his ass. Bribing local politicians for tax breaks, illicit business practices, that kind of thing. None of it provable."

"Good God," I muttered. There were moments when I wished fervently that Stitcher was just a pathological liar with Tourette's Syndrome and that everything he described was an elaborate, dark fantasy. But then reality washed back in like a wave of cold water that smelled of raw sewage.

"Everything was going great until this raid. Why the fuck would this asshole do this?"

I thought back to my first uninvited visit to the Washington, DC factory five years ago. "Is it possible Lyle Nunez is his informant?"

"Lyle? That nervous rat-bastard? You think he talked to the feds?"

I tried to picture that. "I doubt it. But he did point me to the DC factory, remember that?" Lyle somehow had worked his Latino connections to get the job at the DC facility. He could just as easily have repeated that west of the Rockies.

"Motherfucking fuckity fuck. How would he have known about the West Coast?"

There was a blurry line between what Lyle knew for sure and what he thought he knew. "Remember, he's resourceful. He tracked medical waste to the DC factory, and then got hired there. Not to mention talked me into sneaking in there to gather samples."

Stitcher sputtered. "But now we're routing supplies through a food distribution company we set up, to be more subtle. You promised me that he wasn't a loose end."

"He isn't." I don't know how much I believed that, but I couldn't let Lyle die by having some ghoul suck his soul out of his nostrils. "He didn't find anything out from me. We haven't talked once since then."

Stitcher groaned. "I thought that asshole feared the government more than he feared us. Could he really have gone to the FBI?"

I laughed. "What am I supposed to do, John? Invite him out to lunch and ask for his latest conspiracy theories and contacts? He'd head for the hills, totally disappear if I did that. He thinks you guys bought me off and that I'm another evil corporate tool."

"That's goddamn fabulous. Because right now, we're fucked if Pierce and that Hispanic shit are working together. It means whatever I do could pull Pierce that much closer to the actual truth. Financial shit won't interest him if he thinks we're tossing goddamn medical waste into food. Fuck!"

"Pierce thinks he's hot on the trails of an industry-wide conspiracy. He doesn't know what the conspiracy is about though." I shivered in the rain. "I don't want to know about this cloak and dagger stuff."

"Because you, Elaine, are Phase Two. Lyle knows who you are and what the lab professes to research. I left clues for Pierce that lead him to your lab."

"Us? I'm bait for screwing with the FBI?" I shook my head. God, he was such an asshole.

"So sorry, but I needed another misdirection and I didn't have a lot to choose from. We're leading him into a cul-de-sac that will be an embarrassing waste of time for the Bureau. When it blows up in his face, we should be done with him."

"And what if it blows up in ours? What if he outsmarts you again?"

Stitcher laughed nervously. "Don't worry, I'll figure out a backup plan."

"Have things backfired like this before?" I didn't want another bulls-eye on the lab because Stitcher felt desperate.

"Remember *Fast Food Nation*, Elaine?"

"Of course." It was the classic muckraking book about how the fast food industry operated.

"Motherfucking bingo."

I rolled my eyes. "You mean to tell me that the industry set that book up as misdirection? That Eric Schlosser was a tool?" He may as well have blasphemed the Pope.

"No. Schlosser is a true believer, but he followed our bread crumbs. Remember the bad guy in his book? The fast food *restaurants*. Not the food *companies*." Stitcher belly-laughed.

I said, "You mean to tell me that you guys threw the fast food companies under the bus to divert attention from the agricultural and food processor sectors?"

"There is an eternal fucking war between the restaurants and the food supply chain, Elaine. The more people who go out for dinner, the less buy groceries. We can twist the wants of millions of individual consumers, but the restaurant industry is a club of fucking economic giants who would make us eat shit if they gain enough leverage. When restaurant chains are the biggest potato buyers in the world, they get fucking pushy."

"The things they don't teach you in school."

"So every once in a while we have to knock them the fuck down a peg. Family farmers versus the fucking fry cooks."

"Okay smart guy, what about Pepsico? They own restaurant chains and sell stuff in grocery stores. Them backing a slap at fast food restaurants would be like punching themselves in the stomach."

"Not a problem. The meat division in one company pretends to throw the fast food division into the razor-sharp maw of the health press poodle to divert attention from some colossal fuck-up, like mad cow disease. The victimized division fires up its lobbyists, rides out the negative press, usually doesn't suffer a drop in earnings, and then it's back to business as usual for everyone."

I held up my hand as sleet pelted my face. "I am in the heart of the obesity conspiracy, and I'm finding it hard to believe that fake intra-corporate scandals are actually tools to misdirect public anger."

Stitcher chuckled. "It's classic corporate public relations misdirection. The corporation can set the agenda, the media will eat out of their hands as the routine scandal/expose storyline plays out, and it sucks all the oxygen out of the room for the issue the industry would rather avoid. It's the same thing as when Reagan invaded Grenada right after the Marine Barracks were bombed in Lebanon. They fucking practice this shit in corporate war game exercises at executive programs at Wharton and Harvard Business."

My mental wheels spun so fast I felt dizzy. "So what about the *Food, Inc.* documentary? That was a corporate set up too?"

Stitcher replied, "No, that wasn't us. That hurt like a bitch. Our lobbyists earned overtime that year doing damage control. Sometimes when you feed an attack dog, it takes a damn chunk out of your hand."

"Okay, John. Like I have a choice." I ran back into the doorway, hugging my chest with a shaking, wet arm. "I have to go."

[28]

The directors of our labs in Brussels, Chicago, and Silicon Valley stared back at Betty and I on the teleconference TV screen. They looked as concerned as I felt.

"Do you know why Donald called this meeting?" asked Stephan from Brussels. It was early evening there already.

Anna pursed her lip but didn't say anything. Ben in Silicon Valley looked green around the gills. But it was morning out there still, and he often looked like death until the afternoon.

Betty and I exchanged a look. I shook my head and said, "He just said it was urgent. That was enough for me to call all of you."

Donald hustled in and sat next to me. "Thank you for all making the time to talk on short notice. The climatology projections are much worse than they were six months ago. And we're not the only ones who will know about it."

He looked at me significantly. This wasn't just a science problem, I felt, it had to be a conspiracy problem. "Anna can explain more."

Anna's lab in Chicago did the lion's share of our oceanography research. She shook her head of short, white hair back and forth. "Donald, those are new projections. We're still reviewing them."

"I know, I know. But just show them."

She shared her laptop's screen with us on a second monitor. It showed a global map of ocean temperatures with a lot more blue on it than it should have. "Over the last two decades, as projections of global temperature changed, sea level and ocean acidification have been growing worse and worse. What's known publicly are the most conservative, highly-vetted projections. But they are not the most likely, partly because the latest projections may be the most accurate since the situation keeps changing. This map is the the most likely sea levels over the next fifty years, assuming a temperature global temperature rise of four degrees Celsius."

"But the Paris agreement was to keep the increase to an average two degree increase," Ben said.

Anna glared at her camera. "That voluntary approach has been an utter failure. China, India, and Russia have missed their own targets year after year. And our government just keeps cooking the books to make it look like the U.S. is on schedule. Meanwhile, the projections show the average temperature increase could be in the four to five degree range. This is the bottom of that range."

Anna's time-lapse map showed New York, New Orleans, Venice, a good chunk of Indonesia, coastal India, and southeast Asia disappear under the waves. Inland flooding in the Mid-Atlantic riddled it with swamps and lakes. Meanwhile, the Midwest and Southwest underwent full-scale desertification.

"Didn't the projections already get worse a few years ago?" I asked. My whole adult life seemed to be a series of increasingly gloomy forecasts of the ozone hole, global warming, ocean acidification, and rising sea levels. Each one was worse than the previous one.

"There's a five year lag in new projections being vetted and ultimately accepted," Anna explained.

"Have you double-checked the numbers?" Betty asked with a tang of fear. Betty and I had been through this many times. My people always double-checked their numbers. But she needed to hear it from them each time, face to face, especially when she couldn't freaking believe what they were saying. I was having a hard time believing it myself right now.

Ben held up his hands. "I only run these models, I didn't build them."

Betty raised an eyebrow. "Donald? Anna?"

They both nodded. Anna said, "Checked and double-checked. Plus validated with other research. What we thought about sea levels in 2010 is now the most optimistic case. The extreme estimates from a decade ago are the new norms. And it's because the polar ice cap melting has accelerated. It's not that our scientific projections have improved that much."

Stephan still looked puzzled, but added, "It gets worse when we incorporate people's reaction. We ran the behavioral model on top of the new sea level scenarios. Svetanka is our Chief Social Scientist here in Brussels. Let me get her in here." Stephan left his office.

I turned to Donald. "What do you know that they don't yet?"

Donald whispered. "It's how everything adds up. You'll see."

Svetanka was a frosty-blond in her mid-forties, one of the first Slavic hybrids. If you've noticed a ton of Eastern European mathematical and computational geniuses floating around, it's because Brussels ramped up it's hybrid production by something like 400 percent in the early 1980s. They knew the Wall would fall before Gorbachev came to power in 1985 and that hybrid babies would flood the western world, making it easy to conceal a couple of thousand hybrids supposedly adopted from the East.

Svetanka appeared on the video conference and said in an English accent, "We project a flight from the coasts, away from the cities. A massive disruption to the energy and food industries: gasoline refineries, farming, and the power grid are highly susceptible to weather events and are not easily relocated or rebuilt. The ensuing economic and political fallout would worsen fossil fuel use, increase military conflicts, and degrade air and water quality."

The map showed sea levels swamping the coastal areas. The population snuggled up against the Appalachians in the east, away from the Great Lakes in the north, and away from the Gulf Coast. The economic effects would hamstring government response to natural disasters, and the wheels would slowly spun off of everything, it looked like to me.

"Without substantial protections, New York, Boston and Washington, DC will become uninhabitable within 25 years. We ran a scenario where we added seawalls and other protections exogenously to see what would happen," she added.

The digital map of North America ran forward in time again, but the population density stayed roughly constant. Superstorms lashed the East Coast every three years, causing massive blackouts and economic disruptions. Catastrophic flooding outside of the cities' protected areas caused

147

southern New Jersey, the Outer Banks, and Long Island to become economic wastelands.

"However, the costs of seawalls and other protections are so high that it is very unlikely that they would be built. To protect half of the most vulnerable coastal areas would require about over one percent of the 2018 global GDP. That's over ten trillion U.S. dollars."

"That doesn't sound so bad," Betty said.

"That is more than the U.S. Government's entire budget," Svetanka replied. "Raising that much would require a massive tax increase or expansion of national debts around the world to finance. And the political will for that, which is already lacking, would evaporate even further."

Betty sighed. "And that dog don't hunt," she said in an exaggerated Southern accent. "These questions are above all of our pay grades. But we must have some possible solutions."

Modeling anything was speculative in nature and I just felt extra skeptical about putting too much faith in it. "Svetanka, what are your models assuming that drives these results?"

She blinked rapidly for a second. "The climate changes themselves. We estimate economic and political conditions, population growth and migration, and a simple destruction indicator. The behavioral reactions driving the migration patterns are all long-validated and peer-reviewed. We've done sensitivity testing on the behavioral components. It is all, how would you say, many flavors of bad."

Betty nodded. "And without any changes, your model was showing that this wouldn't happen until later this century, until this latest update?"

Svetanka nodded. "The economic estimates are drawn from the estimates of financial damage from the last 50 years of extreme weather events. It is the economic drag that makes the U.S. and other countries unable to invest in the needed preventative measures. The political drag on infrastructure spending compounds the damage."

Donald brought up a table on the screen. The table showed carbon emissions, atmospheric CO2, sea levels and average temperatures from his latest projections versus the latest near-consensus estimates from 2018. Donald's estimates started off worse and got incredibly worser.

Anna gasped. "Where did these come from?"

Donald replied, "My meta-modeling team studied these already dire

148

projections and found they are too optimistic. For two reasons. We haven't accounted for the fact that the delays in scientific research have consistently underestimated the rapidity of changes that are occurring. Everyone's projections, including ours, continue to underestimate sea levels, average temperature increases, and all the rest of the bad news. The second reason is that Svetanka's behavioral model indicates that the response to increasingly bad news will be to give up, eventually. In some way, the Paris agreement from five years ago was a subtle beginning of giving up. If we align the baseline projections to account for these two related-factors, what we feared happening by 2100 now happens by 2040."

"What is this meta-modeling team?" Stephan asked.

Donald waved a hand. "A bunch of hybrid grad students in physics, statistics, quantitative psychology and applied math. They test out model methodology to look for weak points. They have begun to re-estimate model results based on systematic biases in the models themselves. They're about three years ahead of teams at MIT and Stanford who are picking at the climate models."

Ben pointed at the end of the table. "What happens in 2100?"

"The planet will be uninhabitable before then. Not entirely, but huge swaths will be too hot, or too desertified, or underwater. Life will survive, but our current state of society probably couldn't handle the shocks to fresh water supplies, electrical power disruptions, and refugees. Not to mention the military, political, and economic ramifications. And before anyone asks, we have triple-checked this."

The room fell silent.

Betty cleared her throat. "What do we have on tap to address this?"

Fifty years ago, the food industry established AgSol with the sole purpose to avoid a future predicted by the Club of Rome's horrific projections of resource depletion and global catastrophe. The industry leaders back in the 1970s believed that advanced technology was key to avoiding such a grim future. Cleaner energy would improve the air and water, higher crop yields would feed the growing masses, improved medical care would slow population growth via birth control and make people healthier.

But the industry leaders had made their plans assuming that the Club of Rome's estimate was accurate of how long the Earth had to right itself. And the estimate was an overestimate. They didn't know about the feedback effects of focusing on better resource extraction on the environment. And their modeling of political and economic behavioral responses was positively crude compared to what we could do now.

Now it looked like we surrounded ourselves with cool gadgets so we could take selfies while we drowned. What we needed instead of thinner phones was genius political consultants to sell the world on building lots of old-fashioned seawalls.

"So, it's likely that our existing plans are garbage," Anna said. "We could have ten times the scientists and engineers working on this and we wouldn't be able to head off these threats in time. Assuming we could 'science' our way out of any one of them."

"Don't be so pessimistic, Doc," Ben said. "Look at where the internet and computing was ten, fifteen years ago."

I held up my hands. "The internet is not waterproof."

Betty was spooked too. She had been in this business a lot longer than me, and watching her turn a gray shade of pale didn't boost my confidence. "Now would be a good time for someone to make the case that we are not totally screwed," she said.

"The best approach would be to prevent the ocean levels from rising that much," Donald suggested without much confidence.

"Right. The rest of the world is chain-smoking coal and gasoline. We'd be better bet on seawalls, if you ask me," Ben said.

"Part of the problem," Svetanka said, "is that the clean up costs of storms and the floods that will precede the sea level rise. They will eat up the money for preventative measures."

Anna said, "If I may, one way to deal with this is to reverse the flows of rivers, like they did here in Chicago. The Mississippi, Hudson, Los Angeles, Potomac. If we create estuaries to desalinate the water, we could pipe in fresh water to the Midwest, Ohio Valley, even the Southwest. Make the sea level rise help to fix our drought problem."

"You're talking about a national water grid. It would be the greatest public works project ever done," Svetanka said. "It would take a massive federal government effort, and your Congress in Washington would never agree to that. America is obsessed with impeaching each new President these days. Even if that did happen, what about the rest of the world? India, Russia, Brazil, China?"

Anna cleared her throat. "Most of Asia, outside of China, doesn't have either the money or a government effective enough to protect itself. There will be an increasing frequency of flooding until eventually, the coastal areas will become permanently submerged."

Betty tapped a finger on the table and looked at Donald. "Which means what?"

Svetanka brought up another chart. "Millions of deaths. Unrest and rioting on every continent. Massive economic disruption. Wars over water rights, huge migrations. A drop in arable land that will shock the food supply system. All much sooner than we estimated five years ago."

So it was a political and economic problem after all. The arenas that a bunch of nerdy scientists like us had no traction in. Could we do anything more than watch the hammer fall and maybe get an early start in running and shrieking in terror?

After a long, depressing pause when no one spoke, I said, "Okay, we have two, maybe three years before others discover these new estimates on their own. Betty can handle the Board, and I'll talk to Stitcher. The best we can do is push for these new estimates to hit the street later, while we try to figure something out."

Ben furrowed his brow. "Wait, shouldn't we publicize this, and get the warning out sooner? That may spur more serious action."

Svetanka shook her head. "No, no. Most major countries put economic health over the environment. They won't get more serious about this. They already think we're past the point of no return, they just won't admit it publicly. There would be very negative feedback effects that happen when this news comes out."

"But that hasn't happened before," Anna replied.

"The behavioral modeling is not linear. There are hyperbolic curves to the response algorithms. People reach a tipping point," Svetanka made an upside down 'v' with her hand, "and then they disregard the estimates."

"I don't believe that. People are not crazy," Ben said. "But what do I know, I just run the server farm, right?"

"She's right," Donald said. "Every additional step to address environ-mental damage has become more difficult. The scientific community has to make increasingly bigger efforts to convince people, including politicians, that the science isn't wrong. That's something else the meta-modeling team factored in to their alignments to the model results."

"Ten years ago, it was just a few in the U.S. Congress who didn't believe the projections. Now, it's substantial minorities in the parliaments in Europe, India, China, and most of Africa. We may be past the tipping point on the behavioral response making the problem worse."

God, that sounded just as horrible coming off my tongue as they seemed to take it. And with that, I ended the meeting, because I had a burning need to dump this all in Stitcher's lap. I hoped to hell he had a contingency plan ready for this situation.

[29]

My cellphone rang from my purse, in my desk drawer. I was deep into tweaking the latest report that documented how useful we were to the food industry. "There's been a murder," Stitcher said when I answered. "Get your ass on a plane to Vegas."

Just when I thought today couldn't get much worse. We had a procurement snafu with liquid nitrogen that ate up the entire morning, followed by a parade of lab staff needing face time and feeding of egos. I had been out of the office a lot lately and that compounded with people worried about the lab's future made my introverted staff actually make use of my open door policy. Hanging above it all was the existential threat unveiled by Donald's meta-modeling team.

"Where are you?" I asked, thinking about the NSA flagging this call because he uttered the m-word. That was, if Pierce wasn't tapping our phones directly.

"Busy not being in Vegas. Someone died in a strange way there. One of our friends may be involved."

'Friends' was code-speak for a hybrid. This was strange because they were peaceful people. They were raised by scientists and were very smart. They rarely got into trouble intentionally. Accidentally, well, that's what kept Stitcher employed.

"I need you to fly out there and deal with it. Especially the Feds."

I'm not a forensic scientist, lawyer, or a detective. But if Stitcher needed me, he wasn't kidding around. I didn't have to ask if it was that bad.

I had an overnight bag stowed under my desk. I could be gone in a few minutes. "Okay. I'm heading to the airport. Are you going to tell me what the hell is going on?"

"Somewhat," Stitcher said. "I'm sending another friend of mine to help. Malachi Cleek. He'll meet you at the airport. Text me when you land."

Unfortunately, Alex's personal jet was flying him over Germany right now, heading back from a tour of the facilities his company owned there.

I was able to jump on an already-scheduled charter flight to Vegas. The executive jet company filled the niche for corporate executives whose shareholders frowned on buying jets with corporate profits. Me and ten other business people were in the air a few hours later, headed west as the sun went down.

I pulled up Stitcher's notes on previous calamities. He handled them in person, often coaxing local officials to look the other way, or to defer to industry or government officials who had been he had won over to his point of view. After all, that was how I had met him.

It wasn't often that the food industry got into criminal or civil trouble that involved the police. Nothing as serious as murder, notwithstanding the episode with the Fiesta additive a decade ago.

Malachi Cleek found me at McCarran airport. He looked like another ghoul: tall, gaunt, colorless skin, a corpse-like demeanor, and fragile, thinning hair. I don't think he had smiled or bought new clothes since the Ford Administration. Rather than shake hands, he simply nodded and chewed on a toothpick. "Dr. Cassano, it's good to meet you. John has told me a lot about you."

I looked at him warily. "He's never mentioned you to me at all."

I was hoping to tease a smile or some sign of humanity from him, but his mouth stayed set in a grim horizontal line. The toothpick reminded me of an uncle I had in Philly. Uncle Gio drove a city bus, ran numbers on the side, and always had a toothpick in his mouth. "That's as it should be. I done security work with him in the past. I called a taxi to take us to a motel not far off the Strip."

My shoulders tensed. "Why are we meeting in a motel room?"

154

"No possibility of being spied on." Malachi took a step and then realized what I was really asking. "We're meeting a private detective there. He insisted on it. It's okay, I know the guy."

I wasn't really reassured but Stitcher told me to trust the guy and I wasn't used to working on a murder. The motel had a fresh coat of white paint but everything else about it looked like it hadn't been updated since the Rat Pack roamed the Strip. Every window was blocked by faded gray curtains.

Malachi paid the driver from a roll of bills he fanned out like they were playing cards. "Are you going to be okay with this?"

It occurred to me that all I knew about Malachi was Stitcher's mention of him. Maybe Stitcher had planned my murder and my soul was a gift to his pal Malachi. The thought was ridiculous, but I had reasons to be afraid of strange ghouls. I tightened my hand on my go-bag. "I'm fine."

The motel room door was opened by a tall, good-looking WASPy man in his late thirties with dark hair. Malachi introduced him as Tim, and me as Elaine. No last names. "Tim has worked with the LVPD before and has good contacts in the department. Elaine is my boss and she knows some science."

"The police found a guy dead in a back alley," Tim said as he closed the door behind us. "The ME says that the body was artificially decomposed." He looked at notes on his phone.

"Artificially decomposed? Maybe someone tried to dispose of the body?" I still wasn't understanding why Malachi and I were here.

The detective looked me up and down. "Artificially decomposed in that his body was treated with a chemical that affected it. It removed all of his adipose tissue. That is, um, fat tissue."

"Adipose is fat tissue, yes." I looked at Malachi.

Malachi was watching me for a reaction, but I didn't give him the satisfaction. "Who was the victim?"

"Alonzo King, forty-two years old. Worked in construction, mostly. Had an ex-wife and a ten-year-old daughter. Does that ring any bells?"

I shook my head no.

Tim continued, "ME thinks the cause of death was asphyxiation, possibly an asthma attack. The victim did have a prescription for an inhaler, but none was found with his body. But the chemical burns messed up a lot of the analysis. They don't know if the body was treated before or after death." He looked at us. "You know what this is."

"I wouldn't say that," Malachi said. "Could be that someone strangled this guy and then tried to cover it up with high school chemistry."

Tim looked at me and then back at Malachi. "You two are not normal investigators, are you? I've seen a lot of weird stuff around this town, and I can tell when people are suspecting 'the other.'"

"The other what?" I asked. I was only half-playing dumb.

Tim's eyes darted between me and Malachi. "The other stuff. Unexplainable, unless you believe in a literal translation of the Bible, that Stephen King actually writes nonfiction, and that H.P. Lovecraft was a reporter."

Malachi chewed his toothpick in quick bites.

"Well, I'm a miracle-believing Catholic," I replied to cover for my new ghoul partner. "But we're not ghost-trackers, if that's what you mean."

"No, what I mean are ghouls, succubi, golems, and demons." He looked pointedly not at Malachi. "Walking around like they're the same as us."

"You sound like that is based on personal experience." Suddenly I wanted to bone this guy. Any man who could look the occult in its dead eyes and be so nonchalant made my insides feel like warm butter.

Tim smiled at me but Malachi spoke up before he could say anything. "This is a straight-up murder with a strange circumstance. There's no fang-holes on the victim's neck, is there?"

"The neck melted before anyone could see," Tim pointed out.

Malachi grinned a little. "Fair enough. My point is: why are you going occult on us?"

Tim held up his hands to apologize and smiled. "Sorry about that. I worked with a psychic last week, and the mental cases all seem to involve Satan, hookers, and a secret plot by pot sellers to take over the world."

"It's okay," I said. "We're interested in the chemical analysis the ME did."

"Yes," Tim said. "Malachi said to bring a paper copy. Here it is."

He held out several pages of test results. Before I could take them, Malachi swooped in and took them. He placed each one under the lamp on the nightstand between both beds. He took out his phone and carefully took pictures of each page.

Satisfied, he emailed me a copy and turned to the private investigator. "Have you heard anything about suspects?"

Tim replied, "Nothing solid. They probably have DNA from where the body was found, but I'm guessing that there's no match in the databases. You asked me earlier to see if the department will go hard on this or not. We get about eighty murders a year here and nearly all of them are gunshot victims. Not a lot that asphyxiate and then are melted down very carefully to remove a certain kind of tissue. This is strange enough for them to chase, but also weird enough for them to let go of. I would guess it's a 50/50 chance."

I looked at the ME results. "The corpse was liquified. And the body fat percentage was close to zero."

Malachi nodded. "What about where they found the body? Any leads there?"

"They wouldn't tell me." He looked at me and Malachi. "Do you want me to investigate on your behalf? Do you have some connection to the victim?"

"No," Malachi said. "We are curious about how the murder happened, and who did it. And why. You don't get a lot of corpses like this around here, do you?"

"None," Tim said. "And there's the possibility that the victim died of natural causes and then someone else did this to his body. But if the melter didn't kill Alonzo, why mess with him?"

Something occurred to me. "Have there been cases of bodies altered after death? Surgical procedures, strange mutilations, that kind of thing?"

Tim gave me a crooked grin. "This is Vegas. Absolutely. But we haven't hosted a mad scientist convention in years. I can check on that, but I usually hear about the more occult and strange cases. There's usually a murder or two where someone carves up their spouse and sticks them in the freezer. But you mean something more like Jack the Ripper, or organ-harvesting."

I nodded and he made a note on his phone. "Anything else?"

Malachi put his hand on the doorknob. "You've been helpful, Tim. Thank you. We'll be in touch if we need anything else."

Tim looked at us like we were nice but crazy. He didn't seem upset that Malachi was leaving, but he gave me a wink as I headed out. I smiled politely but kept going. There was something about him that both aroused me and gave me the willies. Weird.

[30]

Malachi and I started walking back to the Strip. He claimed he wanted to stretch his legs so he could think. I needed fresh air. The air wasn't fresher so much; the night air was like walking into a hair dryer set to low speed.

"That detective was kind of creepy," I offered, more to myself than Malachi. "No wonder the police go to him for the weird cases."

Malachi replied, "Tim Marduke is not with the police no more. He's private. He has seen some strange things in this town. He doesn't like having his full name tossed around, if you know what I mean."

"Sure." We walked another block and it seemed like the Strip was only further away. "Why is Stitcher so concerned to send us out here?" I asked. There wasn't enough info to scare me into thinking I had to fly out here. Chemical burns can destroy adipose. So what?

"Stitcher called me when this body was found. This chemical uh, wash, just flushes all the adipose out of a body. Liposuction can clean out a spot, like a pot belly, but for the biggest bang for the buck, you go for it all. I think we have a hungry, hungry hybrid on our hands."

I shook my head. So Malachi knew about the hybrids. What else did he know? "A hybrid wouldn't do this." They were law-abiding, dedicated citizens, not grave robbers.

"Who else wants a body's worth of adipose? Don't tell me that it has

158

some black market value. I've heard the tale about those gangs in Peru." Malachi shook his head. "When someone goes after adipose like this, it's one of our special friends."

"The simplest explanation is that the killer wanted to destroy any incriminating evidence," I said.

Malachi shook his head. "Then why not wait until it was completely decomposed? Why not use a chemical that would fully decompose the body instead of turning it to bones and goo?"

"I think we're jumping at shadows," I said. Stitcher had not been wrong in the years I worked with him, but either he was holding back some information from Malachi and I, or to err was also to be undead. "Would one of our friends come to Vegas, play the slots, and then do this?"

"Our supply of special gouda is tight out here, in case you haven't heard. Enough for a normal-sized adult, but they ain't all normal-sized." Malachi gave me a side glance and whispered, "Have you heard of the superhybrids?"

Ignorance was plastered all over my face.

"Right. Some of our special friends have been experimenting with heightened abilities beyond the brainy stuff. A group of them have found that more high octane gouda adds more muscle. Like a steroid, but you still have to work to build it and maintain it. Like those ball players did with steroids back in the 90s."

There followed a lengthy explanation by him of all the crooked baseball players who juiced themselves to home run records and World Series victories. I won't repeat it here.

"None of my scientists have ever mentioned these hybrids," I said to turn the conversation back to what mattered. Did Donald know? I guess I didn't keep up with the hobbies and interests of the hundreds of thousands of hybrids all over the planet.

"The supers are not highly respected by the nerdy types. Most of them dropped out of college." Malachi waved his long-fingered hand to brush away a fly. "Besides the point, really. They're gym rats and their protein needs are like double or triple to maintain their physique. Not a problem when the golden gouda was flowing."

I covered my mouth with my hand. "Oh no."

"Where are they gonna go if they can't get more, right? This is what Stitcher has had me looking into. Not a lot of sources for this stuff."

You know, I thought that I had been Stitcher's only errand girl doing all the crappy jobs. He'd been going easy on me, as it turns out.

"So let's go talk to Henry Ota," Malachi said. "Hybrid, 1992 class. Has had some problems. He lives here in Henderson, just outside the valley. He's a professional card player and a weightlifter. One of the dropouts. Hell of a card counter though. We should see him before the cops reach him."

"Why would you think of him?" I asked. "Why would the cops think of him?"

Malachi shrugged. "Because Murphy's Law says they will. It may be DNA strands, or an eyewitness or a security camera. Henry is not the most careful or thorough kind of guy, unless he's playing Texas Hold'em. Not all the hybrids are geniuses."

So they had played cards together? Malachi got around, I have to say. Maybe he personally knew each hybrid.

Malachi looked at my legs. "Do you have any other shoes?"

I scowled. I was wearing dark blue flats, the epitome of business casual, and they were cute, damn it. Was he one of those self-appointed women's fashion critics? "Are we going to a gym?"

Malachi scratched his head. "If he's not at home, yeah. And I'm not one for running. Given my condition."

I looked him up and down. "But you're tall and lanky."

He raised an eyebrow, telling me that I know what he was referring to. "Let's skip the bullshit and agree that I know that you know about me. So let's talk contingencies," he said. "If Henry did this, we may have to let him take the fall."

I didn't like that at all. We didn't have a policy of no hybrid left behind, but it rankled that we would just step aside because a hybrid acted out of starvation.

"But what if he might tells the FBI about the hybrids? We have to protect him so he protects us."

Malachi wasn't buying that. "He's mentally ill. And they'll not believe some story about being part alien and needing to consume human fat. They'll get him a psych eval and a shitty public defender."

"Can we afford to lose even one hybrid's skills and expertise?"

Malachi shrugged. "He's never really been part of Project Rogers. He gets his dietary supplement and that's it. He's a professional card player."

He hailed a cab and we took off out of the city, holding our tongues along the way. Contingencies. The word had taken on a distasteful connotation in the years since I had become Stitcher's errand girl. It always involved ugly choices, underhanded activities, moral compromises, and other things no one would want to tell their kids.

Night fell completely as we climbed out of the valley. Henderson was on the outskirts of Las Vegas, a town of condos and townhouses and of course, casinos. The cab dropped us off at a gated townhouse community with a random-sounding desert oasis name.

Malachi buzzed Henry's apartment. "Hi, I'm a cousin who just came into town. The *family* wants us to have a chat. 83,518,679."

The intercom hissed with the sound of an open line, but Henry didn't speak. The gate swung open to admit us though.

"What did you tell him?" I asked as we walked in.

"His hybrid ID number. Anyone who uses it signals that they need to talk to the hybrid ASAP. Don't you know these rules?" Malachi looked around as we walked down the street under bright white streetlights. "But still, be ready if he tries to run."

Malachi's paranoia was a thing to behold. We were practically family with Henry, right? Why would he bolt, especially if Malachi had used his hybrid number? At this point, I was highly skeptical that some weight-lifting gambler would resort to murder, much less run from his 'family.' Even still, Malachi rolled his undead shoulders as we turned up Henry's street, girding himself for confrontation.

As I expected, when we knocked on his door, Henry Ota answered it. He opened the door wide and gave us the once over with a passive nonchalance. Then he grumbled and let us in.

Henry was a massive, husky Asian-American, like a Samoan version of Superman. He stood over six feet tall and his muscles were huge. He weighed about two Malachis or one and a half of me. His thick black hair was a ruffled mess and he had a crappy gray t-shirt sporting a dopey IT joke that had a URL as its punchline. I didn't see an ounce of fat on him.

His living room consisted of bookshelves filled to overflowing with books on math and fitness. His family room was an online gambling den. At least

161

three poker games were in session on three different laptops. The news whispered from a small TV in the corner and an old superhero movie was playing on an old-fashioned laptop.

"Can I get you something?" Henry muttered as he opened the fridge. It was full of protein shakes and vegetables like chard, broccoli, and cauliflower. The door was a mass of tall water bottles.

"We're good, thanks," I replied. I didn't want to put Malachi in any uncomfortable eating situations.

Henry unscrewed the cap on a water bottle. "If you're here about me going back to school, I'll tell you the same thing I told the last dozen people. Hell no, I won't go."

"We're not here about that," I reassured him. "How have you been doing with the rationing of the supplements?"

Henry looked at the floor. "I'm doing okay here."

Malachi folded his arms. "There was a strange death in the city. Guy had all of his adipose melted off of him. And you're the only super-hybrid in Vegas."

"So?"

"So… did you kill him, Henry?"

"What?" Henry scowled. "No. I didn't kill anyone."

"Then how are you keeping up your size without the usual level of supplements?" Malachi asked.

Henry shrugged his massive shoulders. It was like two bowling balls rolling around under his t-shirt. "I've been bulking up on normal food. Yeah, I've lost a little weight, had to drop a few reps. It's been tough, but I'm managing."

Malachi held his phone up at arm's length and tapped at it. "Your lifting competition last month, you weighed in at 320 pounds. That was before the supplements were cut back to survival levels. Should we do a weigh-in right now or you could just be honest and tell us how much you weigh."

Henry sighed. "Okay, I'm 345."

Malachi put his phone away and looked at me. I guess I was playing the good cop. "We're here to help you. Can you tell us what you did and why you did it?"

Henry shuffled out of the kitchen, avoiding eye contact with us both.

162

Either he was burning up with guilt or he had some emotional processing problems. Not unusual for a hybrid.

"I'm out of food," he grumbled, knocking an empty pizza box off of the counter. "I can't live like this any more."

Malachi clucked his tongue in disapproval. "You can't substitute for the good stuff in your diet, can you?"

Henry walked into the living room and we followed. He moved very gracefully for such a large man. "I was starving. I got all the money I could ever have, but I can't feed myself."

"I don't understand, how much above the daily supplement requirement do you need?" I asked. "The daily amount is what, ten grams a day?"

Henry looked at me in bewilderment. "An adult can survive on eight. But for people like me, we need twenty-two to thirty."

"Thirty?" I looked at Malachi. "Why do you need triple?"

Henry pulled a sleeve back and showed us a bicep. "Weight training is my job, other than cards. My muscle fibers are about one and a half times stronger than a normal human's. I need the supplements to build it and maintain it."

"This supply problem is only going to last a short while. Why not take a break from being a huge palooka?" Malachi sniffed disdainfully. "Fake an injury or something."

Henry cleared a pile of debris off his couch, sweeping it behind an end-table. He offered us seats on his couch. "Weight-lifting is more than my career. You've heard of the super-hybrids, right? We're trying to find our maximum physical fitness levels. I'm almost thirty, so I'm already fighting muscle loss. If I give it up now, I'm finished."

Malachi didn't take a seat. He wandered around the room, looking at the books on the bookshelf. I sat down, trying to be polite. Henry sat across from me. He didn't sit by falling on the couch, he performed the sitting operation like he was squatting a bar full of weights. You could land a plane on one of his thighs.

Malachi's eyes were open a little wider than normal and his toothpick wandered across his lips. I don't know if a ghoul can have a stroke, but if any of them could, it would be Malachi. He peeked out of Henry's back windows. We couldn't talk here too long.

163

I tried not to fold my arms in a skeptical pose. "What happens to you if you don't get over twenty grams of the supplement?"

"Hunger. Insomnia. Decreased cognitive function. I get cranky. Sometimes I get the shakes. And then I start losing at the card table."

Malachi straightened his head. "That sounds like withdrawal symptoms, not hunger."

Henry ignored him.

I stepped forward. "Henry, could you be addicted to the supplements?"

Henry looked at me in shock and then slowly shook his head. "No, how can that be? That would be like being addicted to protein or water. If I'm addicted to anything, it's being a super."

I felt a headache coming on. We had created the obesity epidemic to feed hybrids so they could help us save ourselves. And now we had overeating super-hybrids who needed large amounts of human fat, during an acute human fat shortage, who may have resorted to killing a human to get it. It was a full-circle fuck-up.

"You should only need ten grams a day," I said. "You may have become more dependent than you should be. People do get addicted to water and food."

"Not me. I've experimented with forty, even fifty grams a day. I got diminishing returns, you know, as far as fitness goes. And I started feeling sick. I am part human too." Henry sat completely still, his beefy bare arms resting on those giant quadriceps. He had a calm energy.

Between his icy calm and Malachi's undead eyes bugging out, I felt tense. I wanted to go see the crime scene, maybe have a peek at the body. Perhaps Tim could spring a police file for us. "So you had nothing to do with a body being melted of all its fat here in town?"

Henry looked me straight in the eye. "I never said I had nothing to do with it. I said I didn't kill the guy." He had a great poker face.

"Did you ever kill anyone to obtain adipose?" I asked point-blank.

"We need to help the hybrid who did that, before the cops get to them," Malachi added.

"This guy was having an asthma attack outside a gym I go to in North Vegas. Homeless guy, always got a bag of food from White Castle. I gave him his inhaler, but it was out." Henry scratched his chest absent-mindedly. "He died right there in the street. Really big guy, over two-sixty."

"How did you remove the fat tissue so exactly?" I asked.

He looked at me like I was dumb. Excuse me, but even smart people aren't well-versed on how to make a homegrown super-dieting pill or play chemist with dead bodies. "I watched some videos on liposuction. Made my own rig and did it. I doused the body with hydrochloric acid to destroy the evidence, and then dumped him."

Malachi and I just stared at him.

"So you didn't kill him, you just failed to report a death and then defiled the corpse," Malachi said in disgust.

Henry looked Malachi up and down. "And *you* think there's something wrong with messing with dead bodies?"

Malachi held his hands out. "What can I say, I'm real old-fashioned. This poor man deserved to be treated respectfully. Not like a hock of ham."

"Then give me my thirty grams a day," Henry said in a low grumble. "Me and the rest of the super-hybrids. We're just as valuable as the brainy ones. You don't believe that, do you Elaine?"

Unlike Henry, I have a terrible poker face. These super-hybrids weren't doing anything to advance technology or science or solve our exploding list of problems. But that was beside the point. "I don't think weight-lifting or card-playing will help solve global warming."

Henry pushed his hair out of his eyes. "I know I'm an apostate in the church of the greater hybrid nerd. But super strength isn't useless. Who you going to want there to help when a bookshelf falls on a kid? A spindly meteorologist or someone who can squat over 600 pounds?"

I had a tart reply on my tongue but swallowed it like a sour patch candy. "You probably should leave town," I said. "Because if the cops get interested in you, you'll have zero grams to eat. I don't think the county lockup has a special diet for men addicted to human fat tissue."

"It will kill you," Malachi added.

"The cops won't figure out that I had anything to do with it."

"You have to consider the contingencies if they do," I said quietly.

Malachi tapped his lip with a finger. "Where'd you get the acid?"

"I bought it. On the internet." Henry's icy calm held for another second until the distress emanating off of me and Malachi penetrated his skull. "What's wrong?"

"Come with us," Malachi said. "Talk to our lawyers about a strategy. You

165

don't want to get put in an interrogation room. It's best if you disappear and the cops forget about a homeless guy's body being melted. Burned."

"I think I can hold my own against some junior college graduate with a badge," Henry said.

I folded my arms. "Oh, is this a poker game to you? Are you going to bluff your way past them? They hold all the cards, these are worse odds than at a casino. And the stakes are not just your survival, because you're going to die in jail. It's the entire hybrid program. The goals of our program. You have to think about *your family* and what could go wrong."

Finally, an emotional reaction from the super-hybrid. "I hadn't thought about it that way."

"We're leaving right now," Malachi said. "Take whatever you need to survive for the next couple of days."

While Henry trundled off to his room to pack, Malachi said, "What do you think we should do?"

I wanted to kill the fat bastard and bury him in the desert. I don't know where that anger had come from so suddenly. Maybe that another short-sighted hybrid had risked the conspiracy, and his own life, all just to bench press more. "We need to get him out of here quietly. Let's fly him out of town." I could take him with me back to Tennessee and see if we could stash him somewhere.

Malachi shook his head. "I'm not sure I want you with him." He indicated my breasts, hips, and legs, and then motioned to his own skin-and-bones frame. "To him, you probably look like a puff pastry." When I scowled at the implied insult, he shook his head. "I'm not kidding. I should drive him myself over the state line. Airline passenger records are run through federal databases."

"Should we take his car?" I dreaded the idea of a late night dash across the desert, but getting back to my high school kid in Tennessee didn't sound like a good enough excuse.

"No, too easy to track. A taxi or bus, and then a car rental." Malachi patted his back pocket. "I can rent a car without leaving a trace. Come on Henry, shake a leg," Malachi yelled at the bedroom door.

Henry shuffled out. He agreed to the plan and I left ahead of them, as Malachi suggested, and walked down to the gate, looking for a cab. The gate opened and three police cars barreled past me with their lights running but no sirens. I texted Malachi 'run!' but it was probably too late.

I let myself out of the gated compound. The street was deserted, with no sidewalks, and high walls running in both directions under sparse street-lights. I couldn't turn around and go back to Henry's.

I walked quickly toward the next intersection, looking for a cab company on my phone. I had to expect that they would escape the police. And then a car pulled up behind me and slowed down. A sinking feeling formed in my gut.

"Elaine?"

It was Agent Pierce's voice.

[31]

"Are you tailing me across the country?" I asked, taking the initiative.

He didn't smile. "I'm assisting the local police with a raid. A disturbed man lives here who may have brutally killed someone and mutilated their body. I have to say that it is very odd to find you so close by, and so far from Knoxville."

"And you suspect that I am somehow involved?"

Pierce looked around, his hands still on the steering wheel. "You want to tell me why you just happen to be on the same street in Henderson, Nevada at the same time that we arrive?"

I rolled my eyes. "And it seems to me very odd that I come all the way out to Vegas and the same FBI agent who is poking around my lab just happens to show up on the same street. You must be following me. Tapping my phone, maybe?"

He put the car in park but kept the engine running. "Do you want to tell me why you're here? You know what, never mind. I'll just try to follow up on it and we both know whatever your alibi is that it will fall through, right?"

Alibi sounded like indictment sounded like arrest. Fear twisted my guts but I was simply walking down the street of a suburban town. I decided not to give him the satisfaction. "Are you going to keep throwing vague accusations around or will you actually suspect me of something?"

168

"I'm always suspicious of you, Dr. Cassano," he said. "You keep showing up where trouble is. You're walking down the street by yourself. Looks like you could use a lift."

I sighed. There were a dozen reasons I could give for not needing a ride, but he wouldn't believe them. Before I could answer, his radio crackled.

"Suspect is on the run, heading west inside the community."

My eyes met Pierce's. Clearly, I wasn't the suspect they were referring to. I grabbed the car door handle and yanked it open before he could pull away. "Let's go."

Pierce grimaced. He gunned the engine and whipped the car around the empty intersection. He radioed in that he was outside the community, headed west. He turned on the solitary red light on the car's dash.

"I'm not your prisoner," I said, more to reassure myself than to set him straight. "I just need a lift."

"Right," he said.

We passed another entrance to the community and at the next intersection we swung left. Pierce parked the car by the corner. The gated community had a cement wall that rose ten, twelve feet above the sidewalk. A similar wall of another gated community across the street turned the street into a concrete canyon. We could see at least half a mile down the straight street. The only sign of life was a car crossing the street four blocks away.

"This is Pierce. I'm on the road along the west side. No sign of him."

Tinny voices responded on the radio about the suspect still running west. One of the other cops said he lost sight of him, which made me doubt that they were after Henry after all. He wasn't easy to lose sight of.

"If anything happens out here, you stay in the car," Pierce instructed. "For your own safety."

"Yes sir."

Halfway down the block, a massive figure dangled over the wall and dropped ten feet to the sidewalk. He landed gracefully, like a cat. If I had done that, I would have sprained my ankle or broken a foot. But Henry hit the ground running and scooted across the street faster than I would have imagined. I guess all that muscle, plus adrenaline and fear, were responsible.

My breath caught in my mouth. I couldn't act like I knew this suspect, could I? Or was that ruse already up? I bit my tongue.

Pierce threw the car into drive and floored it. Henry turned and ran away

169

from us. He was fast, but he couldn't outrun a sedan for half a block. Pierce raced ahead of him and cut him off by pulling up on the sidewalk.

"Stay here." Pierce jumped out with his hand on his gun. He radioed for help and took a stance behind his door.

"Henry," Pierce shouted in a low, commanding voice. "I'm FBI. Stop and put your hands up. Do it now!"

Henry looked right at me as he raised his meaty arms. His face had gone into that slack, hyper-calculating mode. He was weighing whether to call, raise, or fold.

My hand tightened on the door handle, afraid to move, afraid to not move. What could I say that would help here? Look back on this moment now, I realize that I had already said too much at this point.

"We need to talk. That's all," Pierce continued. "I know, you're scared. Just do as I say. I want you to kneel down on the ground." Pierce was moving around the front end of the car.

My phone began buzzing in my purse with a text alert. I ignored it, my eyes glued to Henry. I don't mean that my eyeballs were literally glued to him. I hope whoever is reading this knows what I mean. I'm not a great writer.

Henry took a step back.

"Don't move. I want you to help me out here. I need you to kneel down on the street and put your hands on the back of your head."

Henry turned around and ran. I don't know what he was thinking. He didn't have a chance of getting away.

Pierce chased him on foot. I popped my door open but Pierce waved me back and I hesitated.

Henry dug something out of his shorts pocket as he ran. It could have been a handgun. It could have been a phone. The streetlight only showed a dark object.

Pierce yelled, his gun up and pointed at Henry's back. "Freeze. Lower that gun."

On the next block, a police car careened around the corner and came racing towards us.

"Elaine, get back in the goddamned car," Pierce yelled over his shoulder.

Somehow I had come out of the car without realizing it. I looked at

Henry. He did have a snub-nosed handgun. What the hell did he think he could do with that?

"Drop the gun, Henry. No one has to get hurt."

The barrel of Henry's handgun dropped a millimeter at a time. I gripped the frame of the door, wishing he would toss it away.

The police car pulled up on the sidewalk, boxing Henry in.

"That's good, keep lowering it and place it on the ground," Pierce said in a commanding but encouraging tone.

I didn't see Henry moving at all. The gun's barrel hung there in mid-air, with his huge hand engulfing the grip.

Police officers were scrabbling up the far side of the concrete wall of Henry's gated community. I could hear them panting and grunting.

"On the ground now!" Yelled a cop from the cruiser's PA system. He was out and hiding behind his door, his service weapon out.

Henry looked from the cop to Agent Pierce. Finally, he looked at me. I motioned for him to lower the gun. He blinked at me and his face looked sad for a brief second.

He raised his gun.

Pierce and the police officer fired two quick bursts at the same time. The thunderclap of the guns firing echoed like an artillery barrage in this concrete-enclosed street. Henry slowly sunk to the sidewalk. He tossed the gun aside as he laid back on the sidewalk.

Pierce was breathing hard, sucking in huge breaths and trying to steady his gun as he approached the downed super-hybrid.

Henry watched as Pierce kicked his gun away. The police officer chattered into his radio, calling for an ambulance in a high-pitched voice.

I looked up to see cops struggling over the wall. One dropped to the street and grabbed his ankle in pain. The others stayed on the wall and drew their service weapons. Pierce did a quick search of Henry's pockets, looking for any other weapons.

"Looks like a terrorist," one of the cops said. "Who works out."

"Elaine, see what you can do for him," Pierce said as he holstered his weapon. "You're a doctor."

I'm not a medical doctor and Pierce knew that. But I didn't hesitate a second. I ran over to the big guy and kneeled down.

The police officer was pulling gauze from a compartment on his belt while his partner ran for the first aid kit. I could smell blood and gunpowder. Henry wasn't talking but was breathing fast and shallow. His eyes were shut.

"I've got a wound in the upper chest and in the neck," the officer said. He clamped a purple-gloved hand on Henry's neck.

"Henry," I said, "Can you hear me?"

He opened his eyes and looked at me and then the cop. "Sorry."

"What the fuck were you thinking?" I normally don't swear, but the insanity of what just happened had landed on me like a dog jumping on my back.

Henry's eyes rolled back in his head a second. "Trapped. No escape. Like you said."

I wanted to slap him in the face. Malachi and I had said that to twist his arm. He didn't believe us then, why would he sacrifice himself based on that now? We could have done something else to say him. Stitcher could have swooped in and saved the day. Trying to shoot a cop was the dumbest thing he could do.

"Hang in there," the police officer said, "I think we missed everything vital." He shoved gauze into my hand and guided it to Henry's upper chest. Henry's oversized t-shirt was wet and slick there. The cop cut it away. I found the bullet wound in a giant pectoral and pressed hard. Henry didn't react. He didn't flinch when the cop cuffed him either.

A very loud motorcycle turned onto the street, wailing a siren as well. It was a paramedic on a speed bike. More sirens wailed in the distance.

The paramedic ran over while digging in an enormous duffle bag she had pulled off the back of the bike. She handed me an IV bag and told me to hold it up while she found a vein in Henry's arm.

"What's your name? Henry? I'm Amanda. Can you help me out and stay awake," she asked as she leaned over him. She handed me another set of bandages to press against his wounds.

Henry's chest was rising and falling irregularly. He passed out. I was surprised how little blood was coming from his chest wound.

"How's the neck?" she asked the cop.

"Bleeding," the cop said neutrally. He had both hands on the side of Henry's neck. "This guy is huge."

The ambulance screeched to a halt and killed its siren. The paramedics that boiled out of it forced me away from Henry. I stepped back, watching, helpless.

Henry was bathed in blue white light from the paramedics' headlamps. They were doing a lot of things to him with a quiet, focused energy. The third paramedic brought the stretcher and collapsed it to ground height.

"He's a suspect," the cop said. Cops were arriving in droves now. A crime scene van pulled up. More unmarked cars.

"Shit," the motorcycle paramedic said. Paddles came out and they zapped Henry's body. Twice. I couldn't see anything other than a cluster of dark blue paramedics with bright white light sneaking out between their arms, legs and torsos.

I held my breath.

Finally, they sat back. "I'll call it," said the motorbike paramedic.

A cop stepped in between me and Henry as the paramedic read off the time and the location. "Ma'am, this is an active crime scene. I need you to put the IV back down, right there is fine, good, thanks, now please step back and let them do their work." He led me back to where Pierce was throwing up quietly in the gutter.

There wasn't any more work for the first responders to do. Henry, bathed in harsh white lights, was a giant scarlet and white angel in deadly repose. I put my hand on Pierce's back as he heaved, not knowing what else to do.

[32]

"Ma'am, let's get you cleaned up," said a female police officer. She lead me over to a police cruiser, donned purple latex gloves, and went to work on my hands with moist wipes. She tossed each bloody one into a plastic bag. An evidence bag. Henry's DNA was in the evidence bag. It was also all over the street.

"You were in the FBI agent's car, right?" she asked, almost nonchalantly.

My hands felt wet and cold and shook a little as she wiped the blood off. "Yes." She let me explain what happened.

I realized that I needed to explain what I was doing there and why. It was an interesting question I hadn't thought about for several minutes. I didn't have an answer ready for Pierce, and I hadn't had any revelations since I got in his car. This was going to be a problem.

Done cleaning, the officer took my statement, making me repeat everything again. She walked me through every moment of the shooting. The statement was as much for the shooting investigation as anything else.

"Why did the FBI agent pick you up?" she asked me again.

"We uh, know one another, from Tennessee. He has been investigating me for a while."

"And he ran into you on this street here in Henderson tonight?" she asked.

174

"He has been trying to pin something on my science lab for years. I came out here on business and he must have followed me. I was pretty freaked out when I saw him."

"According to your statement, you're saying that Agent Pierce had a good reason to shoot Mr. Ota," she stated.

I nodded. "Was that his name? Yes. The other man had a gun and was raising it toward the FBI agent."

"You're sure?" she asked.

Well, this was an interesting opportunity. I could throw Pierce under the bus here, imply that it wasn't a clean shoot, and that could get him off of my back for a while. But this may be the wrong kind of push, the kind that would make the Bureau look closely into Pierce's allegations, into who and what Henry was, and what he had to do with a bizarre killing out here. Stitcher would have my head for trying to play this too smart.

"I'm sure. He was defending himself. The dead guy had a gun and was pointing at Pierce." I thought for a second. "Is the agent going to be okay? I want to see him."

She looked at me under hooded eyes. "I'll see what I can do." She walked away. I could see Pierce in the distance, by the ambulance, talking to a quartet of cops and FBI. They probably didn't want any chance of us coordinating our statements.

The earlier text was from Malachi. He had said that Henry had bolted from him. I texted him back.

[Henry was killed

I'm a witness]

[God

Keep me posted]

Pierce came over to me. "How are you?"

I didn't know, actually. I wouldn't know for a few hours. "I'm okay, I think. And you?"

He put his hands on his hips and looked down at the asphalt. "I won't be."

I wanted to put my hand on his arm, but something stopped me. He was the enemy. He wanted to throw me in jail. He was also a pawn in our conspiracy. And he had just killed an innocent man. A hybrid who could have done great things, eventually. Henry wasn't a murderer. "I'm sorry."

175

"This is not my first time. They say," he motioned to the cops poking at their phones a dozen yards away, "this was probably suicide by cop. I'm not sure that changes anything." He looked up at me. "You know anything about why this guy would do something like that?"

I didn't say anything. I kept my mind blank so my face or my chakras or brain waves didn't betray anything. "Gambling debts?"

Pierce grunted. "You need to come with me back to the police station. They'll want to do another round of statements. And then you and I need to talk."

It took another hour, but eventually Pierce and I got a ride from the Henderson PD to a City of Henderson police station. It was a sandstone-colored building with bright blue garage doors, ablaze with bright LED lamps among the palm trees.

I updated Malachi after they sat me at a detective's desk, waiting to do an encore recounting of what happened. After an hour of waiting, it was now almost midnight, a tough-looking blond cop with massive biceps named Matthew interviewed me. Luckily, with Nevada three hours behind Tennessee, I wasn't tired yet.

The cop didn't press me on what I was doing in Henderson, or how I knew Agent Pierce, which I thought was odd. He walked me through every minute of the shooting and asked for the oddest details. Then he took me into an interrogation room and left me there with coffee in a cheap paper cup. I waited another half hour before Pierce came in.

For some reason, I was feeling confident. We were both in an awkward position here, but I wasn't the one who had just killed a man.

"I take it they're not charging you."

Agent Pierce shook his head. "It was a clean shoot. They still have to go through the motions though." His voice nearly cracked. I had hit a nerve. Good, I wanted my interrogator to be off-balance. "What are you doing in Nevada, Doc?"

"I could ask you the same thing." I folded my hands together.

He frowned. "I don't have to tell you. FBI business. But you showing up here right as we make a move on Henry Ota. Come on. It's been a long night, why don't we level with one another."

I smiled back, implying that I didn't have to tell him what I was doing here either. "I just met Henry tonight. I was hoping he could give me some

176

tips on playing poker." I paused. Pierce didn't believe a word of it. "People tell me my poker face is no good. Why were you after Henry?"

Pierce raised an eyebrow. "Henry Ota was wanted for questioning about a gruesome murder that happened in Las Vegas. Do you want to hear why it was gruesome?"

"A murder? Not really."

He put his chin on his fist. "How did you know him?"

"Sorry, that's a trade secret."

"Are you going to stick with that answer when I tell you that the murder involved chemically decomposing a body to remove the fat tissue?"

"Why would someone do that? There's more efficient ways to dispose of a corpse."

"Do tell, Dr. Cassano."

"Incineration, acid, there's plenty of ways. Why would you suspect that Henry did that?"

It was Pierce's turn to play coy. "I can't reveal details of an ongoing investigation."

"No, I suppose you can't. Well, Agent Pierce, we seem to be at an impasse. You may not like that I showed up, but I am the only witness that exonerated you in a police shooting. Of a minority. So why are you interrogating me?"

Pierce shook his finger at me. "That's all true. But Elaine, I know that you, or Stitcher, or someone on your side heard about the murder. And that's why you came halfway across the continent. And like the LVPD and the Henderson police, you went straight to Henry. You can't tell me why?"

"I wanted to talk to him about computational science work we're doing on in our Palo Alto facility. He was a math savant, from what I was told."

"So you must have talked to him. You were walking away from his neighborhood when I saw you. You didn't think I'd remember that, huh? So what did you find out?"

"We had a riveting discussion of matrix math and protein folding."

Pierce sighed and rubbed his face. "You do have a pretty bad poker face." He pulled his phone out and brought up autopsy photos. "Someone killed this man and tried to decompose the body for some reason. Probably to cover it up. The local police have good reason to think it was Henry."

I shrugged my shoulders. "Could be. I didn't know him that well. Just

177

heard he liked to count cards and lift weights. Maybe he was a killer. He didn't seem like that to me."

"Kind of odd, you visiting this guy at his home, at night, by yourself." Pierce narrowed his eyes.

"He's not my type. And since he made his living with online poker and weightlifting, I couldn't visit his office."

Pierce rolled his hand. "Go to a restaurant. Coffee shop. A library. Some place in public. Some place safe."

Shit. He was picking apart everything I was saying. I cleared my throat. "He was the type who really didn't like doing that. Crowds, noise, I don't know. These savants are like that, you know, on the spectrum. So why does a local murder merit the attention of the Bureau's finest?"

Pierce kept his face neutral. "Stop fucking with me. You know why. Your people are behind something awful. We're going to find odd substances in Henry's basement. DNA tests will connect him to the victim. And you're looking like an accomplice, or at least a person of interest."

"Then read me my rights and I'll wait for my lawyer to arrive," I said. "You know my lawyer. He likes to embarrass the Bureau."

Pierce narrowed his eyes but I saw the fear flash across them. In the years since I had joined Stitcher I had caught hints and glimpses of how he screwed with nosy government bureaucrats.

"Did you see how Henry dropped down from that wall? He was a huge man, even for a body-builder."

I gave him a so-what look. "Maybe he was taking steroids. Or he was in some competition. Or was just one of those gym-rats."

"Here's the thing though. You keep popping up on my radar, Elaine. I've heard you're connected to the whistleblowers causing so much grief for the food industry. Like you did back in the old days at Agriculture. And yet you act like John Stitcher, a tool of the industry, is your own personal savior. Maybe he doesn't know that you're stabbing his industry in the back. Maybe he won't want to be your guardian angel."

Well shit, Pierce knew more than I figured. He connected the dots wrong, but not too far wrong. I was supposed to be leading him back to the industry jerks Stitcher wanted out.

I looked down at the bare metal table and swallowed audibly. "Look, you think the industry is one cohesive group, but it's not. There's factions, companies and divisions of companies in furious competition with one another. Just like any large organization."

"Give me details." His eyes had widened a little and his voice had climbed an octave. He was itching to know more.

I shook my head. "I can't. Trade secrets and NDAs."

"But you can help whistleblowers bust their NDAs. That doesn't seem allowed either."

"I manage a lab. I'm not a corporate spy. I just testified to Congress."

"Elaine, I know you've been playing gopher on a lot of these insider leaks from inside certain companies. Stop dicking around with me. Was Henry Ota another informant?"

"No." God, this guy was all over the place connecting all the wrong dots. "Something completely separate. I'm trying to walk a fine line here talking about things you care about, understand?"

He leaned forward and nodded.

"Okay. Follow the earnings growth in the big companies. The domestic market is mostly zero-sum: one brand stealing market share and earnings from another. Each brand trying to keep ahead of the latest fad, including efforts to fight the obesity epidemic and wrap bacon around everything. Exporting such a mature market is the money tree. Okay? That's all I can say about it without lawyering up."

Pierce's eyes flitted back and forth. Would this dribble of insight prompt him to look at the efforts to create an obesity pandemic? I didn't know. He was very astute one moment and completely lacking in sense the next.

He stood up, keeping his long fingers pressed firmly to the table's cold gray metal. "Okay. Good. This has been helpful."

"So will that get you off my back for a while? I have a teenager who shouldn't be left alone overnight."

He smiled. "Yes. Thank you, Elaine."

[33]

When I got home to Knoxville, normal life settled in for a few days, except for flashbacks to Vegas. I still thought about Henry a lot when I was awake too. Our adipose shortage loomed large in my head and I pushed Donald to find a viable substitute.

I found myself reliving that night when Charlie yelled something from upstairs but I didn't hear him. I was in the basement swapping summer clothes for winter ones.

I hate getting into screaming matches between floors. He could wait till I came back upstairs. If the house was on fire, I figure he would come get me.

"MOM!" He yelled from the top of the basement stairs.

"Come down here if you want to talk," I yelled back.

Clomp clomp down the stairs. He was really putting his heels into it.

"Mom, couldn't you hear me?"

"No, if you want to talk to me, get within speaking distance. How many times have I told you that?"

He ignored that. "Ugh. What'd you do with all the good food?"

"Oh." I pulled sweaters from an old chest that once belonged to my father, "I got rid of it. And I'm not buying more junk food."

"I'm just going to eat more bread then," he retorted.

I put the clothes down. "Are you intent on being overweight? Is there a prize you're trying to win?"

"Yeah, Mom, that's exactly it. Fattest guy gets all the girls. No, I'm a teen boy, I'm adding muscle mass. I learned that in health class."

"Cookies and chips are not muscle-building foods," I pointed out.

"Funny. You can't starve me like this."

I focused on stacking sweaters. Sometimes, I've found with angsty teens, less eye contact is better. "Remember what I said about the meeting I had at your school? I didn't ask for that meeting, they sprung it on me."

"I'm not overweight!"

"Charlie, don't argue about the facts. Your BMI is too high. If you think that it's wrong, we can weigh you and measure your height right now."

"I'm not as big as the other kids at my school," he whined. He knew that wouldn't fly with me. "You should see the other guys in the robotics club."

"Then you have less to do to get down to a healthy weight than they will."

He put his hands on his love handles. "Dad is a lot easier to live with."

I shook my head. "Good luck with that guilt trip. I'm not competing with him. I'm trying to keep you healthy. It would be easier if you helped me."

He huffed indignantly.

"But I can see that your teenage brain is incapable of adequately evaluating the risks of a poor diet. So I have rebooted the food selection at home; more vegetables, fruit, and leaner proteins. No salty and sugary food with good mouth-feel."

"I'm just going to eat more crap when I'm out of the house." He crossed his arms.

"You're not sounding as mature as you think you are," I retorted. "The obesity problem is an epidemic, especially here in the South. It will wreck your life. And that will break my heart."

He stared at me in disgust. I resisted the urge to slap him across his smug face.

"How many kids do you know who have Type II diabetes?" I asked.

Eye roll. "We don't compare our health records at lunch time. It's not a nursing home."

I took a deep breath. Getting through his teen years required a lot of deep breaths. But I said nothing and waited him out.

181

Finally, he shrugged. "Maybe ten. Aidan just found out last month."

Aidan. A sweet kid, really respectful, called me "ma'am" and always offered to help around the house when he was over. He had a puppy dog crush on me.

He was also really overweight. Always had a twenty ounce soda in his hand and could put away double the amount of food I could, even though he was still shorter than me. His parents were morbidly obese too.

"Aidan is wrecking his entire cardiovascular system. His life expectancy is a lot lower now, and his life will be much more miserable along the way." My voice caught and I could feel tears sliding over my eyes. "You know what I've said happens to kids who get Type II."

Charlie nodded and looked down at the cheap basement carpeting.

I pulled him into a hug, mostly because I needed it. "I have to protect you, it's my job. I do it because I love you and I can't stand to see you hurt. But the older you get, the less I can do and the more you have to do to protect yourself."

He sighed. "I love you too, Mom."

I squeezed him tight and then let him go.

"Does this mean that if I pace myself on cookies and chips that you will let them back in the house?"

I flashed a quick, insincere smile that said funny, but no way. "When we eat outside the house, it's hard to avoid the bad stuff. That's just the way it is. Let's have an oasis here, where we can get away from the temptations."

He grinned. "Then we'll just eat out more often!"

"Where's that maturity I was hoping for? Seriously, kid, the world wants to fatten us all up. It's not an accident. We have to fight it."

"But you work for those guys who are making us fat," he said. Jesus, he was still arguing with me.

"Teenager discovers hypocrisy, news at eleven, right?" I said and shook my head. "It's because I work for them that I know this. And it's not as hypocritical as you think."

His arms dropped to his sides. "Come again?"

I chose my words carefully. "The food industry is both happy and horrified by the obesity epidemic. I don't think they expected the country to get so dangerously fat. The reason they fund my lab is because they realize that the public is in serious trouble and they want to help correct it."

He squinted at me skeptically. "There's more to it than that. But I get the gist."

"Good, now carry these clothes upstairs," I held out a pile of thick sweatshirts and sweaters.

He grinned slyly and backed toward the stairs. "Nah." Clomp clomp up the stairs. The twerp.

[34]

Donald appeared in my office doorway wearing an overcoat and a devilish grin. He looked like he had just run in from the parking lot. I gladly set aside my administrivia to see what his rush was. Generally, science was not a sprinting activity.

"We have partially deciphered the message in the meteor," he said, almost hopping from one foot to another. I waved him in and he closed the door.

"Take a breath there. Just tell me what you did."

"It's only a partial translation. Even with the translation key, we made only slow progress." He showed me a picture of the crystals with a small red sliver that indicated the proportion that had been deciphered.

"The code uses minute dislocations in the atomic structure of the meteor's crystals. The pattern wasn't random. Each crystal is a different document, and each dislocation in the structures is a word."

"And how did you see a pattern that small?" We had no instruments in-house that could do that kind of work.

"We borrowed time on the TEM and SEM at ORNL," Donald said. ORNL was Oak Ridge National Laboratory, for those not local or not in science. "TEM and SEM are electron microscopes, transmission and scanning."

184

The hairs on the back of my neck stood erect. "Did they know what you were doing?"

He shook his head as if the question was silly. "They were just happy to have the business. They charge a lot per hour. Operational security wasn't threatened."

I made a mental note to see later how he had that expense paid for.

"We transcribed those dislocations into a digital 3D map. It turned out to be an encrypted message. So we have been trying to crack that code."

"The aliens didn't want to make it easy, huh?" Make it was the secret formula of some kind of space Coca-Cola.

"No, they didn't," Donald replied excitedly. "They must have wanted only an advanced civilization with a certain amount of knowledge and computing power to decode it. We couldn't figure it out ourselves. We went to another outside group to crack the code."

"An outside group?" I shivered. "Who?"

He smiled proudly. "We used an open source alternative reality game about aliens conquering Earth. The code was something the players in the resistance had to crack to understand the games aliens' communications."

As usual, he was incredibly ingenious and incredibly dumb at the same time. I could feel a headache coming on. I kept my voice calm and low. "Tell me more about this game."

"The aliens are space Nazis who worship a tentacled monster god; the game is based on a Charles Stross science fiction spy novel. The code was presented as an occult, 21st century equivalent of the Enigma machine that Germany used in World War II."

"I don't know anything about science fiction," I said. "I get enough of it at the office. I don't know much about World War II, except that it was horrible and we won. But the bottom line here is that there better be enough misdirection to cover us."

Donald nodded. "Once the players cracked the code, the game producers gave it to us and then started building it into the story's narrative."

How would I explain this to Stitcher when it blew up in our face, as it probably would? "You don't even know what the message was? It's the first proof of alien intelligence and you're having it come out in a video game? That's a huge risk that it wasn't something clearly not from a game."

Donald just stared at me with a grin. It was his way of being nice to people he thought were playing dumb. It took me a second to realize that he was waiting for me to think about this some more. So I did.

"You figured that whatever the message was would not seem out of place in this game. And that the players would naturally assume it was fiction."

He kept grinning. "No worries, right?"

I shook my head. "You've opened us up to someone asking questions. Don't the game producers wonder what the code was and how you came by it? And if you don't know what the coded message was, why would they let it in their game? It could be incredibly offensive."

Donald shook his head. "The producers wanted something random, and something really hard to crack. A lot of the players are programmers and know encryption. It had to be really good, very realistic."

I sighed; he wasn't understanding me. "Let's say that a player calls his buddy at the NSA about this tough code in this online game. His buddy looks at it and is amazed because he's never seen anything like it. Now the government's national security guys are interested. They ask the game producers who came up with it. They point to you. So they come knocking on your door, handcuffs in one hand, job offer in the other, and ask how you came up with this unusual encryption. And what do you say then?"

Donald licked his lips. "I say that I based it on the DNA of various biological specimens and the molecular structure of cheese product and fast food chicken nuggets."

"You snow them, you mean?"

"Yes. They would leave us alone after that. Their eyes would glaze over."

"That is wishful thinking. What if they had top geneticists refute your story?" I folded my arms.

He didn't have an answer.

"At this point, the best you can tell them is that you created it, which will they will see through when they investigate you. And that will likely lead them right to the lab and to the hybrids and our real research. That is a huge risk."

Donald knitted his brows and sat on the corner of my desk, thinking. "That all must have a very low probability of happening," he stated.

I shook my head. "That's your wishful thinking."

He winced. "What should I do if they come by?"

"Say it was a personal project. Or say you mashed up a lookup table at random. But whatever you do, it has to encourage them not investigate further." Even as I said this, I realized that Donald pulling off such a conversational feat convincingly was unlikely to an extreme.

"You're going to tell Stitcher?" Donald looked apprehensive.

"Hell yes. Maybe he can run some interference so they don't hook you to a polygraph. Or get ahead of the story somehow. Also, he may tell me I'm overreacting."

Donald's face clouded over. "I'm sorry, Elaine. I thought I was being careful."

I leaned forward. "You were being careful. Quite devious and ingenious, in fact. And it will probably be fine. But we need to be three times more careful than that. Run these things by me first, okay? No more outsourcing anything about hybrids without asking me first."

He stood up and waved his tablet in the air. "Now can I show you what we found?"

I grinned. "I wouldn't let you leave this office until you did."

[35]

Donald held up his tablet. "It's a message, to anyone who can decipher it. I'm sending it to you now."

A text file appeared in my email. The message was paragraphs long. It seemed kind of verbose, with long sentences made up of numerous dependent clauses. I started to skim. The opening lines sounded like a grand pronouncement, beginning with, "To the sentient beings who have reached the adequate level of advancement for making the necessary implements to discover this message, we convey greetings and positive wish-thoughts."

I asked, "How much of this is a direct translation versus an interpretation? Because it looks like bad English to me, which would be highly improbable."

Donald chuckled. "Direct translation to English. It took us a while to decipher the language, but not as long as you would think. They included a translation key: that's what the game players cracked. We simply had to program a translator to apply it to the entire message."

"How long have you been working on breaking this code?" I asked. I had a feeling it was a lot longer than since last Wednesday.

"I started when I was in graduate school. But I've been planning on it since I first saw the meteorite when I was a little kid."

"That was what, almost thirty years ago?" I said. I shook my head and continued reading.

The message went on at some length explaining who the people were who sent it and how old their civilization was. It also explained the various achievements of their civilization, including powered flight, clean energy, and genetic engineering. I was surprised they didn't mention eliminating poverty or eradicating disease.

Well, there was proof that we weren't alone in the great big dark. Donald's ancestors weren't just highly-advanced bacteria that had hitched a ride on an interstellar crag of rock.

"So, this means that intelligent life exists in the universe," I said. "Your DNA being on this meteor was not an accident. This is the discovery of the millennium." Visions of intense publicity run ran through my head. Would we even want that kind of attention? Would it be smart to mention it, or would it reveal the entire conspiracy? No, on second thought, we wouldn't want any of that attention.

Donald nodded impatiently. He thought I was joking, since we were both ears-deep in a conspiracy where extraterrestrials were not the most shocking part. "That's not the most important thing. Keep reading."

I stared at him, trying to get my head around the idea that the discovery of extraterrestrial life was not the biggest revelation in the message. Sometimes Donald completely missed the larger point and had an odd perspective. I opened my mouth to remind him of this but he waved me off.

"It's not that there are others out there, it's why we haven't heard from them." He nodded at my tablet.

Well, that was academic, wasn't it? I am no astronomer, but even I knew that the distances involved would mean transmissions and signals of other advanced civilizations would be lost in the universe's background noise. Delivering the message snail mail like this had to be incredibly slow but still more reliable than hoping that a beamed message would make it intact across light-years.

I kept skimming; when I see a lot of important text for the first time, I skim it to become familiar with the major sections, the shape of the paragraphs, and to get a taste of the prose. On a second pass I actually read for comprehension. That little trick was how I got through graduate school.

The message had several parts. There was a section about who the message senders were, why they were encoding a message, and finally, what the message was.

"We are an advanced biological species of beings that have mastered many fields. We have orbited our planet and explored other planets. We have mastered the animal and plant life of our planet. We have developed nuclear technologies." There was a long list of the technologies they had invented, some of which I didn't understand. They were advanced, maybe even beyond where we were.

Fifteen paragraphs later I found their explanation of why we hadn't heard from them before. The message said, "Our civilization is dying. Not because of wars, or achieving immortality or transforming into another species type.

"The technologies, industries, and lifestyle we have developed have also poisoned/damaged the atmosphere and even our planet's mantle. We realize now that this is not the first time this has happened on our own planet. At least two other species overpopulated our world and changed either the atmosphere or the liquid bodies to a degree that caused their own extinction. Perhaps this is the desired manner of the universe.

"We have tried to remedy this damage, but after 200 revolutions around the star we realize that it is too late. The damage cannot be reversed. Our planetary resources have become depleted to the point where we have less power over our planet than we once had. Our biome's ability to sustain us is compromised. Some of us in the science and biological disciplines believe that our people will become extinct within a number of centuries."

And here was the warning: "That is why we have prepared this warning for other advanced civilizations. The people behind this message and the genetic code captured inside this spacefaring rock are concerned scientists and philosophers dedicated to warning other sufficiently advanced civilizations. This communication device only reveals itself to a sufficiently advanced civilization like yours. If you are not, then our doomed fate should serve as a cautionary tale.

"We assume that you are similarly vulnerable. Please heed our warning. Advanced civilizations do not fall because of war, or exploding stars. They fail because they foul their own planet to the point where even their own bodies break down. It is a slow process, but observable by those who study the air, the food, the plant and animal life. While we have failed, we hope that this warning can help another civilization across the stars to avoid our fate. Do whatever it takes to stop chemically transforming your world."

The message continued in vague generalities on what a civilization should do to avoid an environmental apocalypse. It read like generic health tips: don't smoke, don't overeat, get proper nutrition and sleep, etc. Finally, it finished with a mention of the genetic code that we had grown the hybrids from.

"We hope that you do arrest your planetary decline before it reaches an irreversible point. If you do, the signs of progress will be observable early on. We have included samples of our genetic material in the space rock in case you do. Even though our civilization will reach its end, we hope that you can bring our species to life once again. Our desire is that our kind will learn from your lessons and can live on a planet that has succeeded in maturing and growing beyond where we have failed. We now make <appreciative noises> at you."

I looked up. "How did they know we would have to be sufficiently advanced to find their message?"

Donald stuck out his lower lip. "They embedded the message in the crystalline structure of the meteor itself. The arrangement of the rare elements in various patterns was a big hint; we would never find something randomly occurring in nature. The molecular structure had to be carefully designed, tested, and placed inside the meteor. And only a civilization with highly advanced diagnostic tools, like electron microscopes, would notice the structure."

I scratched my head. "How old is the meteorite?"

"Probably over a billion years old," Donald said. "Carbon dating it has not been conclusive. Given the millions of years it would take for a meteorite to cross from one solar system to another, we have to assume that the aliens are long, long dead."

I pursed my lips. "I'm sorry, Donald. You don't have any other of your kind to share this with. You're the oldest of the hybrids, so it is probably worse for you. Especially since they are talking to you, in particular. At least in a way they are."

He held up a hand. "No need. It's not much different than you feeling sad while looking at cave paintings by early humans."

"What's the rest of this?" I asked, pointing to the pages and pages of material that, even in English, still looked foreign to me. "Did they provide any science or technology that can help us?"

Donald looked at his tablet. "The last section of the message is highly scientific and the terms they use could be misinterpreted."

The meteor was probably sent with the best of intentions. It was a warning, maybe a help manual, plus a vehicle to perpetuate their species.

"They have included an instruction manual," Donald replied. "on how to genetically engineer the DNA to recreate their species. I think that is the primary reason that they launched this meteor into space."

I tapped my finger on my desk. "So if we had deciphered the code when the asteroid landed, we would have been able to pump out hybrids much earlier. Or maybe even the full-on aliens themselves. And without all of the deadly failures that happened early on."

Donald nodded slowly, sadly. "It appears so."

"Huh. At the same time that they wrote off their entire planet, their entire species, they still wanted to give someone the ability to bring them back." I shook my head. "That's incredibly hopeful on their part."

He nodded. "Yes. Or egotistical."

I cocked an eyebrow. "How so? It's just perpetuation of the species."

Donald frowned. "They must have believed that their mistakes were not fundamental to their species. Blasting their DNA into space is predicated on a belief that they weren't responsible for the mistakes they made in planetary management. Or that they could avoid making those mistakes again."

I put my tablet aside. I'd read the rest later, maybe after Donald and his team deciphered the rest of it. "Maybe if we can bring one back, there is a happy ending to the story after all."

"The preface says that this is a warning to those who may have followed their path of doom. There is no happy ending, if we are as far gone as they were." Donald sighed. "But. I want to bring one of them back, without human DNA." He looked at me with unblinking eyes. "Honestly, that is really why I have pushed so hard to make progress on vat-grown substitutes."

"Oh, I don't know if we'll ever be able to do that." I shook my head. "We can barely feed you hybrids right now. Plus, they may not look as human as you do."

Donald scowled. "We'd be fools not to try."

192

I felt like shit for sounding so defeatist. There was too much running through my head right now. Extraterrestrials, planetary apocalypses, messages sent through outer space. God damn. "I'm sorry. Don't listen to me, Donald. You're right." I smiled at him. "See, you're smarter than me."

He grinned as he left my office. "Naturally. We'll see what we can pull from the scientific section. Maybe the key to avoiding their fate is all written out for us."

[36]

"Elaine, grab a shovel. We have a big fucking problem."

I looked at Charlie sitting at the kitchen counter, waiting for my help on his biology homework. It was getting late on a school night. I rolled my eyes at him, pointed at the phone held to my head, and went into the living room. "What is it?" I had a feeling that I would be heading to the airport soon.

"Grab your coat, and a shovel, and plug this address into your directions app," Stitcher said. "I'll explain on the way."

The address was out in the sticks. "John, what the hell is this about?"

"It's a fucking 5-alarm fire and this is other duties as assigned."

I lowered my voice. "A shovel? You need to be straight with me. What are we doing?"

He ignored me. "I'll call your cell in two minutes. Jeff Ewell and a few others will meet you there. Leave Charlie at home."

"John. John?" The call ended. I stared at the phone for a second. What the hell? Did he find buried treasure? Had he killed someone? I turned towards the kitchen. "Uh, Charlie, I need to go out. Something happened at work."

Charlie looked at me suspiciously. "This late at night?"

I shrugged helplessly and pulled my coat out of the closet.

"If you have a date, you can tell me," he said.

The dating thing again. Sometimes I wonder if he and Ma conspired

194

behind my back. "Would I go on a date dressed like this?" I indicated my old jeans and ratty t-shirt.

He turned sulky. "Never mind. How am I supposed to finish this homework?"

"The internet." Every academic subject now had a number of lectures online at all different levels of learning. I had told Charlie a million times that if I had the modern internet when I was in high school, I would have made straight As.

He groaned. I got it, helping with homework was time we could spend together. But I would make it up to him later.

I hurried to the garage. I tossed a shovel in the back of my minivan and grabbed a flashlight and fresh batteries.

Stitcher called just as I left my subdivision. "Tell me you're on the road."

"I'm on the road," I said. "What the hell is going on?"

"Goddamn Agent Pierce has discovered an old lab secret. As lab director, you're on the clean-up crew to remove the evidence before he gets there."

I gulped. "I don't like the sound of that."

"Well, early on in Project Rogers, somebody didn't fucking follow through on a critical task and now, somehow, it has come back to bite us in the balls," Stitcher said through gritted teeth. He must really be angry.

"Remember I told you that during the hybrid experiments back in the 70s, there were a lot of uh, failures. The leftovers were supposed to be incinerated, but someone, for reasons which fucking escape me, decided it would be better to bury them up in the mountains, in the lab's dumping ground."

"Oh God, John, are you kidding me?" He was talking about hybrid fetus corpses. Donald Meers wasn't the first hybrid grown, he was just the first to survive infancy.

"I wish. Now someone must have discovered what we dumped there and called that FBI dickwad. He called the state troopers' crime scene squad, and luckily I have a friend there who warned me. You need to get the leftovers out of there before Pierce and the super trooper squad find them."

I gripped the steering wheel. This sounded perfectly awful. "How the hell are we going to do that? Ask Pierce to stand aside?"

"Don't worry about it. I have the state trooper crime scene team dragging their feet; they don't want to rush around for a fed. God bless the fucking Confederacy. They will probably get to Pierce in the next half an hour. He's

195

waiting out by the main road for them; I'm sending you in the back way. You'll have to get in and out before Pierce gets there. Oh, and there isn't a cell signal within two miles of the site."

"Why didn't the lab take care of this 40 years ago?" I yelled, more out of frustration than anything. I wanted no part of this.

"Someone fucked up, what else?" Stitcher replied.

I exited the highway and continued down roads that became progressively darker and more sparsely populated. Within two minutes I was on a two-lane road with no streetlights. I switched on my high beams. "Isn't Pierce going to see me and Jeff coming? There's no other lights out here."

"The address I gave you is on the back side of the property. You'll have to hike through the woods a ways," Stitcher said. "There's no way they'll see you from the main road."

"How the hell did Pierce find out about this?" I asked, slapping the steering wheel. I was afraid that a herd of deer would come charging at my car in the black gloom. The green pinpricks of my headlights reflecting off of animals' eyes did nothing to settle my nerves.

"Beats the shit out of me. I only found out when Pierce called this in. Friends at the state police tipped me off because the site is on lab property. They fucking owe me a dozen favors."

"This guy is like a monster in a horror movie. Why is he in Tennessee?" I asked.

"He must be a very determined asshole, I'll give him that," Stitcher agreed. "I can locate his cell phone now since he called from such an isolated location."

"You have friends at the phone company?" I asked.

"I have friends fucking everywhere, Elaine. I belong to the corporate espionage union and we all help each other out and jerk each other off on the weekend. It's not your concern. I'm texting you the address of the place to take the leftovers so it's not our goddamn problem ever again. Download this before you lose your cell signal or you will be well and truly fucked."

"Okay. I'll talk to you later."

"Call me the first second you're back in cell range. I'm dying over here not knowing what's the fuck is happening. If Pierce gets ahold of the leftovers, well, that could be the beginning and middle of the end."

"I'll keep that in mind when I'm digging in the dark."

196

I sighed and pulled over to do that. As it was I almost had no signal on my phone. Stitcher wanted me to take the 'leftovers' to a funeral home up here in the mountains. It confirmed my worst fears about what the 'leftovers' were. I had hoped that we would be unearthing boxes of paper files rather than dead hybrid infant skeletons or body parts.

I started driving again and for several minutes saw nothing but tree trunks, and the occasional deer. The woods were so thick it felt like driving through a tunnel.

My navigation app announced that I had reached my destination. I recognized Jeff's silver pickup truck parked in a small clearing off the side of the road. I parked behind it and was chagrined to find that Jeff didn't wait for me. I had to run through the dark woods by myself.

[37]

I grabbed my shovel and flashlight and used my phone's GPS to orient myself. I had to march straight into the woods to the right.

I kept my flashlight pointed low and thrust my way in. The undergrowth was over my head, tangled and dense. I had worked my way around some dead ends. I wished I had a machete to hack through it all. If it weren't for the phone, I would have been lost.

After ducking under what seemed like a million branches, I found my way to a spot where the trees were tall and the undergrowth was no bigger than a fern. Without Stitcher cursing in my ear, I couldn't tell if I was late or ahead of schedule. Instead, my heart pounded with the fear that we would be caught. At least Jeff was ahead of me.

I was careful to not step in a hole or trip over a moss-covered log. A twisted ankle or broken foot out here could be really bad.

I still didn't see or hear any sign of Jeff. The ground sloped down to a stream and I poked along its bank looking for a way across with my flashlight. This late in the year, at this time of night, I was not getting my shoes and clothes wet, nor was I taking my chances with bare feet on a stream bed in the dark. I had to walk, or run, out of these woods on these feet.

About thirty yards to my left I found a series of rocks I could cross. The ground rose again and I ran into another thick tangle of towering, dense undergrowth. When I found the southern edge of that tangle, I could hear the distinctive slish of a shovel carving through dirt.

Jeff and three other guys were digging in a pool of weak light aimed at the ground, not more than fifty yards away. I stepped over a series of fallen branches to them, snapping and cracking an announcement of my arrival.

Jeff looked up and hurried over. "Oh good, you made it. And you brought a shovel, great. I'm going to send out my boys to create a diversion."

He introduced his sons Clancy and Tim, and Tim's partner Kevin, who looked like a body builder. All three were in their 20s, wearing camouflage, night vision goggles, and goofy, enthusiastic grins. These young guys thought this was a fun game. They reminded me of Charlie.

"So what do you mean by 'diversion'?" I asked. I didn't want these guys tangling with the FBI and the state police.

Jeff waved away my concerns. "They'll dig a couple of holes closer to the other road. The cops will stop and take a look at them before pushing all the way in here. It should slow them down."

I was so scared I was ready to pee myself. "Are you sure getting closer to the cops is a good idea?"

Tim Ewell replied, "We're not taking any lights with us. We can see just fine as is. And we're bringing this," he hoisted a gravestone. I shined my flashlight on it and saw that it was a Halloween decoration, a blank tombstone. In the dark it looked real enough though.

"All we need to do is buy some time," Jeff said. "The boys'll give us a heads up when trouble's coming."

I shook my head. "How? My cell phone has no signal."

Jeff smiled and held up a device the size of a smartphone. "Ultrasonic bat detector. They have a dog whistle."

I hefted my shovel. "Fine. Let's get this over with."

The boys ran off into the woods, making a lot less sound than I did coming in.

"Let me show you what we have here," Jeff said.

I had the sense he didn't want the boys around for this. There were dozens of little bundles lined up in a hole that was a shallow grave about three feet deep and ten feet wide.

The four men had worked fast. But they hadn't pulled up the bundles yet.

"It's better if you don't look at them," Jeff mentioned, his voice quivering.

I was tempted to shine the light in his face to see if he was welling up like I was. But I didn't.

"We need to put them on this tarp here. Each of us will drag one tarp out, okay? Let's dig."

We shoveled furiously under the bouncy headlamps, careful to avoid splitting any of the lumpy white plastic sacks. I found a corner marked off by a black plastic border and worked my way around the edge. I had sweat running down my forehead when we finished digging.

Then Jeff and I hurried to move the bundles from the hole to the tarp. I had no idea how we would move all of them. I found they were heartbreakingly light. Some felt like a loose bundle of sticks. Others felt squishy and still others seem to have metal parts clanking inside. It's just old lab parts, I told myself.

A twig snapped to our right and I tensed. But it was Clancy. "The cops just pulled up. But they haven't come in the woods yet. Tim sent me back to help you."

Jeff nodded. "Put these bags on the tarp. Be careful. They're really old - we don't want them breaking open."

The three of us formed a bucket brigade from the hole to the tarps. We were three-quarters of the way done when the bat detector blinked red and vibrated.

Clancy barely flinched as he handed me another bundle. "That means the cops are headed for the pits we dug. We only need to worry if Tim sends us three short blasts."

"Aren't the police going to see him and Kevin?" I asked.

"No ma'am. Tim and Kevin are sneaky guys. They'll just lay low if they can't run and walk out tomorrow."

The bat detector flashed three times and vibrated. I sucked in a breath. There was still so many sacks left.

Kevin came running up. "Let's go," he said.

"We should fill the pit in," Jeff suggested. The bundle I handed him ripped open and the contents tumbled out like a bag of chopsticks.

"Damn it," I uttered and pinched the bag closed before anything else could fall out.

"I'm sorry, my fault," Jeff said.

Someone swung a flashlight on it and I really wished they had not.

Resting on the dead brown leaves was a tangled pile of little femurs. And sitting atop it, upside down, was a human skull about the size of a tennis ball. But it was not completely human; it had ridges and protrusions in odd spots. The tiny bones didn't look right either. They had a bluish tint. I shoveled them in the bag.

Behind me, Clancy retched.

"We need to go, right now," Kevin said, grabbing a tarp and folding it into an impromptu bag.

"Did you get them all?" Jeff asked me in a shaky voice.

I swept the ground with my flashlight. No horrors appeared. "Yes."

"Tim and Clancy, start filling in the pit over there while Elaine and I finish over here," Jeff said. "Kevin, you good?"

Kevin hoisted two tarps over his immense shoulders. "I'm already gone, Mr. E."

Tim and Clancy shoveled dirt into the far end of the shallow trench. It occurred to me that this area would look all dug up in plain daylight. Hopefully Pierce wouldn't come back in the morning and find anything.

Jeff and I finished filling the remaining tarps with the remaining bundles. Then we swept the ground with our flashlights once again to make sure no bits were left behind.

"Lights off," Tim whispered. "I can see their flashlights."

The gloom settled in but once my eyes adjusted I could just barely see what I was doing. I didn't see any flashlights in the distance, but I wasn't wearing night vision goggles. I tied up each bag while the other three shoveled furiously.

"Let's go," Jeff whispered. "Elaine, take the shovels."

Clancy and Tim did something to erase our tracks around the pit, spreading leaves and debris around. I winced at the sussing, crackly racket they made.

The men each carried a tarp. Kevin was ahead of us in the dark, snapping an occasional twig. Clancy brought up the rear, covering our tracks as we went and keeping an eye out with his night vision goggles. I struggled to maneuver straight shovel handles through the crooked confines of undergrowth and tree branches without clanging them together.

We took a short break at the stream to catch our breath. My arms were tired from the shovels and so Tim and I exchanged cargo. The plastic tarp I slung over my shoulder had ghastly little bumps and knots that sickened me when they dug into my back.

Clancy rejoined us, wiping our footprints away. "They're moving faster. Their flashlights are pointing up too much, not looking at their feet. They probably have heard us."

We splashed across the stream in a hurry and gave up covering our tracks. Hopefully the high-treble hiss of the stream would mask our noisy retreat.

My legs felt cold, wet, and numb from the shins down as we climbed up the far bank. Running through the woods in the dark, even on relatively flat ground, became a squishy, painful slog. I tried to follow the steps of Tim in front of me so I didn't break a leg or catch a branch in my eye.

There was a loud, sharp gunshot. It echoed off of the tree trunks like the report of a breaking baseball bat. Then came a rustle of feet through leaves far off. Everyone began to jog. Low hanging twigs and spiderwebs grabbed at my face and I ducked my head down and focused on keeping up with the legs in front of me.

My knapsack of horrors swung, banged and crunched against my back as I ran. At least it didn't smell - all I could smell were moldy leaves.

We reached the thick brambles that I had been caught up in earlier and caught our breath, again, as Tim looked for a way around on his night-vision goggles.

The rustling of feet through leaves and a rapid crashing through underbrush echoed through the woods.

Tim took off to the left. He ducked down into a hole in the bramble. He threw the shovels to the ground, crawled through, and dragged them after him.

This was crazy. These flimsy tarps could catch and tear open. We couldn't stop and collect anything that spilled without getting caught. But leaving any evidence behind would be almost as bad.

I dropped to my hands and knees and dragged the tarp behind me. Every scrape of a twig, any resistance I felt when I pulled convinced me that the tarp had split open. After what felt like ten minutes, with a crackle of breaking twigs, I finally pulled my bundle free of the forest. I ran my hands over the tarp to feel for tears. There were none, but the feel of bony protrusions were enough to make bile mix with the cool night air in my mouth.

I breathed through my nose, hoisted the bag over my shoulder, and ran. I could only hope the nausea would hold off until we were away.

We sprinted through the field towards the road. Kevin rushed back from the cars to meet us. He silently took the tarp from my arms and hurried ahead of me. I nearly fell down without the weight pressing me forward. I stumbled and planted a knee deep in the soft dirt. Behind me I could hear voices in the woods. I turned and saw flashlight beams flailing around in the trees.

I ran, not looking back again. I made it to the road just as the guys loaded the last tarp into the back of my minivan. I swallowed vomit back down as I jumped in my van. We left in a loud hurry, but with our lights off. I followed the darkened rear end of Jeff's truck down the total darkness of the back country road.

[38]

I was so intent on following Jeff's truck that I had forgotten about Stitcher completely until my phone rang.

"Yo," I answered.

"Mom?" Charlie said.

"Charlie? Oh. I'm almost done, babe," I said. "Just go on to bed. You have to get up for school tomorrow."

"No way I'm going to sleep in this house by myself," he said.

There was only one reason he would say something like that. "Did you watch another horror movie?"

Silence. And then my phone beeped, with a call that was probably Stitcher.

Charlie cleared his throat. "It was *The Shining*."

"Holy crap, really bad idea. I'll be home when I'm home. Gotta go, love you," I said quickly and then switched to Stitcher.

"We made it, John," I said.

"Jesus Fucking Christ, that's a relief," he said. "I couldn't delay the crime scene guys any longer because Pierce's flight landed early. Did those donut-fuckers see you?"

"Yes, they saw us. They chased us across a field. But I don't think they could identify us. It was dark, they had flashlights. They were too far away."

"I will give Jesus a rim job if you're right. Are you sure you got all of the leftovers?"

"As best as we could do at night, and in a hurry."

"You're not pumping me full of hope here, Professor," Stitcher replied. "Are you heading to the disposal point now?"

"Yes. Jeff ran a really organized team here. Night vision goggles, camouflage." I left out the bat detector.

"Jeff and I have been through scrapes like this before," Stitcher explained, but didn't elaborate. "Pierce is fucking relentless. Are you sure he couldn't ID any of you?"

I relived the chase in my mind while I absently followed the pickup's taillights. "I'm sure they knew we were there, they could probably hear us, but we were at least fifty yards away, in the dark, with trees and other bushes in the way. Plus, they were running through the woods with flashlights, so their night vision was shot."

"Let's motherfucking hope so. I want you to make sure that the stuff is completely disposed of. Completely."

"I got it," I said and hung up.

The funeral home that Stitcher directed us to looked like a colonial plantation house dropped into the wilderness, with white columns bathed in floodlights. The lights inside were off and there weren't any cars in the parking lot.

Jeff knocked on the side door while we all waited in our cars. An old woman answered and the two talked. Jeff waved us around back. Of course, we looked completely conspicuous, a couple of vehicles idling out front of a funeral home late at night. We pulled behind the building and the old woman let us in a back door.

She looked at our wet feet, the young guys' camouflage, and chuckled. "The taxidermist is down the road," she said as she held the door open.

When no one laughed, she said, "John Stitcher sent you folks? Good, I owe him my arm and leg. This should pay the bastard back, I reckon."

We brought the bags in and piled them on a stretcher by the door. She began to close the door but I stepped forward.

"We need to see this through to the end," I said. "Make sure there's no loose ends."

Jeff nodded.

"Oh," she said, and let us in.

Jeff's phone rang. He answered and gave me a look; it was Stitcher.

"No, we're there now," Jeff said. "Yes, we're doing that right now."

He looked over his shoulder at me. "Yes, she's here. No, I'm pretty sure. Okay. Bye."

"John is nervous," Jeff said.

I nodded. "This has been much too close, even for him."

We followed the stretcher into the room they used to prepare the bodies. It looked like a doctor's examining room or an outpatient surgery suite, but with extra sinks and hoses.

The old woman turned on a series of bright white lights, washing out much of the color in the room. We blinked until our eyes adjusted.

Kevin looked around the preparation room like we were going to tie him down and vivisect him. Clancy noticed that at the same time I did, exchanged meaningful glances with Tim, and jabbed a thumb at the door. "We'll just go wait in the truck."

Smart boys. The old woman upended the bag under the bright white lights.

And they spilled out, bluish-white bones and tiny skulls. Most were clean of any dirt or debris, while others were streaked with dirt and clay.

I couldn't take my eyes off of them. "Can anyone do a DNA test on cremated remains?"

The old woman shook her head. "No ma'am. We had a state's attorney in here last year who tried that. We humored her, but the lab couldn't find any trace of DNA."

She continued dumping the bags into the plywood box. Tiny femurs, skulls, ribs, pelvises, and finger bones grew into a mounting pile.

Jeff and I watched, like witnesses to the unearthing of a mass grave which we had a hand in producing. Mass graves were usually filled with human adults. This was semi-human infants.

"Funny looking bones," the woman remarked.

I didn't know whether to throw up, cry, or look away. I did none of that. I just stood there, wet, cold, and mute.

The box began to fill and she had to spread the bones around to keep them from overflowing. The finger and toe bones fell through the spaces between the bigger bones. One of the little skulls rolled and stopped with its little eye sockets staring right at me.

"Follow me," she said, a bit sadly. This was probably more than all the children she had buried in several decades.

She pushed the gurney out of the room down another hallway to the crematorium. It was simply a large stainless steel box with a door and a control pad.

We helped her shove the box into the steel crematorium. I kept my eyes on Jeff rather than look down at the remains. Jeff's face was a road map of anguish. "Now what?" he asked as the woman punched buttons and a whooshing began inside the box.

The woman wiped her hands on her jeans. "It'll take four hours, I reckon. Normal body takes about two or three, but this is all bone. We grind up the ashes and any fragments."

She looked from Jeff to me. "You folks aren't going to sit around waiting until it's done, are you?"

Jeff and I looked at one another. "We should see this through to the end, right?" He said. "I'll stay."

I was afraid that Pierce would show up, shut down the crematorium, and remove the remains. I was jittery and feeling like anything that could go wrong would. "You don't have to do that. Your sons and Kevin are waiting in the truck."

Jeff shook his head. "You have a younger child waiting for you at home. I won't take no for an answer. My guys are already snoozing out there. I'm sure."

I didn't want to stare at a stainless steel box for four hours with cold and wet legs, but I was the lab director. I couldn't let Jeff do this while I scooted home. But I knew Charlie would be gnawing his fingernails all night waiting for me to get back. I was responsible for him, not for Jeff or Stitcher.

"If you want, you can go lay down on the couch in the office," the old woman said. "There's nothing else for you to do. Honestly folks."

We turned to go.

"One other thing," the old woman said. "What do you want us to do with the remains?"

Jeff motioned for that to be my decision. Shouldn't I take possession of a bag of incriminating evidence? I looked at the woman. "What do you usually do with the body parts that you remove?"

She rolled her eyes. "Oh, that's medical waste. We have a truck come around every week and haul it away."

I smiled weakly. "Pray tell, which company is it that takes it?"

She looked at me warily. I must sound like a total obsessive compulsive. "Medshine."

I looked at Jeff and tried not to ralph. Medshine was one of the medical waste companies that supplied liposuction-produced human adipose that were processed into the hybrids' food supplements. Medshine probably wouldn't mix cremated remains with human fat. Or would they? I believed in recycling, but not like this.

"I'll dump them down the drain," Jeff said. I had no idea if that was legal, or ethical. But the DNA would be completely destroyed and then scattered through the sewer system.

The old woman nodded solemnly and took Jeff to find him a couch. I left the crematorium, verified that Jeff's crew was snoozing in the truck, and went home.

[39]

Charlie spent Veteran's Day weekend with his dad while I attended a conference on childhood obesity in chilly Boston. I was presenting several papers and wanted to get an ear to the ground on this issue, in no small part because of Charlie's brush with it. Money was pouring into childhood obesity research, in part because we as a country were running a gruesome natural experiment in the lifelong effects of obesity.

It was an experiment that more than ever I wanted to bring to a premature end. Henry Ota and kids like Charlie's friend Aidan were fresh reminders why I pushed our guys so hard to develop a human adipose alternative to feed the hybrids. I was certain we could do it soon and could end this terrible sacrificing of our kids' health.

My panel was on how diet affects childhood obesity. The room seated 50 and I saw many familiar faces, some of them friendly, some not. I presented a paper on the metabolic effects on mice of various food additives. I know, ironic, huh? The other papers were on correlations between obesity and celiac disease, and an updated results on which foods increased insulin-resistance fastest in a lab setting.

My discussant, a well-known Ohio State professor, was rigorous but gracious. The moderator asked for questions.

A researcher from Harvard Medical School gave me the classic 'you-should-have-thought-of' criticism. I acted like they were good suggestions that we were already planning to incorporate into future work. The reality was the paper was a spinoff of our work to find an additive mix that made people feel full when their stomach was only three quarters full. We were making progress, but it was proprietary progress.

"This is also for Dr. Cassano," said the next questioner, who looked young enough to be a grad student. "I have a hard time accepting the findings in your paper. I mean, you and your co-authors are funded by the companies that make these additives. I'd like to hear your thoughts on how this is not a conflict of interest."

This type of question was another reason I attended these conferences. I was there to show that we were a legit lab and interested in working with others. I leaned toward the microphone. "Every researcher is funded by someone who is interested in the kind of work they do. Not every funder has altruistic motives, and not every scientist who takes the money cares what the funder's interests are." I smiled. "I was not on the food industry's Christmas list for a long time. I'm interested in the science, whether it comes from the industry, the government, or academia. Furthermore, our lab's website makes clear who our funders are, and each paper lists its funding sources, if any."

The questioner persisted. "That may be how you view this, but what do you say to those who believe your research is tainted?"

I held up my hands in surrender. "All I can say is that these issues were near and dear to my heart before I left the USDA and they still are. In my five years working at AgSol, I have never seen the industry try to interfere with our research."

The moderator interjected, "Are there questions for the other papers? And by questions, I mean with a question mark, not a comment."

There wasn't and the panel broke up. I was relieved I wasn't accosted by any anti-corporate types who wanted to yell at me, like my old pal Lyle. In fact, no one approached me as I packed up my things and the next session's panelists came in. Being ignored happened sometimes. You couldn't expect future collaborators to be sitting at every presentation you did. But it still felt like not being picked during speed-dating at single's night at church.

I was almost into the hallway when I heard, "Elaine, long time no see."

I turned around. It took me a second to recognize the man, because he was out of context. Way out of context. "Agent Pierce, I'm surprised to see you here."

He smiled. "I'm trying to get up to speed on obesity, nutrition, and weight-related diseases." He held out a tablet. "I'm even reading a biology textbook."

We walked out into the hallway and I tried to find a quiet corner where we wouldn't be overheard. "This may be jumping into the deep end of the pool while wearing ankle weights," I replied.

"I'm a quick learner. I need some idea of what you all are talking about. And I still haven't figured out why a man would kill someone so they could siphon off the victim's fat tissue."

"How are you doing, after what happened in Henderson?"

"I'm doing as well as can be expected. Thanks for asking, Elaine." The iota of warmth in his voice dropped away. "I still have a lot of questions about what Henry was up to. And why you happened to show up right before the police moved in."

Meaning, he was still on the case and I was still under his microscope. "Well, it may concern folks here to know that the FBI is snooping around," I shot back.

He shrugged. "I registered with my affiliation." He showed me his conference badge. "Don't worry, I'm not going to arrest anyone here, in front of their colleagues."

Or shoot anyone, I wanted to say. But I didn't blame him for shooting Henry. I blamed Henry and myself. "But harassment and stalking are fair game," I said.

"I'm not here for you or your lab, Doctor," he said sharply. His face clouded over. "I didn't even know you would be here, to be honest. This isn't an abstract academic subject for me. I have a nephew who is morbidly obese; already has Type II. My mother lost a foot to Type II and died early. My brother has heart trouble and he's barely in his forties. So I have a personal interest in making sure the food corporations are not deliberately fattening us up."

I swallowed. "I'm sorry. I had no idea."

"I can't imagine anyone thinking that tricking people into becoming overweight was worth another dollar in share price, if they saw the human cost. But that's business, right?"

I indicated the people around us. "You have some of the smartest, most caring, dedicated people here trying to figure out how to stop it. That's business too."

Agent Pierce nodded back towards the room my presentation took place in. "You got some tough questions today."

I smiled. "Those weren't tough. I'm hell on people compared to that. There's a lot of sloppy work out here, a lot of people looking for the controversial headline or the next grant. It's not all benevolent geniuses trying to solve the world's problems."

Damn it, I almost winced at that Freudian slip.

It was okay; he missed it. "Why don't your scientists present their own work? Most of the papers presented here are by the authors, not their bosses."

"Oh," I said smoothly, "they do. But we can't all come to a conference like this. We put all of our resources into the work. And I do have a direct hand in the papers I present."

What I didn't say was that I realized that many of the harebrained ideas my staff latched on to came from their inability to sort through the deluge of discussions and stray thoughts that came out at conferences like these. A lot of oddballs and kooks, like Lyle, hung around these things. Some were looking for funding for their crap project, others were trying to sell some solution or lab equipment. Our alien cannibal nerds were geniuses, but the business and networking side of these events was an unsolvable puzzle to them.

Pierce nodded. "Used to be us feds couldn't go to any conferences. But I noticed that you've presented almost all of your lab's work the last two years. Some might say that sounds like a glory-hog. Someone who likes to fly around and stay in hotels."

"Ah, well, if that were so, I would be listed as first author, but I'm third or fourth. I'm a single mother of a teenage boy - trust me, I would rather never travel for work again if I could. Presenting the work lets me do the networking, and the fundraising. My scientists would rather stay in the lab."

He nodded. "Right, right. But here's the thing. They're not getting the interaction, that exchange of ideas that is so critical to research, I'm told. And yet they keep doing all of this great research. How does that happen?"

He had this intense look in his eye that gave me the willies. Just here to learn, my ass. He thought I was guilty of something, and he was politely poking around for a way to figure out what I was guilty of. Despite the fact that we were standing among a couple hundred scientists, I felt like we were locked in an interrogation room.

I hefted my conference materials. "I don't know what you're getting at. We just work differently. As an industry-funded lab, we are different than the academics or government scientists."

"Yes, I guess that must be it. Or maybe I'm missing something," he waved his hands at the people milling around, "being new to this work. I majored in economics in college, became an accountant. That's how I got in the Bureau - being able to uncover the discrepancies, no matter how long it took."

I nodded, but the hair on the back of my neck prickled. "My people keep in touch with their colleagues. About a quarter of our papers presented here are by co-authors from outside AgSol. And I don't go to the conferences that are outside of my expertise."

He spread his hands. "Fair enough. Well, I won't take up too much of your time. Another session is starting soon."

I watched him walk away. I wanted to follow him, and see if he attended any other sessions, or if he was just here to confront me. But there was a session on parental interventions that I wanted to catch, and not entirely for professional reasons.

Still, I had to know if Pierce was after me. I would only be a little late. I kept him in sight as he passed one conference room after another. The hallway was jammed with people.

Pierce headed away from the conference rooms and towards the poster session off the main lobby. He stopped at each one, studying the poster and chatting with the author.

"Elaine? How are you?" It was Felix Cho, a neuroscientist I co-authored with in the days before my stint at USDA. Back when I really did systems biology at the agency I won't name.

"Felix, it's been forever." I maneuvered around him to keep Pierce in sight over his shoulder. "Are you still at Baylor?"

Pierce stopped at the one poster that was a project in which Donald Meers was a co-author. Pierce took out his cellphone and took a picture of the poster.

213

"I'm visiting at Hopkins' Bloomberg School for a year," Felix said. "I can't believe you took an industry job."

I looked back at Felix and laughed. "It was a wonderful opportunity. Actual money, no micro-managing advisor or manager, really good scientists and the pay raise didn't hurt."

Felix handed over his business card. When I looked back up, I had lost sight of Agent Pierce. Shit.

"Hopkins is great," Felix said. "They let me poke around in microbiology and bug the child health PhD students."

Felix and I joked about the pluses and minuses of academia, government, and the private sector. I was barely paying attention as I kept searching for Pierce. Not knowing where he was made me nervous.

I extracted myself from talking to Felix and searched the halls for Pierce. The next session had started and there was no sight of him. I had a plane to catch back home anyway.

I just couldn't wait to tell Stitcher that misdirecting Pierce was going *so well* that the FBI had nearly figured out that my scientists were oddly abnormal, even for scientists.

[40]

About a week later, Betty burst into my office with tears in her eyes. "John Stitcher is *dead*."

"Of course he is," I said slowly, surprised that she was learning this just now.

"No, I mean *totally* dead. His neighbor found him and called the police. They called his law office and his secretary alerted us."

A lump appeared in my throat. I took a couple of breaths but it only got worse. I had just been yelling at him a few days ago about Pierce stalking me at a conference. Had that killed the undead ghoul?

It dawned on me that for all of Stitcher's worrying about protecting the conspiracy, one of the weakest links in the conspiracy would be losing him. He was the glue that kept the whole thing together. I hoped he had a contingency plan for his own death, even if I never found out what it was. Otherwise, the next problem would spiral out of control.

My voice went rock-climbing in my throat. "How did he die?"

"I don't know; I just got the call. The Board wants you to deal with this. They said Stitcher left instructions on what to do if he passed away."

Oh. I was the contingency plan. I closed my eyes and opened them again. What would Stitcher do in this spot? "Where's the body?" I asked.

"The body?" Betty said. "I don't know."

"We can't let anyone get to the body. A coroner is going to estimate time of death as sometime in the Reagan Administration. That will raise a bunch of questions."

"We need to get that body," Betty agreed. "Maybe we can revive him."

"Do you have any idea how they did that?" I asked. "Because I don't have the first clue." Undead voodoo resurrection or whatever had never been covered in grad school.

She shook her head. "Our lab didn't have anything to do with reviving dead people."

If Agent Pierce found out about Stitcher's existence as a ghoul for decades, it would point him at the real conspiracy rather than the new one percolating amongst our enemies in the food companies. It would undo all the misdirection and probably toss us all in jail. "Okay," I said.

Betty left to call people while I tried to figure out what to do next. I wanted to call Charlie, but it was the middle of the school day. I'd have to reach him later.

Betty texted me that a chartered plane would fly me to DC as soon as I could get to the airport. Knoxville to Washington was a hellish long trip through the dregs of the domestic air system. I drove to the airport with no change of clothes, no toothbrush. A corporate jet was waiting on the tarmac for me. It's amazing how cursory security is when you're boarding a corporate Gulfstream.

As soon as the wheels were up I started making phone calls. I began with Stitcher's neighbor, who recounted how he had found the lawyer facedown on the sidewalk and called 911. Next were the paramedics who pronounced Stitcher at the scene and carted him off. Next was the DC medical examiner's office. Not being next of kin, I couldn't stroll in there and carry Stitcher out over my shoulder. I tried to make a case for that, but was given an earful about rules and regulations for releasing remains.

Betty's secretary emailed me Stitcher's will. It named me as executor and stated that Stitcher's lawyer would handle legal matters. I called the lawyer as my plane descended towards Reagan National Airport.

"Elaine, Stitcher wanted me to handle the legal aspects of the will. He hoped that you can handle the details on the ground."

"Like planning the funeral?" I asked with a wince. I remembered what my mother went through handling my father's affairs.

216

"There won't be a memorial service, just a quiet burial. We need you to run interference on dispensing with his property, signing documents, that kind of thing. But the absolutely most critical thing today is to get the body released to you. Take it to the funeral home that Stitcher specified in his will. Do *not* allow the DC coroner to autopsy him. Is that clear? I'm told it will be obvious that his tissue has not been alive for some time."

"How do I stop an autopsy?" I asked.

"We're working on that. Usually a medical examiner doesn't press if the decedent had a medical condition and the death is not unexpected. We hope to use that loophole. I'll call you with more instructions as needed." He promised to email me his contact information and hung up.

When the plane landed, a courier was waiting for me on the tarmac with legal documents. The courier was also a notary public and I had power of attorney before I got in a black Lincoln that Alex's lawyer had sent for me.

Sitting in the Lincoln's backseat was Bob, Charlie's dad.

"Elaine, how did you get yourself into this mess?"

"Stitcher chose me I guess."

Bob leered at me.

"Fuck you. I didn't sleep with him."

Bob shrugged, not believing me. "How's Charlie?"

Charlie. Who didn't know I had left town. "He's hanging in there. Freshman year can be tough." Should I mention the meeting with the gym teacher? Or our son's emerging sexuality? What are the parameters for parents talking about their kid when they hate each other?

The car headed north on Route 1 towards the District.

"He's overweight," I said.

Bob laughed and grabbed a generous roll of his belly. He was definitely buying his suits from a big and tall store these days. "Everyone is. Except you. Of course."

"This is serious, Bob. You know the lifelong health ramifications."

Bob waved off my comment. "It runs in the family."

I glared at him. "Why, may I ask, are you here? Along for a ride in a nice car?"

Bob sighed and looked out the window. "My firm has been called in to help take over Stitcher's work. He was kind of a lobbyist, attorney, jack of all trades. We get the lobbying work he was doing. And since I know you, the partners wanted me on this."

I shook my head. "What do I have to do with this?"

Bob looked surprised. "You're the new Stitcher. Come on."

"No, I'm not," I shook my head. "I'm a scientist. At a lab. I have a full-time job. And a family."

Bob laughed. "The lawyer sent us instructions too. I'm your lobbyist contact."

He was pulling my leg. This had to be one of those frat brother things where you tease ugly girls and nerdy guys just to see how long they'll fall for it. But was he that much of an asshole to do something like that, at a time like this?

"I'm just taking care of some of the funeral arrangements. There has to be some kind of misunderstanding," I said.

"They sent you to take care of Stitcher," Bob replied. "It was in his will. You're already doing his job."

"And Stitcher thought that you and I would work together?" I shook my head. Stitcher had been strangled to death by his wife, before he was resurrected by the conspiracy. Maybe he thought Bob needed strangling as well. "This will never work out, you know that. I may have to kill you."

"If you trust me with Charlie, you can trust me with business," he retorted. "Stitcher did in the last year or two."

How much did Stitcher tell him? I assumed that Stitcher played things close to the vest with the lobbyists. Did they even know about the obesity conspiracy? The hybrids? The environmental collapse? Or did Bob just mean the secret about Stitcher's undead condition? I would have to feel things out so I didn't reveal something that shouldn't be revealed.

We crossed the 14th Street bridge into DC. "I'm not sure what I'm supposed to have you doing at the moment," I told Bob.

He waved his hand. "Don't sweat it. It's your first day. This is just for us to get acquainted again about business."

Oh, that.

"What have you been doing for him?" I asked.

Bob listed a dozen different lobbying efforts, including fighting food-labeling regulations, pimping corn subsidies, and throwing industry weight behind EPA rules on carbon emissions.

"And we're rattling cages about this FBI investigation into the food processing industry. We've done a second round of calls, threatened to set up meetings. The Justice Department is giving us the runaround, saying they don't comment on ongoing investigations, that kind of thing. But they get that we're pressuring them and they may leak something. The sympathetic staffers on the Hill are ready to make calls on their own for us."

I nodded. None of the lobbying had worked really well apparently, given that Pierce had chased us through the woods in Tennessee and shown up at my conference presentation. Then again, Agent Pierce hadn't interrogated me, raided the lab, or shut down any other adipose processing plants.

My phone rang. It was Alex's lawyer. "John was under a doctor's care for a heart condition. His death was expected. We're emailing you some medical records from his doctor. They shouldn't feel the need to conduct an autopsy if a known disease was the likely cause of death."

"Okay, but what if they insist?" I asked.

"Call me then. Given his age, address, and occupation, they probably won't suspect foul play." He hung up.

We arrived at the DC morgue at the end of Massachusetts Avenue, Southeast. It was a couple blocks from RFK stadium and the DC Armory. The prison was nearby, which I thought was ironic and sad. Our Lincoln Town Car stood out like a sore thumb amongst the dinged city vehicles and low income folks waiting for the Metro bus.

"You want me to come in with you?" Bob asked, indicating the not-so-Georgetown, not-so-white people outside.

"I'm not going to get mugged at the morgue," I said, but then saw the look on his face. He was trying to be gallant. "Fine, come in with me."

The receptionist in the lobby gave me forms to fill out and then we waited. Someone from the ME's office came to escort us to an interview room. They scanned my power of attorney paperwork and they told me to wait. Again.

The ME staffer returned, not showing any sign that something was amiss, and asked if I could identify the body before it was released.

She guided me down a hallway to a room that overlooked a lab. Stitcher's corpse was blanketed by a white sheet and under a bright white light.

Before they could lift the sheet, the door opened and a bleach-blonde in her fifties scooted in on high heels and fake boobs.

219

She looked at me and I looked at her.

"Who the are you?" she asked.

"Elaine Cassano, one of the executors of John's estate. Who are you?"

She sniffled and put a hand on her hip. "I'm Barbara Stitcher, John's wife."

[41]

"His wife?" The one who smothered him when he was passed out drunk at home? Ho man, the stories this lady could probably tell.

"Thought he was dead a long time ago," I said, wondering what her reaction would be.

She nodded. "We buried an empty casket, but I received an inheritance from the law firm. Never considered that he wasn't dead." She looked away. "God, I need a cigarette."

The coroner's assistant joined us in the room while her coworker pulled the sheet back. I almost expected someone else to be under the sheet. But no, it was John, looking like he was asleep under the harsh, bright white light.

"Mrs. Stitcher, is this your husband?"

Barbara nodded. "Yes. That is the sonuvabitch."

The assistant didn't know what to do with that response and left us alone again.

"So is it going to be like last time, you and the firm clean up all the details and I get a check?" Barbara asked.

"I'm actually a scientist, not a lawyer. A friend of John's and I are named executors of his will. I'm not sure what you may be getting, if anything." The will was sitting on my phone, but I didn't see any need to refer to it at the moment. Not until I had the body safely somewhere the hell else.

221

Barbara put a hand on her hip. "I better get something. Clearly this asshole faked his death to avoid an expensive divorce. Paid me enough to go to rehab and kick coke. I wonder how much the fucker put away in the years since? I'm getting some slices of that pie. I should have the whole damn thing."

I held up my hands. "Maybe you will. I don't know anything about that. I'm just here to see to the funeral arrangements."

"Thank God. The last time his firm took care of it."

At least I wouldn't have to fight her for possession of the corpse. When the coroner returned, I said, "When can the funeral home come for the body?"

The coroner assistant frowned. "I'm sorry; we have to do an autopsy, which we haven't done yet. We can't release the body until then."

Here we go, I thought. Bob said, "Why? He had a heart condition. He knew this could happen. He got his will in order, made arrangements. This is not an unexplained death, like it said on the form."

My hand wrapped around my phone, ready to speed-dial Stitcher's attorney.

The assistant looked at the form like she had never read it before.

"That's not what I was told," the assistant said in a huff. "I have to go check on this." She left the three of us standing there.

"Do you need me here any more?" Barbara asked. Apparently she had better things to do.

I shook my head. "No, I don't think so. I'm sorry for your loss. I wish we didn't have to meet like this."

She gave me a polite smile and left.

"What a bitch," Bob muttered.

I gave him a look. "She *was* married to Stitcher."

He snapped his fingers. "Good point."

The assistant came back with a doctor in tow. He was an annoyed little man with thick glasses.

"Are you next of kin?" he asked in a heavy African accent.

"No, but I am an executor of his will and have power of attorney."

That didn't impress the good coroner at all. "This man was found dead on his front steps this morning in a sweat suit. I did a cursory examination and he appears to have been dead for a lot longer than just one night."

"He was walking around just yesterday," Bob said.

"Are you next of kin?" the doctor asked.

Bob shook his head. "But I talked to him two days ago."

The coroner turned back to me. "You say that he had a heart condition. Was under a doctor's care. Do you have some proof of that?"

"Geez, doc, you itching to do an autopsy today?" Bob asked nervously.

The coroner gave him a sharp look over his glasses.

I forwarded the medical records to him. He read them over for a full minute. He looked at his watch. "I'd like to call the deceased's doctor and discuss this. I haven't seen a case like this before." He asked the assistant to get the doctor on the line.

Bob and I exchanged a glance. I wasn't even sure that Stitcher had a doctor. Did the conspiracy keep doctors on staff to cover for ghouls? I guess we would find out.

The coroner's phone buzzed. He looked at it and sighed. He excused himself and took the call out in the hallway.

"I wonder what John's EKG looked like at his last visit," Bob said.

"Shut up," I said.

Bob held up his hands. "Sorry, I joke when things get too depressing."

"It's amazing Stitcher didn't strangle you with your own shoelaces," I replied.

He didn't know how to respond to that.

The coroner stepped back in. "His doctor confirmed what the records show. But something about this is fishy. I really would like to do the autopsy."

I folded my arms. "And I would really like to get that body released today. He needs to be buried within twenty-four hours."

The coroner nodded. "I understand. But the law is clear that religious practices don't trump any legal need to determine a cause of death through autopsy."

I nodded at the forms he was holding. "The cause of death is right there." The coroner's phone buzzed again. "It doesn't sound like you have time to deal this anyway."

"Four teens were killed in a drive-by shooting in Northeast," the coroner said with a sigh. "Okay, I have to release the body to you. Heart failure will be the cause of death on the death certificate, as per the medical records

223

indicate." He scribbled a signature on the form. "I'm very sorry for your loss."

The assistant returned to the room with the completed documents. "Who are we releasing the body to?" she asked.

I pulled my phone out and started scrolling through the will. The funeral home was listed, along with a contact and a note to make sure that the funeral home knew it was picking up John Stitcher. I imagine that meant some kind of special treatment. Did ghouls need embalming? I don't think the law covered these situations.

After a couple more forms were filled out, they handed over Stitcher's clothing, phone, and house key. The funeral home texted me that they were sending a hearse. Bob and I left the morgue and blinked in a sunny DC afternoon. NASA headquarters was across the street and 395's roar of traffic echoed between the office buildings. As we climbed in the town car, we saw four ambulances pulling up, their lights and sirens off.

John Stitcher's last favor for us was to drop dead in a city prone to spasms of deadly violence, so the coroner wouldn't have time to autopsy him.

[42]

As the car headed for the funeral home on Capitol Hill, I looked at the medical records that had sprung the body.

"Oh shit," I said. "You have to be kidding me."

Bob looked over from across the seat, trying to read my phone. "What?"

The doctor's name was Donald Meers.

I called the number, which of course was his office number at AgSol.

"Donald, did you just lie to a medical examiner that you were Stitcher's physician?"

"No. I was Mr. Stitcher's physician. Heart failure is how we referred to his condition."

"What exactly was his condition?" I asked.

"Advanced decomposition due to heart failure," Donald said. "Did you have the remains released to you?"

I rubbed my forehead. "Yes." I was about to ask how we had kept a dead man from completely decomposing over thirty years. But Bob was sitting right there. "How did you treat that?"

"Chemistry. I don't know how he was revived, but it was done before any substantial cell death happened. He slowed the decomposition with a solution that mixed a preservative for his tissues with a medication that kept his

225

brain and nervous system functioning. Don't ask me how it worked, because he never let even me see it."

I squeezed my eyes shut. This should all be giving me a rip-roaring headache, but I felt serene. "Listen, is there anything else that Stitcher told you to do? Or any other secrets that you're keeping from me?"

"No, Elaine."

"I'm not mad at you Donald, I just am, surprised. Let me know if you plan to pretend to be anyone's physician again, but before you do it."

He promised to do so, and I hung up and looked at Bob. "It's a surprise a minute around here."

At the funeral home, the undertaker greeted me with a wink when he heard Stitcher's name. Apparently, ghouls got some kind of different treatment. Stitcher would be cremated as soon as they received his body. We signed more papers, and I put paid for it with my credit card.

When we got back in the car, Bob gave the driver an address on Capitol Hill and a second in Georgetown. "Stitcher wanted you to clean out his house and office."

"We'll get to that," I said, annoyed.

"You need to get his files right now. He didn't want them falling into the wrong hands."

I hefted Stitcher's phone in my hand and wondered if the old guy had kept any of his information anywhere else. He was a jerk full of secrets, so it was best to cover all the bases. "Okay."

Stitcher had a cream-colored brick row house on Capitol Hill near Lincoln Park. The living room looked like a home-decorating show room that had been abandoned in the 1990s, and was now dusty and faded.

The kitchen was the same. "Guy worked his ass off for the agricultural, food delivery, and food processing industries and it doesn't look like he ever ate at home," Bob remarked.

I raised an eyebrow but said nothing as we headed upstairs.

The only parts of the house that Stitcher used were his study, the bedroom, and the bathroom. Did the undead sleep? The bed was messed up and there was an alarm clock on the night stand, so that seemed to be a yes.

"This place is really dusty, and that says a lot coming from me," Bob said.

"Not home much, I guess," I mused. But it occurred to me that Stitcher may have shed skin cells faster than a living person. And if he was decomposing even faster at the end, that would explain the dust buildup. No wonder he could see the end coming - he was literally turning to dust.

The study was ringed with cherry bookshelves crammed full of books on management, leadership, and the environment. The desk was blank except for a tablet. Bob and I went through the drawers and files, piling up everything that looked important. It wasn't a big pile.

"We need to eat lunch," Bob pointed out.

"Order something," I said, not wanting to be distracted. But I hadn't eaten since breakfast and it was getting to be late in the afternoon.

Bob ordered greasy subs from a place by Eastern Market. I wiped down the kitchenette set so we could eat on it. I tried not to think of where the dust had come from as I munched on the provolone and prosciutto sandwich Bob ordered for me. Fifteen years after a one-night stand, and he still knew my favorite foods.

I ate quickly and then descended into the basement. I found a box marked 'property' that had the deed to the house, the paperwork on a sports car, and his bank account numbers. We would need those records for handling his estate, but it could stay in the house for now.

We grabbed Stitcher's keys and tablet. We loaded up the car with the files worth keeping, locked the place, and left. It was only when I held his cellphone and tablet in my hands that it hit me that Stitcher was really, truly dead. I buried my head in my hands and wept. I even let Bob hold me while I cried.

[43]

We crossed town to Stitcher's office in Georgetown as the sun began to dip behind the Lincoln Memorial. It was a very DC moment to be in the backseat of a car like this passing between the Mall and the White House. This was what power looked like in the movies. I wondered if everyone in this iconic, Hollywood moment failed to enjoy it because of the real world worries and responsibilities that had tossed them in these leather seats. I, for one, was too busy wiping my snotty nose.

I tried calling Charlie again as we wormed through the evening rush hour. Thank God he picked up.

"Charlie, I'm in Washington, on an emergency work thing that came up. I'm with your father."

"Hey screwball!" Bob called out.

"Tell Dad I said hi. What are you doing up there?"

"Dealing with a small crisis. Can you manage things by yourself for a little while?"

"Sure. When are you coming home?" Charlie asked.

A great question I didn't have the answer to. "Probably tonight."

"You don't have a flight booked? Or did you drive?" Charlie asked.

"I can catch a flight back pretty quick," I said. I didn't want to mention the Gulfstream or everything that it came with. "Why so curious? You going to throw a party while I'm away?"

"Great idea! It would help me make friends," Charlie said.

I grinned. "Just keep in mind that I could be home at any moment, smart-ass."

"Gotta go Ma, I gotta sign for the keg delivery."

Bob laughed hard when I told him about his son's signoff line. Okay, maybe my son inherited a few charming traits from his father. Not that there were a lot, but there were a few.

The driver dropped us off in front of Stitcher's office. Law firms occupied most of the prim brick townhouses on this quiet, tree-lined street.

"Elaine," someone called as we walked up the front step.

It was Agent Vernon Pierce, strolling up the sidewalk with his hands in his pockets.

I'm sure the blood drained right out of my face.

"I heard John Stitcher died today," Pierce said. "I'm sorry for your loss."

"What are you doing here?" I asked.

Pierce nodded towards the townhouse. "Waiting on a warrant to search the premises. I can't let you go inside."

I put my hands on my hips. "I'm the executor of his estate, and I need to secure his belongings. Don't you think you owe me one after Henderson?"

Pierce shrugged. "Why don't we make this easy, huh? You could let me in and we can get both of our jobs done."

I narrowed my eyes and climbed the first two steps. "When you get that warrant, Vernon, make sure you knock rather than bust the door down. We'll open it for you."

"Elaine, you can't remove anything from the premises," Pierce warned. "That's obstruction."

I kept walking up the steps. Bob followed me. I turned back towards Pierce. "What's the warrant for? What investigation?" I asked.

Pierce looked at Bob and then back at me. "Bribery, blackmail, fraud, among others."

"That's not an investigation - that's Lyle's imagination run wild. Now, the guy just died this morning, why are you hassling us about this today?"

Pierce cocked his head to the side. "You claimed his body really fast.

Wished I could have examined it before it was cremated. I heard John Stitcher was a marvel of modern medicine."

I shook my head. "Some marvel, his heart gave out. Why would the FBI want to do that? The medical examiner had no reason to do an autopsy."

"Because you twisted his arm," Pierce said. "The ME thought Stitcher's body was in an 'unusual state.'"

I paused. "DC is not a state. Let me know when you get that warrant."

Pierce huffed and made a call as Bob and I went inside the house. I closed the door and locked it.

"What are we going to do?" Bob asked. "Is that guy a cop?"

"FBI, actually. We are going to get Stitcher's files out of here. Let's hurry."

Bob put his hand on the door to Stitcher's office in the back of the town house. "That's not so smart. He could arrest us for obstruction if we trash the place, especially since he told us that he's got a warrant coming."

I smiled at Bob. Between the two of us, I didn't think that I would be the risk-taker. But he also was a lawyer by training. "I don't think he has a warrant on the way. What probable cause would he have? Stitcher being a profane ass? His death?"

"What if he's still standing out there when we come out with boxes in our arms?"

"No warrant means we walk away."

"Pissing off the FBI is not a smart move, Elaine. What's Charlie going to do if we're both in jail?"

I turned to him. He was sweating a lot. "You're scared, aren't you? Don't worry, if I'm the new Stitcher, I'll make sure we get bailed out. And you won't lose your job."

"Stitcher could pull that off, I'm not that confident in you," Bob admitted. "No offense, but you today is your first day in the job."

We passed the abandoned receptionist desk; Stitcher's secretary had passed away over a year ago, and apparently didn't have a clause in her contract to be revived.

Stitcher's office was almost exactly the same as the last time I was here. A single tablet sat on the clean desk. No paper files, law books or anything else.

"We can't take the tablet," Bob said.

I picked it up and poked at it. It wanted a password. Luckily, Stitcher had put that in his will. I sighed and entered 'monkeyfucking ass clowns" and the tablet came to life.

"Destroying incriminating evidence is just as illegal," Bob pointed out.

"Do you know of any incriminating evidence or activities that Stitcher was involved in?" I asked.

Bob opened the cabinets. "No. I'm just the lobbying end of his operation."

"Then relax. Look for any hidden papers or files. This may be our only chance to get them if they exist."

Bob hunted around the office while I went through the tablet's contents.

"This guy didn't even have a phone in here," Bob said.

"Of course not, he only used his cell," I said. Other than a large collection of punk and heavy metal music files, Stitcher had nothing stored on his tablet. He had a number of apps for file storage, digital security, and an open-source office software app. None of them would auto log in though.

Bob was right: legally, I couldn't take the tablet or destroy anything on it. But if all of Stitcher's files were online, then I didn't have to worry; I just needed the logins for the apps.

"This will take a few minutes," I said. I pulled out the tablet I took from Stitcher's house and logged in with the same password. The house tablet did have the login info. I didn't need his work tablet at all. Pierce could sweat his balls off about it, and never think that it was a ruse.

Bob groaned and went to see if Pierce was charging into the building yet. He came back. "That agent is still on his phone."

I laughed. "He was bluffing. Let's go."

Agent Pierce was surprised to see us leaving Stitcher's office empty-handed. I smiled as we came down the stairs. "It's all yours, Agent. Give me a call when you get that warrant and someone will come to unlock the door. We don't want a broken front door, even in this neighborhood."

Vernon Pierce glared at me in a cold, hateful way. "You don't want to tease me, Elaine."

I smiled at him as Bob and I climbed into the car. I told the driver to take me to my mother's house in Silver Spring. I couldn't swoop in and out of town without stopping in to see her.

Agent Pierce watched us drive away and I turned around to see him punch the air in frustration. I wish I felt as happy as he was upset, but the whole thing just made me shaky and want to pee.

Bob had the driver drop him off at his chic townhouse a couple of streets over. "You know where to reach me, boss," he said as he heaved his frame out of the backseat.

"Huh?"

He grinned his 1,200 watt smile and nodded at Stitcher's tablet. "You've got Stitcher's job now, right? You've got a lot of studying to do. Call me when you need something from me." As he closed the heavy car door, he started whistling in a carefree manner because the world had fallen on my shoulders, not his.

Stitcher's job. Managing the conspiracy, screwing with the FBI, taking on food industry executives, handling the Board, worrying about the chemical industry. The idea of doing all of that made my skin crawl. And it wasn't something to think about today. Stitcher had just died. Someone else could step in and take on the role.

Bob could be such an asshole, trying to rattle me like that. But deep down, I knew he hadn't been joking. Which meant, on top of everything else, that I had inherited him from Stitcher too.

I sat back and watched Georgetown scroll by. As we turned on M Street I had the urge to stop at a cupcake shop and eat a box of them. A battle between my willpower and an emotional craving to coat my grief in sugary icing erupted as we waited at a light a few blocks away. My willpower failed utterly, but then my phone rang.

It was Betty. "The board wants to meet with you about Stitcher. Teleconference, as soon as you're back in the air. We have a secure line on the plane."

The car rolled by the pink cupcake shop. The moment had passed. I said yes and hung up.

[44]

By the time I was strapped into my seat on the Gulfstream, I was dialed into the conference call. It was even stranger to meet the board on a faceless phone call than in the dimly lit bank meeting room. I couldn't identify anyone other than by voice.

"Elaine thank you for joining us," said the gruff voice with a German-sounding accent. "I wish we didn't have to meet like this. It's a tough time for everyone, especially those of us who knew John for decades. How are you doing?"

"You all have made a terrible, terrible mistake," I blurted.

They laughed, not expecting that.

"We didn't choose you," said a man with a quiet voice. "John made a convincing case that you were the best choice. You will be able to marry the technical expertise with the wits to keep things running smoothly, he said."

"He didn't make that case to me," I pointed out.

"I'm sure he had his reasons," the old woman said. I could tell it was her from her voice quavering and warbling. "You need to get over that and focus on the task at hand. Time is short and we're at a critical juncture."

I shook my head. "I don't see how I can do this. I am running the science programs at our labs. Stitcher was working a job and a half by himself."

"We realize that Stitcher was overcommitted and under-resourced. We suggest that you build a team of counterparts to help you. You already have Bob."

I raised an eyebrow. "Bob wouldn't be my third choice. I don't trust him or like him."

"He has an intimate knowledge of the activities that Stitcher had him doing," the gruff voice said.

"And you are both in regular contact because of your son," added the old woman.

I bristled. They knew about Charlie? Suddenly, I felt threatened. What else did they know? Would they use it against me if I failed, or didn't follow orders? I flashed back to the night when a ghoul tried to choke me to death in my own bed.

"Relax, Elaine," said an Indian woman. "When John presented you as his successor, he explained a little about your family situation. We don't know anything more than that."

"You have me at a disadvantage," I said. "I don't know all of your names and faces."

"We understand. Some of us worked with John for almost forty years. But rest assured that we have families too, and we'll make sure that yours is supported and protected."

I sat up straighter. "Protected from what?"

"The government. Various other... factions that oppose our efforts, mostly because they misunderstand our intentions."

"I was attacked once, by one of John's kind. John said something about the chemical industry. He was worried that someone may try to kill me when I broke into the adipose factory in DC. Who is after us - the people who oppose us?" I asked.

"There are some corporate executives in the chemical industry who think destroying the environment is a business opportunity, not a threat. They see our efforts as a threat to their businesses. They will protect those businesses by any means necessary," the old woman said.

I made a face. The chemical industry and the food industry launched ghouls at each other's conspiracies? Finally, I snickered and immediately felt ashamed to do so. I recovered and said, "So what do I need to do about that?"

The gruff voice sighed. "Nothing yet. We're working on it."

The brushoff made me mad. "Unless they happen to attack someone else, right, in which case I'll have to clean it up. Have they killed anyone on our side yet?"

"Not that we know of," the old woman said. "But that is our problem at the moment, not yours."

"Fair enough." Except I knew it wouldn't be just their problem for long. I'd get pulled in eventually. "What about Stitcher's legal expertise?" I asked. "He used the law like a weapon. I'm not a lawyer."

"That is one of the holes you will need to fill on your team."

My team? "How much should I tell my team? About the conspiracy, you all, the hybrids? This is what I mean by not knowing what I'm doing," I said sharply.

"It is up to you. But your primary responsibility is to protect our efforts and their secrecy," said the Indian woman. "You should train a replacement for yourself though and you can brief them more fully than John briefed you."

I nodded. Cover all possible contingencies, like Stitcher had said. "Besides assembling a team, and getting up to speed, my highest priority is misdirecting the FBI away from our labs and adipose facilities, right?"

"Yes. Are you continuing John's plan to deal with Agent Pierce?"

I smiled. "Of course." I needed every crutch in the conspiracy-running business I could use until I figured out how to become John Stitcher.

"What kind of funding do I have?" Replacing a ghoul who could work around the clock with a team of humans with bills to pay would be expensive.

"John used several Swiss bank accounts. The information is in his files," said the old woman. "We can pay you a salary for your efforts."

I made a face they couldn't see. "Eh. No thanks. That kind of financial connection would raise some eyebrows. I expect that the FBI will keep an eye on my tax records and bank accounts."

"Very good. That's reassuring that you're thinking ahead like that," said the German man. "You see, Elaine, there's several areas where we think you'll do better than Stitcher."

"Better?"

"Stitcher quite enjoyed handling emergencies. Loved the thrill. You like to avoid calamities and will be better organized. And you don't bother people

235

like he does. You have proven that you can manage people and can get others to cooperate."

The plane was dropping through the clouds into a rain shower coating the mountains. "Is this meant to cheer me up?"

"We just want to make sure you have everything you need," the old woman replied. She read off a number I could call if I needed anything in the interim, until we worked out some better method of communicating.

"Thanks, all of you. I'll be in touch." The call ended. I looked away from the window, and then slid the shade down. I needed to focus.

[45]

The Gulfstream touched down in Knoxville right after nine and I made it home close to ten. Charlie was still up and had already watched our favorite reality TV show *We Will*.

This season of *We Will* was focused on sex addicts in Los Angeles. A side project was going on about the porn industry and whether performers had psychological problems or were normal people who just liked getting it on. Whether the whole season was essentially one big advertisement for the porn industry was a subject that the show itself decided to cover in addition to the personal dramas of people way too into their own genitalia.

Charlie, not surprisingly, was enthralled.

Typically, I avoided the room while he was watching it. There were just some things I couldn't watch with him. I would hole up in my study and then watch it later with headphones on.

He paused the show when I came in the front door.

"Okay, Mom, you have to explain how you got home that fast. Dad called me and said you were still in DC two hours ago."

"I may have mooched a ride on a corporate jet that runs between Knoxville and DC," I muttered.

"A corporate jet? Sweet."

I kicked off my shoes and wiggled my toes. It felt so good to be in my house. "Well, what's not so sweet is that I may need to use it more often, on short notice. My schedule could get kind of hairy."

He raised an eyebrow. "Science doesn't have emergencies. You always say it's not like it is on TV, it takes a lot longer and requires careful planning."

"Yes," I said, trying to find the right words, "would you believe that it is funding opportunities that I really have to jump on?"

He shook his head no. Rats. "Are you in some kind of trouble again?" he asked.

You know, a being in trouble story wouldn't be a bad idea. Since my compulsion to be honest tended to wear out my welcome, everyone, including Charlie, probably expected I would screw up the AgSol job. I could tell people Betty was holding my leash close, the budget was tight, and so on.

But I had to tell Charlie the truth. "I have to pick up some more job duties. I'm sorry, kiddo, it wasn't my choice. They kind of threw them in my lap."

He knitted his brow. "What about Stitcher?"

"How do you know about him?" I asked in alarm.

"Ma, I met him at last year's Halloween party, remember? He was dressed as a zombie and had all those funny stories."

I nodded. I had been walking on eggshells that whole night, hoping Stitcher wouldn't corrupt my kid. When that hadn't happened, I plain old forgot that Charlie even knew him.

I folded my hands in front of me. "John Stitcher passed away today. That's what I've been dealing with."

"No! I'm so sorry. How did it happen?" Charlie got up and gave me a hug.

I looked at my feet. "Heart attack when he came home from a jog. Instant. It's his job that I'm helping out with."

"How's that going to work?" Charlie asked.

I smiled at him. "We'll make it work. Don't worry."

"Worry? Ha! You'll have to let me drive at sixteen if you're doing all that work." He was totally pumped. God help me.

It may be a mom thing, but I sent him off to bed and made sure he brushed his teeth. Sometimes you just have to regress a little when your kid is trying to grow up too fast, okay?

I called Ma. "Did you see *We Will* tonight?" she asked instead of saying hello.

Tonight's episode was about how a three-way orgy gets choreographed and filmed. "No, God, I can't watch that with Charlie around. I'll watch it later."

"Well, this is one of the wildest episodes yet. I can't believe they show this stuff on television," she said. "You really shouldn't let him see this kind of thing."

"I am a terrible parent, I know. But I'm trying not to underestimate how much of an adult he is about some things," I said.

Ma huffed. "He's still a child. This will make him see women as sex objects."

"Ma, he's fifteen. He is a walking clot of hormones, everything is a sex object. He'd hump a wet hole in the ground if he thought no one was looking. But he has friends who are girls so he seems to function okay."

"Okay, different subject, sweetie," Ma said in a overly polite high pitch. "How's work?"

"I have to take on a project I don't want."

"Yes you do," she replied. "You just want me to make you feel alright about it, whatever it is."

"Among other things," I said. Like jail, death, undeath, and bearing the stress that Stitcher had. I wondered if it turned him into dust that much sooner. If this came along four years from now, I could handle it much easier. "I'm not sure what to do."

"It's a management thing. Could take me away from home a lot. It's on top of my regular work."

"And you're worried about Charlie," she said. "Isn't there some way to get some flexibility on the hours? A family-friendly approach?"

I wish. "No, it's one of those being on call to jump on management crises at any time."

"For a science lab? You always say nothing gets done quickly in science."

Uh, yeah, I had said that. Crap. "You'd think, but some kid gets E. Coli from a burger, or a strange virus appears and they want experts there on the spot."

239

"Like the CDC? Sounds dangerous," she replied with apprehension.

"Yes, it is a little bit. I would have to take a fair amount of precautions. And there is a learning curve that I would have to climb on how to play it safe."

"You don't want to do this, do you?"

"No, but I was recommended by the person who just left the job."

"Have you talked to Charlie about it? You should, since you think he's adult enough to watch porn."

I closed my eyes. "Just a little."

"He will have to handle you not being home more. Unless…"

She wanted me to say 'unless what.' "Unless what?"

"Well, I want to retire. I could come down there and help out. Keep an eye on this teenager when you have to travel. Besides, it's too pricey to live up here on a fixed income, and the neighborhood is turning over."

"Ma, are you talking about moving down here?"

"Not in with you, but to the area. Yes."

Ma was over 68 years old. I always thought my mother would die at her desk in her 80s. She had never mentioned retirement before. In fact, she always disparaged retirement as waiting around to die.

"Ma, is everything okay?"

There was a pause.

"Work is not all it used to be," she said slowly, carefully. "Most of my friends have retired and I'm the dinosaur around there. They want us to use this new software and I just don't like it."

There was something about her tone that made me focus back on why she was saying this. "How are you doing health-wise?"

"Oh, I'm fine, I'm fine. I don't have the same energy I did ten years ago, but who does? But I can definitely keep up with Mr. Charles."

"I would love it if you were closer by. Charlie would too." Where I can keep an eye on you, take care of you, I thought, but couldn't say. The thought that she may need my help and I was an eight hour drive or flight away scared me for the first time. Maybe it scared her too.

"Really? You're not saying that?" This was my mother's way of finally letting herself be happy about getting something she wanted.

"Absolutely not, Ma. I'm part Italian, I need to take care of mi familia. And I may need that hand with my teen son in the near future."

"So you're going to take on that project?" she asked.

Covering the Charlie angle was only part of the equation. Stitcher played a three-dimensional chess game with pretty horrific risks. I wasn't sure I was up for that, no matter the consequences for life on Earth and humankind.

"I don't have a choice," I lamented.

[46]

Taking over Stitcher's job was relatively anticlimactic. There wasn't a secret underground base, no team of experienced black ops specialists and con men, nor a pay increase. I got his cell phone, his computer, a list of passwords, and a bunch of unanswered questions. Unfortunately, people fired questions at me before I had time to review Stitcher's files.

Malachi Cleek visited me at the lab a few days after Stitcher was cremated. "The FBI." He tossed a manila folder on my desk by way of greeting. "Your friend Lyle." Another folder. "Corporate executives." More folders thudded on top of the pile. "Lobbyists." Three more folders.

"What are all of these?" I peeked in the top folder.

"Briefing materials. Flesh out what you got from Stitcher." Malachi frowned when he saw the guilty look on my face. "You haven't looked at his files yet, have you?"

"I haven't had time," I said slowly, indicating the piles of work around my office. But I sounded defensive and whiny, even to myself.

"Wrong answer, doc."

I looked at him, but he simply shrugged his shoulders. "Okay," I said. "The only way I can handle this is to have a team. You need to be on it."

Malachi just stared at me for a second, and then replied, "Okay."

242

I sat back in my chair. "Stitcher probably kept you out of most of the loop, right? Well, that ends now."

"So what's my role?"

I looked around at the pile of folders on my desk. "That depends - where's the folder on you?"

He looked at the folders. "I don't know. I expect Stitcher has one on me but he never let me see it."

"Yes, I get your point." I was tempted to just turn everything over to Malachi and let him sort out Stitcher's files. But I didn't know him. That could be an enormous mistake to make just because of my workload. And to indulge my reluctance to deal with the full extent of Stitcher's probably cringeworthy projects.

"From what you know, what are the things I should be most worried about?"

Malachi took out a notebook, wet his thumb, and flipped through the pages. "FBI. Your friend Lyle. The chemical industry spooks."

I tried to think like Stitcher. "Is there anything you think I need to focus on right now, today, before it blows up in our faces?"

He furrowed his brow. "FBI. Agent Pierce is sniffing around quite a bit. We would be better off if he stopped."

I looked down at my desk. "Okay."

"You going to be okay, doc?"

"I'm beginning to see why Stitcher was Stitcher. I'll call you when I'm ready to talk. Your number… is in Stitcher's contacts, okay."

Malachi smiled, stood, shook my hand, and left.

I stared at the folders. More dark secrets, more intrigue, more plates to keep spinning. They reminded me of the first time I was in this building, when Stitcher drove me all the way down here to show me the Project Rogers files. I wanted to sweep everything off my desk, lay my head down, and take a nap.

I locked the new folders inside the credenza where I kept my purse and other personal things. Next step: adjust my AgSol job so I could take on the new one and not screw up both.

There was a junior scientist, an epidemiologist named Sarahi Muldoon, who Donald had pointed out as someone who was interested in the management track. She was a good human scientist who had a knack for running down grants and minimizing administrative work for her team.

I called her down to my office. She appeared a few minutes later, bearing a tablet and a quick smile. She was short, with dyed blond hair and a thin build. Her father was Irish but her mother was a Kurd, her file said.

I returned the smile but dove right in. "Dr. Meers tells me that you have management potential. And that you don't want to be a bench scientist your entire career. I need assistance. There are workloads I need to delegate. I have a whole bunch of things that fell onto my plate that I can't ignore."

Her face fell. "I see."

"Are you thinking that I want to you to be a glorified administrative assistant, a secretary?" This happened to women in science all the time. They either got pushed out of the lab, opted to bail on the lab's boys-club atmosphere and go teach, or were sent to the least scientific aspects of an institution, where no 'real work' of consequence took place.

"Oh, no," I waved my hands in the air. "I'm not looking for that. I need a deputy who can take over for me when I'm not available. Really, a junior partner. I want to groom you for taking over my position."

Her mouth dropped open but her eyes blazed like she had won the lottery. "Shouldn't it go to a more senior scientist than me? Dr. Meers?"

I shook my head. I had seen too many good bench scientists shuffle off to management because they saw it as the only way to increase their pay or prestige. They were usually bad managers. Few did it because they excelled or enjoyed it, and science was the worse off for it. And I had seen too many of my fellow women in science get shuffled off to do trivial, technician work, denied opportunities in leadership.

"Don't talk yourself out of a promotion. Seniority isn't important. There's a lot more to this job than understanding the science in the research. It takes people skills, decision-making and judgement ability, ruthless organization, which I'm lacking in, and a clear vision. There's surprisingly little time to actually manage the substance of the lab's work itself."

She brightened and thought for a second. "Where would you draw the line between my responsibilities and yours?"

"First rule of management: you often have no choice but to make it up as you go. I'm not a manager by trade and ironically, don't know any management science. There's two things I want you to do. Draw up a transition plan for yourself that doesn't undermine your team's projects. Second, draw up a game plan for the deputy director position so that we are not stepping on each other's toes. Grab time off my calendar when you have both ready."

Sarahi scribbled notes on her tablet. "Thank you for this opportunity, Dr. Cassano."

I smiled. "Call me Elaine, Sarahi. And I'm just as excited about it as you are. I'll make the announcement after I see that transition plan."

She shook my hand enthusiastically and nearly bounced out of my office. Talking to her didn't lighten my load one bit, but I felt better. I couldn't focus on the conspiracy if the lab was flapping in the breeze.

I turned around in my chair, opened the credenza and pulled out Stitcher's phone and laptop. They sat there, inert on my desk, reminders that Stitcher was really dead and gone forever. Without him, they were just objects. I took a big breath and turned them both on. They were mine now.

[47]

When I thought of John Stitcher, I thought of his cell phone plastered to his ear, receiving and transmitting the verbal abuse that fountained out of his mouth. I started with it first.

The Board had given me a password to unlock the phone. It worked, and I felt like I was stepping inside the ghoul attorney's rotten brain. His contacts, his call logs, his internet bookmarks.

The first thing I saw was a note to me. It started, "Dear Elaine, I hope you have not completely lost your shit."

That was it. No heartfelt farewell. Instead, the rest of the note included links to a document full of instructions, descriptions of files, and summaries of relationships.

The first item on my new to-do list was to gain access to a trust I didn't even know existed. Stitcher, the wily lawyer, had created a trust that had only he and I could control. The trust oversaw $5 million in investments and another $2 million in cash. His slush fund, he called it, used at his, or now my, discretion. I had become a millionaire conspiracy runner, like some kind of soccer mom version of Doctor Evil. Great.

"Elaine, the trust is for emergency uses, like when you need to fly out to dipshit town in flyover country to stomp out some stupid-ass thing. It will

246

tide you over until you get reimbursed by the corporate stiffs." More instructions followed on how his secretary obtained the reimbursements.

His contact list was a who's who of the food and agriculture industries. He demanded that I call and introduce myself to every single one of them. Contacts were the lifeblood of this job, he wrote.

I sent the contacts and the call logs to my phone. I needed to know what he was working on right before he died, who he was in contact with. I put all the contacts in a spreadsheet on his tablet and made a plan of attack for calling each one, from John's phone. It would take me days to work through the list.

I prepared a sales pitch about how Stitcher had died and chose me to replace him. I would explain that I had all of his files and notes but wanted to talk separately with that person to explain the relationship they had with John and their recent interactions with him. It was the best way I could think of to jump start a relationship. I practiced it several times on the people in his contact list who already knew me.

Stitcher had written a ton of notes in the last six months. He must have known the end was coming and had started to prepare. That gave me the willies. I hoped that life ended for me all at once, so I didn't have to stew about dying.

I moved on to Stitcher's laptop. He kept everything on there, backed up on several encrypted thumb drives and with one cloud storage company. For a dead guy who would have been in his sixties if he had been alive before he died, he had cutting edge IT. My mother struggled with email.

I had already seen the Project Rogers files, and the ones about the care and feeding of hybrids. He had digitized the contents of those tattered 1960s manila folders he had first shown me five years ago. There were other folders for the food industry, the pharmaceutical industry, the chemical industry, the FBI, and the obesity conspiracy.

He had files on the FBI? I opened those first. He had assessed FBI leadership from the Director all the way down to Agent Pierce. There was a dossier on Agent Pierce that included his history at the agency, his credit report, his performance reports from his previous jobs, and his dating history. Stitcher actually hired a private detective to investigate an FBI special agent. I shook my head at his ballsiness. But why not? Stitcher lived on leverage.

Included in the dossier was a page of notes, updated only two weeks before. It laid out several strategies to neutralize Agent Pierce. Stitcher had chosen the quiet, behind-the-scenes strategy of misguiding Pierce, embarrassing him, and having our lobbyists cry foul about a rogue agent with a vendetta to force the Bureau to rein him in. I wish I had gotten off my ass and read this earlier.

According to Stitcher, the chemical industry had been in bed with the food and agriculture industries since at least World War II. Stitcher had carefully outlined how strong that relationship was. He had leveraged his chemical industry contacts to devise the adipose-infused food to feed the hybrids. He had been part of the cabal that encouraged the chemical industry to create the food flavoring industry. Charlie owed the dead ghoul for helping to create his beloved bacon-flavored chocolate cupcakes. And I wished I could knee the dead guy in his groin for the same.

The file on Big Pharma had dozens of documents. Pharma had done the heavy-lifting on reducing mortality from obesity. I would have liked to think that the conspirators had hearts after all, but I knew better. They wanted their adipose-producers to stick around as long as possible and not give obesity a bad rap by dropping dead at a young age. Big Pharma, of course, had taken this right to the bank with their boutique blood pressure, cholesterol, and heart meds.

His notes on the chemical and pharmaceutical industries mentioned in bold, ALL CAPS font that neither industry knew about the obesity conspiracy. All they knew was that Food had a business interest in stuffing people with as much food as possible and that they could profit from selling more fertilizers in the case of Big Chem, or treating the resulting medical conditions, in the case of Pharma.

Stitcher had begun gathering compromising material on the chemical and pharmaceutical industries. In the last saw five years he saw them becoming potential threats to the food industry as their interests diverged and possibly conflicted.

If you don't believe me, check out the fruit-flavors available for kids' medicines and go eat a bacon-flavored cupcake.

Stitcher worried that the rise of organic food production and would ruin these industrial alliances. Organic food production wouldn't need the massive consumption of chemical fertilizers and pesticides. Organic livestock wouldn't need to consume massive antibiotics. He really understood the financial bonds between these industries. He had played out scenarios to prepare for contingencies.

I was impressed with the breadth of his paranoia and entrepreneurialism. He had ballparked the revenue increases that the pharmaceutical industries would experience as the obesity epidemic spread through the US population. He used those projections in 2017 to pitch both industries on jointly funding a company that provided 'comprehensive diabetes treatment' with prepared meals and medication. He was like an evil Boy Scout, always prepared.

And now, I needed to be just as prepared.

Stitcher concluded his assessment of the chemical industry with reports it running its own covert ops. He only had speculation, hearsay, and coincidence. But he had been shaken when years ago I was attacked by a ghoul he didn't know existed. He never told me who the ghoul was, or who the ghoul worked for, but he suspected, here in his notes, that the chemical industry was behind it. They were the ones who had co-developed the resurrection procedure that kept him alive. He wrote, "Be extra careful with the goddamned chemical industry. They are wily, dangerous motherfuckers."

[48]

My first real test in Stitcher's shoes came with a call from Malachi on a Thursday afternoon. I was at the tail end of a farewell party for one of the scientists. She had been offered tenure track at the University of Minnesota, and given the lab's precarious outlook, took the job. It was probably the beginning of a self-reinforcing exodus, unfortunately.

I stepped out of the conference room and took the call. "We have a problem. The FBI just raided the DC cheese stick factory. The one you visited."

I buried my face in my hands. That was our main East Coast supplier. I was already way behind the curve in filling Stitcher's Florsheim shoes.

I said, "I'll come up there immediately. Where are you?"

"Looking at the smoking ruins."

I put my hand on my forehead. "How bad is it?"

"There are ruins. And they are smoking."

"You said the FBI raided it, not bombed it."

"There just happened to be multiple electrical fires that started when they broke down the door," Malachi explained. "Must have been lots of faulty wiring in the security system we put in place after you snuck in. We were probably in such a hurry after the last break-in."

"Understood." We were talking innocently in case someone was tapping the line.

So, we had to burn the factory to save the factory? I mean, yeah, it made sense to deny Agent Pierce any more pieces of the puzzle. But feeding a fake conspiracy wouldn't feed the hybrids. I wondered if this was something that Stitcher arranged after Pierce raided the West Coast facility.

"Is Pierce still there?"

"No, he and his forensic team left a few minutes before I arrived."

My mind raced. "So he didn't see you. Thank God."

"Thank me," Malachi replied. "I made sure not to show until he left."

"How much does he know?" I sent a message to Sarahi, telling her to take over the lab. I texted for the corporate jet to prep for me.

"I'm sure his team took samples. They may find human remains in the ashes."

Fear gripped my gut like a baby kicking the womb. "Didn't everyone escape?"

"Yes. Everyone is accounted for."

I took a deep breath. I had prepared for this kind of thing. I had cribbed from Stitcher's notes. The cheese stick factories were businesses and involved certain concerns that had to be dealt with immediately. Law enforcement, insurance, the health department, suppliers, and so on. Stitcher had never dealt with those head on from what I could tell. And I didn't have a clue.

"I should talk to the factory manager," I said as I gathered up my purse, files, and my coat.

"I have him right here. He has a checklist from Stitcher for dealing with all the issues that any facility manager would have to. We can focus on the other... externalities."

I nodded vigorously as I changed my shoes. Of course, Malachi couldn't see my fierce nods. "Good, good."

"I'll handle things in DC until you get here."

"Good, I'm on my way. Thanks so much, Malachi. Good work."

"Of course."

I walked quickly to the AgSol lobby and had a new thought. I spun around on the heel of my tennis shoe and marched back to the party. Donald was talking to Sarahi over by the remains of the cake. Yes, we still do cake for parties, even though we know that it can feed obesity. Traditions, you know?

"Hi, Sarahi, can I talk to Donald for a moment?"

"Sure, what's happening?" she asked.

"Nothing to worry about with the lab," I said smoothly.

She raised an eyebrow and looked at Donald. As Donald and I walked to his office, I wondered how tenable it would be to keep Sarahi in the dark about the conspiracy running right through the heart of the lab.

I closed the door. "The DC cheese stick factory was raided by the FBI and burned itself to the ground. That destroys a third of our remaining production capacity."

Donald paled. "Shit."

"Whatever contingency plans you have for this, we need to put them in place."

Donald blinked at me. "We'll cut back consumption to survival levels immediately. Beyond that, there are no contingency plans. I wished Mr. Stitcher was here to tell us what to do."

"I'm Stitcher's replacement," I blurted.

Donald looked at me expectantly. "Are you serious? I can't understand that. How?"

I put my hand on the doorknob. "I need to get to DC. We'll talk later."

I sped through the building, and once I was clear of the lobby, I ran for my minivan. I stopped to throw up on the parking lot median, and then drove like hell to the airport.

[49]

The second I ran aboard the jet at the private terminal, I pulled out my phone and scrolled through Stitcher's contacts. So many people to call, so many loose ends to tie up.

I thumbed Bob's number. He picked up on the second ring. "Elaine, is everything okay?"

"With Charlie, yes. With work, no. The FBI raided our food plant up there in DC. We need to cry foul to Congress, and I need my lobbyists to do it. The FBI is harassing the food industry, and I think it has a rogue agent operating without enough supervision. We need to meet today about this. The backlash for the FBI has to be instant if they are going to crack down on Pierce."

"I can't just drop everything. I have meetings all day," Bob whined. He sounded like Charlie not wanting to do his homework.

We were falling into our typical arguing positions when discussing Charlie, which wasn't good. "Bob, this just moved up to industry lobbying priority number one." I thought back to Stitcher's notes. "Tell your boss that this is a white bricker." Shitting a red brick was bad, yellow was worse, but white was an existential threat to the industry, an emergency. Stitcher created this warning system. It was a metaphor for heat or something. The important thing was that Bob's place would understand. I hoped as soon as I said it that I was not overestimating how bad this raid was for the hybrid food supply.

But we were looking at possible mass starvation of our hybrids if we couldn't get them adipose-infused cheese sticks. And since the hybrids were the key to teching and sciencing our way out of the onrushing environmental collapse, if we didn't act fast, we would screw an already screwed planet that needed hybrids to save our stupid, sorry asses from ourselves. So, yeah, white brick.

I waited until the jet was airborne before I called Malachi back. "Think about how we recover some production, in DC, in whatever makeshift way we can. The hybrids won't survive on what we can produce without DC. Let it simmer in your brain for a while."

"Okay," he said. "Anything else?"

My mind was whirling. "You mentioned the security system went haywire."

"Yes," he said slowly, so slowly that I could tell he was wondering why I was discussing this. A fire was the failsafe to stop the wrong people from getting evidence of what we were doing.

"We can't afford to have that happen again. I would like to review our security systems at food production facilities *like this one*." Meaning, that produced food for hybrids.

Malachi cleared his throat. "That matter has been left to the facilities' own management."

"I understand, but that's not working out well. I don't want a repeat of this if the FBI raids another facility."

"We should talk more about this later," Malachi said. "There are certain *trade secrets* we can't afford to lose, Elaine. You should talk to Dylan Emmerich, the plant manager, when you get here. He is very busy at the moment."

"Got it. Thanks." I clicked off.

The jet was on approach to National and my heart pumped adrenaline out to every nerve ending. I texted the number the Board had given me for emergency updates. I reviewed Stitcher's files for any similar event and how he had handled it. All I found was a health department inspection of the DC factory in 1992 that Stitcher fixed by browbeating the DC health department.

The jet touched down and when it stopped, I raced to a waiting Lincoln Town Car. It was late afternoon before it fought its way across town to the smoldering factory site.

Dylan climbed in the back of the Lincoln Town Car looking like a guilty sheepdog. Until he recognized me.

"You're Elaine? But, you're that woman. Who broke into the factory. Stitcher took you away. What the hell is going on?"

"Stitcher trained me to replace him. Small world."

Dylan rubbed his hair like a mad man. "Jesus Christ."

I handed him a water bottle. "Have a drink and relax. Crazy day, huh?"

Dylan took the water bottle and drank. He struck me as a surfer dude who had reached his forties, put on a bunch of weight, and never quite fit the corporate manager model.

"How are you doing, Dylan?" I asked.

"I'm okay. Everyone got out, but this has been tough."

"I'm not here to fire you. I want to learn what happened here and figure out the next steps."

Dylan took another pull from the water bottle and tried to process that. "You sure have a different style than he does."

"I think people work best when they're not getting screamed and cursed at. How did your interview with the FBI go?"

He put the bottle down. "Okay, the FBI. They got nothing out of the raid because of the fire. So they tried asking me instead. They wanted to know what we make, where the ingredients come from, who we sell to, plus, you know, all the mundane questions. Hiring, environmental regs, taxes, the works."

"Tell me about the mundane questions, in case there is something important buried in them."

"How many people work here, are they all legal, who does our payroll, what will our customers do now, how we'll restart production, who installed the security system, how I got this job; it went on and on. They didn't even care about the answers."

"Have you talked to your bosses yet?"

He nodded. "They want a report on what happened, there's insurance people to talk to, plus planning the rebuilding."

"How long will it take to rebuild?"

He sighed. "I don't know. Maybe a year or two? The factory is pretty easy — just concrete and steel walls, with sheet metal machinery inside. Pretty standard stuff, a lot of it we can order pre-assembled. It's the red tape that

255

could make it take longer. Permits, inspections, construction delays, that kind of thing."

I made a note. Cutting the red tape had to be a Stitcher job. Which meant it was mine. I knew, even as I wrote down this to-do, that I wouldn't have the time or expertise to do it. And the hybrids would all be dead of starvation long before a new facility was producing at a subsistence-level. We couldn't wait for a rebuilt facility.

I raised my eyebrows. "I need you to do what you have to in order to resume production ASAP. You know that there are people on special diets who depend on your cheese sticks for survival, right? Good. We can't let them starve. Here's my number. Call me if you need help. Do you understand?"

He put my number into his phone contacts. "I have a question. The next shipment of medical waste meant for this plant will come in two nights from now. What should I do?"

That fat had to go somewhere else. Somewhere that could turn it into a food-like product for the hybrids to eat. "We need another facility set up before then. We need it turned into some kind of food-like product."

"Well, we treat it first, then package it as cheese sticks or slabs of cheese," he pointed out. "We can do that anywhere, I guess."

I slapped my thigh. "That's it! I don't care how makeshift it is, rent a barn, or move it to your kitchen if you have to. You need to keep production going. There are lives at stake. Can you do that?"

"Um, yeah. Me and the workers just need a place. We won't be as fast. But, you know, we don't have to make regular cheese sticks if we're doing this underground. Yeah, we can do this. If we're not caught."

I patted his knee. "I'll make sure you're not. Thank you. Now get going."

"Um, you're welcome." Dylan climbed out of the car. Every second this car sat in this rundown section of collision shops and cinder block makers made me nervous. I felt like Pierce was watching me already. I had the driver take me to Bob's office on K Street.

Why hadn't it occurred to me to simply set up makeshift production before? Besides the risks of ignoring every health department rule for not mixing in medical waste with edible food for sale. I felt like I was blindly swinging a hammer around at problems as they cropped up.

I breathed quietly for a minute as I wrestled my doubts. This was my first rodeo, I needed to cut myself a break. The car was rolling by Capitol Hill row houses when I called Charlie. I told him I may be late getting home tonight.

I called Donald. "We'll have production started soon, but it's going to be a lot less than before. Possibly for the next couple of years. The feds have now raided both of our major U.S. production facilities."

He replied, "And we have just achieved a new high in hybrid births."

I squeezed my eyes shut thinking of all those hungry babies. I would be damned if I was going to deal with any more skulls. "Is there any adipose substitute that you've found? Any progress?"

"No. I've been spending most of my time on deciphering the code."

The code. I had almost forgotten about that. It seemed like a luxury given an adipose food shortage. Should I have him stop working on it? It almost seemed unfair: he was so intensely invested in it.

"Keep doing that. If nothing is already in the pipeline on the substitute, it'll be too late."

"What are we going to do?"

"I don't know yet. Production will take a hit, but it may only be temporary. We'll think of something. There's human fat everywhere, this is America, right? This shouldn't be too hard."

"I'll start thinking about alternatives," Donald replied.

"Good. Wait." For some reason, the image of hybrids biting into the morbidly obese on the street came to mind, and if I wasn't horrified by the possibility of that actually happening, I'd probably laugh. "You run everything by me first. Even before experiments are set up, understand?"

"Yes, ma'am."

The car was winding its way down New York Avenue in Northeast. There was a lot of obesity on display, sadly enough. "Donald, did we ever run those liposuction clinics in poor neighborhoods?"

"I don't think so. The tour was mostly focused on rural areas and the suburbs," he replied.

"Let's think about the poor urban areas. See if we can partner with local health agencies. They'll understand the health benefits of doing this. And folks here in DC, and Tennessee, could use the help."

The abrupt transition from the grimier sections of Northeast to K Street always startled me. The city was such a collection of jarring contrasts.

The lobbying firm Bob worked out of was on retainer to the food industry. Stitcher's notes said they always answered his phone calls. Bob let them know that I was coming and when the town car pulled up in front of their glass and steel building, he was waiting outside for me.

"So, you're the grumpy old man now," he joked when I got out.

I smiled. He could be charming when he wanted to be. We passed through security and went to the top floor. The partners were a collection of older white guys from WASP central casting and they were waiting in the grand conference room for me.

After handshakes all around I detected something I didn't expect: nervousness on their part. When I sat down, I spread my shoulders confidently, a dominant alpha male pose. Lean in, Sheryl Sandberg had said. She probably never meant to lean in, stretch out, and takeover, but that's what I felt I had to do.

I explained the situation with the factory raids. "I'll be blunt. We have a rogue FBI agent who probably doesn't have support from above. I want you to rattle the politicals above him so they will reign him in."

"Yes, this agent is clearly out of control. We need to handle that," said one partner, an animated smooth-talker who everyone thought was their best friend. "But we have to be ready for when they claim he's working on a criminal case, and they can't interfere with an investigation, and so on."

"To save face, sure they'll say that," said the oldest partner, who sported an old-fashioned suit vest. He reminded me of a 19th century banker. "But that's beside the point, the Bureau will understand that we want this investigation tamped down."

"We have some information on Special Agent Pierce that suggests this may be a personal crusade," I said. "He has a number of obese relatives but he is slim and eats well. He tends to flash his badge and push things when he has little to go on. We have a dossier on him."

"That's great, send us the details," said the vest-wearer. I would have to remember their names eventually.

I nodded. "Look, I don't want to take up more of your time - you are surely billing the industry for this meeting. Truth be told, unlike John Stitcher, I have no legal training and I need to rely on your firm to fill that gap."

The partners could barely conceal their glee, thinking about all of the billable hours. That threw me off some. I hadn't thought about the expenses that

Stitcher incurred and who paid those bills. The industry probably had other, cheaper law firms on tap to help with legal work. I would have to learn more about the financial side of this enterprise and be smart with the trust's money.

"Assuming that the FBI doesn't torch any more of our facilities or cause other political emergencies, I would like to liaise with you through Bob. Stitcher's shoes are hard to fill and I plan to handle his duties with the help of a team. I would like Bob to be on it."

The partners looked thrilled except for the smooth talker, who asked, "We will get to bill for his hours, right?"

"Of course," I said. If Bob was on the clock, hopefully he would continue to be nice to me. "But he can't bill for time spent talking about our son."

The smooth talker grinned. "Sure, sure. Bob are you okay with that?"

Bob nodded vigorously. "This is great, Bernie."

Good. Malachi, Donald, and now Bob. I was starting to feel more comfortable with taking over for Stitcher now that I had the beginnings of a team to help out.

I told the driver to take me back to National for the flight out. I texted the Board a lengthy explanation of what had happened and how I was handling it. I didn't know if they would want to discuss. I didn't even know if Stitcher gave them these kinds of updates. Despite all the material he had left me, even about the Board, he hadn't mentioned little housekeeping details like how much he reported back to them and how much he kept close to the vest.

Then I was wheels-up and headed home to Knoxville. For once, I felt like I was finally getting my head above water. It was a dreamy moment that I should have enjoyed more, before things backfired.

[50]

I hadn't given Agent Pierce much thought after Bob and the other lobbyists descended on the FBI's executives. After not being bothered by him for a while, I figured he would soon be filing fingerprints in some evidence warehouse in rural Iowa.

But this afternoon, Pierce had turned up at Knoxville's airport at Arrivals. He rented a car and left, according to airport spies I inherited from Stitcher.

We didn't know if Pierce was coming to raid the lab. He could have been in town just visiting his niece. So with the sun setting on the pines that towered over the parking lot, I had Malachi call in our security team and headed home. The security team's white utility van pulled in as I left.

Leaving right then may sound strange, but I feared that Pierce was coming to my house. I didn't want Charlie facing a warrant, a badge, and a gun by himself. Charlie was the perfect leverage against me and I didn't know how far Pierce would go to use that. Keeping myself between Charlie and Pierce was high on my list of priorities.

Also, my favorite place to be during the holiday season was in my warm kitchen, baking, with Charlie nearby doing homework or helping out. Go ahead, call me old fashioned and hypocritical for making baked goods. But I didn't want Pierce or the FBI to ruin my night.

My cell phone rang right before ten that night. "He's at the lab," Malachi said. "I just got a call."

I whispered, "You called the police?"

Malachi and the security team didn't like involving the local cops. I know he took it as a lack of confidence in his team, but he knew I wanted the police to catch Pierce. "I called them right before I called you," he replied.

"Good. Don't let our guys confront him. I'll be there soon." I grabbed my coat and purse.

Charlie whirled around on the couch. "Where are you going at this hour, young lady?"

I was tempted to give him a phony teenager answer, but he saw the seriousness in my eyes.

"Trouble at the lab," I said. "Don't worry, I shouldn't be too long."

"Is it serious?" he said.

"They don't call at ten if they don't think it is," I injected some fake weariness into my voice to reassure him that this was more irritating than concerning. He turned back to watching some obnoxiously loud Japanese cartoon.

Malachi texted a video to me. I got in my minivan and played the video clip on the minivan's video system. The security camera showed a grainy black and white image of Pierce, collar turned up and wearing a wide-brimmed fedora. He looked like a G-man from a 30s gangster film, but the hat did hide most of his face from the cameras. I recognized his burly guy-stroll though.

He approached the lab's front door and made short work of the lock. He slipped inside and walked through the lobby and past the offices. The camera showed him heading straight for the labs.

Which was odd, because it would be a lot harder for him to find anything incriminating back there. Parts of experiments weren't tagged with a summary document explaining them. Vials and centrifuges and samples all looked the same, especially when labelled by our own unique barcodes. Unless Pierce had inside knowledge about what we were doing and he was looking for something specific. I wouldn't put anything past him.

The video ended. I squealed the tires as I roared out of the driveway. What did Pierce know? Did he know about our hybrid incubators in the back? Or where the Project Rogers files were kept? I had expected him to

261

make a beeline for my office rather than head for the labs. I drove as fast as I dared.

Stringing along Pierce with enough information to hang himself but not so much to hang us was a tricky balancing act. The whole point of dangling the food company execs' conspiracy to fatten the world was so that he would never stumble into the real one, about the hybrids and saving the global environment. The one sitting in the same building he had broken into.

But Pierce ignored the low-hanging fruit and the easy corporate-mischief headlines his bosses would probably luxuriate in. Instead, he had risked his career to try unearthing the hybrid graves, to track Stitcher's body, and now he was nosing around inside AgSol. Even when we were trapping this guy, he was scaring me senseless.

The streets were empty and wet. Each turn seemed agonizingly slow and I cursed every red light. Finally I pulled up behind the flashing blue and red lights of Oak Ridge's finest, who were parked in front of the lab's front door. I jumped out of the minivan and went looking for my security chief.

He waved me over to the handicapped parking spaces by the front door. There was a police officer next to him tapping notes into his tablet. "What happened?" I asked the cop, trying to sound shaken and concerned.

The cop nodded toward the building. "An intruder tripped the alarm, our officers apprehended him. We're questioning him now."

"Did he destroy our experiments?" It dawned on me that I was in the same position as Dylan had been when I was caught at the DC cheese stick factory years ago.

The cop shook his head. "Cases like these, he's probably looking for a scale to measure drugs with. Every couple of months we get someone sneaking into ORNL or UT looking for scales."

The security chief cleared his throat loudly. "I told the police that sometimes there are trade secrets and high value materials that could be the target."

I nodded vigorously. "I would like to see this intruder before you take him away."

The cop shook his head. "I don't think so, ma'am."

I stepped closer to his personal space. "If he's an industrial spy, we have to take steps right now to secure our data, our experiments, and any trade secrets. I need to know who he is and who he may be working for."

The cop looked down on me. "We have to handle things ourselves from this point. We'll tell you when you can reenter the building. We'll send you a copy of our report."

The security chief gave me an 'I told you so' look. But by calling the cops in first, it had to look pretty bad for the Bureau when the cops caught Pierce red-handed breaking and entering into a private business without a warrant. He would be in for another round of trouble and may even get fired.

The police officer's shoulder radio squawked. Suspect in custody. But the officers inside also insisted that someone call in the police captain. I hoped it was because Pierce had flashed his FBI badge and not something else.

The security chief and I waited in the cold for this police captain to arrive. He finally pulled up and joined the cops, looking irritated. He jabbed a '#1 Dad' coffee mug at his cops to dole out instructions. He gave us an annoyed look, didn't come over to talk, and went inside.

We waited for what felt like hours. Maybe it felt that way because the security chief kept giving me 'I told you so' looks every minute. It turned out to be only thirty minutes, according to my phone.

The cop's radio crackled. "If anyone's out there from this place, send them in. We have some things to sort out."

The cop waved in me and the security chief.

They had Pierce sitting at our conference room table, uncuffed and looking comfy. His badge and gun were at the far end of the table with the captain. There was a police officer in the room and another outside the door. To my relief, Pierce looked mighty pissed to see me.

"This man is an FBI agent," the captain said. "He says he's working a case investigating this lab and several multi-national corporations in the food industry. You look like you know him."

I nodded. "Yes, he's been harassing me and my staff now for months. He's followed me to other cities and keeps trying to steal our files."

Pierce chewed his lower lip and looked away.

The captain pointed his coffee cup at Pierce. "He doesn't have a warrant, but he says he heard someone cry for help, and feared someone was in imminent danger."

My security chief chuckled. "This late, in a science lab?"

I bugged my already buggy eyes out even further. "Isn't this breaking and entering?"

The captain didn't like to hear that. "Not if he thought someone was in trouble."

Our security chief folded his arms. "It's amazing he heard this phantom cry for help all the way out on the street. That's about a hundred yards of forested ground."

Pierce ground his molars upon hearing that. The police captain winced. "Are you going to try pressing charges against an FBI agent?"

Despite the captain's withering look, I had a plan to follow. I needed Pierce off our case. "Yes. And I want his supervisor alerted."

"You're not going to get away with anything, Elaine," Pierce said in a low rumble.

I put my hands on my hips. "An FBI agent accused of breaking and entering. Who has been involved in the fatal shooting of a suspect recently. Who has interfered with funeral arrangements for a coworker of mine who died recently. He has abused his powers to harass and stalk scientists and corporate executives because of his personal agenda."

He made a face. "It's only personal for the millions of people you and your people have fattened up intentionally."

Real anger burned in his eyes and I wished Stitcher was here so I could see what he thought of this. Teasing the feds with a conspiracy to create the obesity epidemic seemed like a double-edged sword with a greasy hilt. Now that I was holding it, I didn't want it taken and rammed up my ass.

I slipped into my best angry mother voice. "Your problem is that you're just right enough to be truly dangerous," I said. "But you don't know the whole truth, and you refuse to see it."

"What do I refuse to see?" Pierce retorted.

"For the last time, the food industries aren't calling the shots, they're hanging on for dear life," I said. "They're not worried that Johnny American eats less junk food. They can sell him diet versions, or ones with extra fat; it doesn't matter to them. What they sweat is bad weather, bad science in the media, and E coli contamination. They're trapped."

"Trapped?" Pierce's eyes blazed. "Pity the corporate executives and their stock options."

The police captain gave the wrap it up sign. "This is all thrilling, but it looks like you two won't work this out here," he said. "We'll take Agent Pierce in, but it's up to the DA if he is charged."

264

I nodded. That was perfect. I wanted the arrest in the system. I did a quick walkthrough of the lab, checking for broken equipment or forced doors. I didn't find any. It was clear the cops wanted to leave and wipe their hands clean of Pierce and the FBI. I returned home and told Charlie that someone tried breaking in.

Pierce never saw a jail cell, Malachi told me the next morning. The police woke up the DA, who refused to press charges and released Pierce. Mind you, none of that upset either me or Malachi. We really couldn't hope for anything better, and this was all we needed.

I called Pierce's supervisor the next day, and ranted about federal agents abusing their power. Bob and a bevy of industry attorneys and lobbyists called the FBI director and several members of Congress, including both of Tennessee's senators.

By the end of the day, Pierce was off the obesity conspiracy case. The Bureau refused to close the investigation, however, Malachi reported. Our careful feeding of insider info to them meant that our opponents in the c-suites of the food companies were still under the microscope. In fact, the Bureau added agents to the case and started bringing in their staff for questioning. I don't know how well Stitcher would have done in the same situation, but I would take whatever wins I could get.

[51]

Thank God my sneaky teenage son was also sloppy. Leaving candy wrappers in the trash where I could see them was not the brightest move in his playbook. I confronted him about it when we had both got home from school and work.

"Hey genius, do you think this is a magical garbage can?" I pointed inside. "Candy wrappers don't disappear when you throw them in here."

He walked over and his face turned crimson.

"You've been sneaking food on me, haven't you? Charles, we *talked* about this."

He looked at his shoes. "Yes."

"Look, I'm your mother forever, but I won't be your watcher for much longer. The food habits you develop now will be yours for life. You lock them in at your age. And your body won't take abuse at older ages like it can now. Believe me."

He cracked a grin. "You're not going to talk about hot flashes again, are you?"

I sighed, folded my arms and waited. Waited for him to listen. Charlie's smile faltered and then fell away in the silence.

"Alright, I hear you. It's as important as wearing a seatbelt. What? What else did I do?"

"I've got to talk to you about work," I said. "I've told you I had some additional responsibilities drop on me that took me to DC. I'm going to have to take more trips, and put out more fires. A lot more. And they will be on short notice."

"Is something wrong?" he asked.

I shook my head. "I will be on call to deal with certain management crises."

Charlie squared his shoulders. "I can take care of myself."

"Yeah," I said.

He got that smartass look on his face again. "What exactly would you be doing?"

"I can't talk about the details. Think of it as rapid response health and biology consulting."

"Is it anything dangerous?"

Where did that come from? "No, it's not dangerous. I'm a scientist, remember?"

He looked at me in a way that made him look a lot older. "You never say much about your work. It's not like when I was little. I'm not even sure what your lab does."

"I don't want to bore a teenager with that kind of thing," I said, waving a hand.

He wasn't laughing though. "I may understand some of what you're talking about."

That was exactly why I hadn't told him much. I needed to say something. "If you want to know more, I'm happy to tell you. But don't accuse me of trying to make it about your weight issue."

He shook his head. "I won't. Is it all obesity research?"

My gaze darted around the kitchen. "We study a number of things. Genetics, brain chemistry, psychology, anything that can affect the human body, really."

"And?"

"And what?"

He wagged his finger at me. "You're getting cagey. I don't know why, but this is a touchy subject for you."

"I don't know what you are talking about."

He squinted his eyes at me, studying me intently. "You're scared of something, Mom."

This is the thing no one tells you about having older children; they turn into highly-perceptive pre-adults and show you how all of your faults have become an open book. Sure, they may be snarky, surly, awkward, and unsure of themselves, but they see things with adult eyes long before they become adults. It completely sucks.

I gulped. "I am scared. It's a big pile of responsibility. I'm not sure I'm up to it and I don't have any one to mentor me. I didn't ask for it, but I have to make the best of it."

He was worried about me. "This may not matter, but I don't think you should do this thing. It sounds bad."

I waved my hand. "The most important thing to me is that I'm here when you need me. But you'll have to parent yourself more."

"What do you mean?"

"Eating right, staying healthy, not partying, and doing your homework if I'm late. Going to bed on time. Acting like more of a grown-up. I need your help for this to work. I need to not worry about you keeping it together when I'm called away."

"Okay. I understand. You could take me with you. I'm old enough now that I can do a lot of my school work remotely."

No way. Nothing I was doing was take-you-kid-to-work friendly. There was a whole other world that I didn't want him to know about. Ever. Ghouls and conspiracies and the ugly truth of how screwed the environment was. I just wanted him to go live his life in the sane world we all think we occupy. That way, I could visit and be away from Stitcher's world. I shook my head. "No way. This is stuff way above your pay grade."

"I could get valuable experience and contacts that could help me down the road. Other kids with successful parents get a huge freaking leg up from them."

"Oh no, you're not turning this into some kind of growth development. The answer is no."

He glared at me suspiciously for a long moment, and that kid looked right fucking through me. He scared me at times like this, because he almost seemed like a grown man.

268

[52]

Donald was talking to a junior scientist when I found him in the computer lab. "Run it again, please," he said. "Just one more time, to be sure."

She curled her lip, ready to retort, but saw me and simply walked away.

"I got your message," I said. He looked at me with a melancholy look I've never seen on him before. "Are you okay?"

Donald looked around at the humming server racks and the technician who was tapping away at a diagnostic terminal. "Let's talk in my office." I followed him back to his office. He sat down, folded his hands, and looked at them for a long moment.

"We've run a number of genetic simulations. Protein folding, cancer cell studies, genomic mapping. We have been modeling how environmental changes affect gene expression for a while now. Genes aren't as fixed as we once believed. Every year the bio-genetics field finds another way in which genes react to environmental stimuli."

This wasn't news. But his voice quaked a little, like something had bit him. He was hardly ever scared like this, he was always calmer than me and Betty. I wanted to get this bit of business out of the way so I could find out who died in his family. It was that bad.

"The amphibian die-off around the world has been caused by the chytrid virus. Recent research shows that pesticides reduce the frogs' natural defenses against the fungus that causes the disease. But those changes are happening in the frog's genes and it gets passed to the next generation."

I nodded. The die-off in amphibian species was alarming. They were a highly sensitive species, with porous skin, and living in water environments. They were our canary in the coal mine when it came to the health of the biome.

Donald continued, "Our genetics team found that a combination of inorganic compounds and hormones activated a number of normally dormant genes that compromised the frogs' immune system. With their immune systems impaired, they couldn't fight the chytrid fungus."

"Our European lab figured out how the environmental conditions, like pesticides, trigger the gene. They replicated it after a lot of trial and error. What happens is that a mix of environmental pollutants and endocrine inhibitors act together to permanently activate the dormant genes. But this isn't just with the frogs and one fungus. It happens to genes across the genome of all living things. And the triggers include dioxin, perchlorate, mercury, the usual suspects."

Okay, now I was getting worried. This was quite the wind-up for a man who usually got to the point quickly. Plus, there were tears in the corners of his eyes.

"We've been running tests of this damage on mice, fruit flies, and a couple of other animals. The genetic damage is permanent and inherited across generations. Even when the environmental stimuli is removed for these later generations. The more exposure to these genetic inhibitors, the more cumulative damage occurs."

"How do we reverse it?" I asked.

Donald looked down. "The Silicon Valley lab modeled what happens when the inhibitor concentrations reach the level we have been seeing in frogs. The genetic damage leads to a gradual die-off of each species. It will happen to almost all organic life. All species. Plant and animal. All over the planet."

I stared at him a second.

"You're shitting me," I said. But he wasn't, I could see it in his eyes. The death in the family was not just a personal matter for him. It was the death of everyone's families.

He handed over a tablet with the tables and charts. I scrutinized them, looking for gaps or methodological errors. "What about humans? When can we start testing them?"

"That's why I'm speaking with you," Donald said. "We'd like to check the gene bank for these same effects."

The gene bank was a collection of genetic information from thousands of volunteers. Medical researchers and other scientists used it to test for various markers, therapies, prevalence of particular gene expressions and the like. The volunteers privacy was guaranteed. Last count, they had over a hundred thousand people in the bank.

I've never seen Donald's eyes look so lifeless. "You already know what you're going to find, don't you?"

He nodded slowly. "There's no way that somehow Homo Sapiens are immune to this genetic damage. We live on the same planet as all the other species. We've been absorbing the same deadly cocktail." He coughed as his voice caught on a snag and cracked.

I ran a hand through my hair. "Yes, prep the paperwork. Dress it up as another study of genetic determinants of obesity."

"We've run the simulations a thousand times extra on this, Elaine, and the same thing keeps happening. This is what the meteor people were trying to warn us about. Once you wreck the genetic code, your fate is sealed; it's only a matter of time."

"But if we dial back the pollutants, whatever that toxic soup is, we can prevent that," I said.

Donald wiped his eyes. "No one has any idea how to remove these chemicals and pollutants from the environment. The genetics team tested themselves and their children. Each person absorbs more as they age, so the concentrations should be higher in older people. And they are. But the absorption rate has increased. In the US, we already passed the critical threshold. Now that we know what to look for, we can see the proof."

"What do you mean?"

Donald pinched an inch of flab and smiled hopelessly. "Obesity, diabetes, high cholesterol, cancer, infertility. They've started increasing in the last decade in places untouched by American food companies or American culture."

"Natural selection can counter genetic damage," I said hopefully. Wishfully.

271

"Evolution moves too slowly. Normal genetic mutations that drive selection need generations to work their magic. Evolution needs centuries, but we only have decades."

More ideas sprang forth in my head. "What was the mix of chemicals?"

"Carbon monoxide, flame retardants, estrogen, PCBs, various toxic chemicals, and other endocrine inhibitors." Donald shook his head.

There was no way to make those go away quickly. Not without shutting down 21st century global civilization. "We could develop new chemicals to counteract their effects. Endocrine and gene therapy."

"Even a hybrid-assisted scientific endeavor would take twenty years to make substantial progress," Donald pointed out. "You know that science is not that fast."

I chewed the inside of my lip. "Are you sure the simulations are right? Remember, the Manhattan Project guys thought they may burn off the Earth's atmosphere with a nuclear detonation."

He blinked at me, his way of signaling impatience. He put his tablet on his desk and turned it around so I could see.

I was looking at a graph titled "Percent of species reaching extinction." The squiggly lines all ended close to 100 percent. There had been a discussion among ecologists for years about whether we were in the early stage of a mass extinction event. But these events took thousands of years to happen. This graph showed it happening in a century.

My eyes filled with tears. That should seem silly, given that this was preliminary findings, uncorroborated or replicated anywhere else yet. But my old researcher instincts were tingling in my head and down my spine. The kind of tingle when I couldn't see any methodological flaws, or crappy data. The kind of tingling that told me that this was right. It wouldn't be disproven.

Donald continued, "We have done triple the number of checks with different assumptions. None of us have any doubt, but I've ordered another round of runs anyway. There's some sensitivity analyses I want to do to eliminate any reasonable doubt."

I shook my head, ignoring my instinctive reaction. "These are simulations. You could have estimated the structural relationships wrong. Or taken a pessimistic approach to nature's resiliency. What did that guy say in the dinosaur movie? Life will find a way."

Donald cleared his throat. "Indeed, life may find a way. It has during the previous extinction event, but each time it took millions of years to bounce back."

"I know. But have you validated these simulations against reality? Shouldn't we be seeing the effects already?" It was a lost cause, trying to nitpick Donald's methodology or methods. In the five years I had known him, I had never found a weak link in any methodology he stood behind. Not a single paper of his had ever been successfully refuted. That was an unusual experience for me. It was beyond human, but that made sense, didn't it?

"Of course, Elaine. We're already seeing the first effects. Cancer and asthma prevalence are increasing, fertility rates are dropping, and extinctions are increasing. It's already started, we just haven't realized it until right now. Do you understand?"

My hand shot to my mouth. All the pieces fell into place. I couldn't believe it, I refused to believe it, but the evidence did fit the theory.

"This is silly," I heard myself say. "This is the problem discovery stage; it's way too early to discuss if potential solutions will fail. We had a long way to go before giving up. Aliens, faster than light travel, nuclear fusion, they were all things that were impossible ten years ago and now were at least theoretically possible."

"Forget peak oil, crop yields, or even climate change," Donald said softly. "We are facing a genetic extinction event. And the obesity pandemic is making things worse, because obesity is helping to activate these junk genes earlier than they would be otherwise by the environmental pollutants."

Tears rolled free down my cheeks. "What do we do?"

Donald shook his head. "I don't know. Nothing seems to change the simulation results."

Even with the help of alien savants. Even with all of our resources. I put my head in my hands. "How long do we have?"

"Maybe 120 years. Depending on whether we understand the interaction effects correctly. Once things really fall apart, they'll fall apart really fast. Food chains disrupted, illnesses spreading quickly through species. On the human side, economic disruption, population crashes, wars, what do you call it? The works."

The works. Also known as armageddon and Judgement Day. All because

273

of the terminal soup we were stewing in. And there wasn't any easy way to drain the pot or season it to make it less noxious.

My first instinct was to call Stitcher, throw it in his lap and watch him curse and cajole our genes to shape up and fly right. But he was gone. It was on me. And I didn't have a fucking clue. I wanted the science community to test Donald's work. But I also wanted to bury it in a hole deep in the woods. "How soon could you publish this?"

His eyes widened. "I wasn't thinking about publishing. We have several papers-worth of material that we have sat on, you know, the preliminary work. It could take years to get all the findings out there. Assuming no one put the pieces together like we have."

I waved away his concern. "I'm not considering publishing, don't worry. Outside of AgSol, who else may have figured this out?"

Donald looked at his desk. "A Nagasaki genetics team is not far behind us on the gene activation. I don't know what they have sitting on the lab bench, or in the pipeline. A South African team of chemists is only maybe two years behind us on the chemical interactions with the genes. There's a woman at Harvard Medical who is on the verge of figuring out how environmentally-driven genetic damage can become cumulative across generations."

"Do you think it would be possible to stop them from publishing their findings?" I didn't want a roadmap leading to the conclusion that he had just dropped on my head.

"Suppress their research?" Donald pushed himself away from the desk like I had taken a swing at him.

Isn't that what Stitcher would do? Bury this stuff so far down that unless someone dropped a fracking oil well on top of it, no one would ever know?

"Imagine the media reaction if this was published," I said. "I think they'll use the word 'doomsday' a lot. You know how they exaggerate findings. It will cause panic, and worse, the knuckle-draggers will take a club to scientific funding. Any chance we have of doing something to stop this will die in the backlash."

"I, I think you're overreacting," Donald said. "This is boring, dry stuff. It will probably be ignored."

Maybe at first. But eventually some smart human would arrive at where Donald and the hybrids had. "That would be great, but it may be too big a risk to gamble on," I replied. "Remember the ozone hole, and the attention it got?"

"And all that attention helped get rid of CFCs," Donald retorted.

"The ozone hole was reversible," I said. "This is the equivalent of an asteroid coming straight for Earth. The social shockwave will take down politicians, medical researchers, and a lot of people who need to help fix this thing. Because we can fix this, right? Tell me you have figured out a way to fix it. That's why you exist."

Donald was looking at me in an odd, hopeful way. Like Charlie used to, when he wanted a cookie and thought he had earned it. Donald was hoping I could pull a Stitcher magic act out of my ass. He hadn't even heard my question.

"Do you think we can fix it, Donald?"

He turned squeamish. "I was hoping we could, at first. And may we can, if we keep trying, hoping for a breakthrough. We didn't think aliens existed a few decades ago, right?"

I had to stop looking into those sad eyes of his or I would lose it. He thought there was no hope. Correction: he knew there was no hope. I looked down at my lap. "Right. Until we have that breakthrough, we shouldn't undercut our effort by publicizing these findings."

"We can sit on our own research, but what about people outside? They are only a few years away, at most, from publishing."

And that's where I failed at being Stitcher, having the answers ready to questions like this. He probably had a scientific research suppression program sitting in his notes somewhere. "I don't know. I have to think about this. This is a lot to absorb." I needed to get out of his office. The back of my throat felt hot and tight. I could picture a genetic asteroid racing closer to our blue air bubble in space. A toxic, DNA-wrecking asteroid that humans had cooked up.

I patted his hand without looking at him. "We'll figure this out." And then I left his office and hurried down the hall to mine, closing the door behind me. I sat at my desk as tears spilled down my face. Something inside me lurched and I grabbed for the wastebasket right before I vomited.

My body was reacting like I had just been given a death sentence. And in a way that was exactly what had happened. Not for me, personally, but for life everywhere.

275

I broke into an open sob as I kneeled next to my wicker waste basket. Deep down, my subconscious knew that Donald was right. It had connected the dots on the coming apocalypse and then hid that truth in a dark corner.

There wasn't a solution. An increasing tide of toxic shit was ripping our genes apart, and there was no stopping it. So now what should I do? How do I prepare for an apocalypse I can't stop?

The End

Before you go...

Mark says, "Please help me by rating this book. Or even better, review it! I would greatly appreciate it because an honest rating or review will help other readers decide if this book is for them."

Find out how to grab a free e-book of the sequel, *The Obesity Apocalypse*

Ancient monsters. Modern horrors. There's always a bigger conspiracy.

Elaine knows how the world ends. All life on earth will die within decades. But she believes she can stop it. If only she and her team can mobilize the world's scientists to tackle this genetic apocalypse.

But going public creates a backlash. There are those who already know about the coming global extinction. They welcome it. They caused it. And they will bribe, blackmail, and summon supernatural monsters to kill anyone who tries to stop them.

All conspiracies end

As the doomsday cult tightens its grip on Elaine, she has to fight not just for her life but for all life. Even if it is a losing battle. Even if she has to endanger her son to ensure he may have a future. Even as she can't escape the genetic damage starting to wreak havoc inside her body.

The truth is everywhere

In the final book of the trilogy, the horror and the heartbreak come at a breakneck pace. Come for the terrifying supernatural monsters, stay for the ripped-from-the-headlines horrors that may be too hard for you to face.

Would you like the *Apocalypse* e-book free, along with Mark's newsletter?
We will only use your information to send you the book and his monthly newsletter. We will never sell it or share it. We will shower you with discounts and early releases. Promise.

Click here to grab the newsletter and *The Obesity Apocalypse* e-book
Or type into your browser: BookHip.com/RSSLTL

ACKNOWLEDGMENTS

(Deliberately presented like movie credits because the author thinks they are easier to skim)

PATIENCE, TOLERANCE, SUPPORT
Wendy Sarney, Karenna Sarney, Jaden Sarney

ALPHA READER
Nolan Smith-Kaprosy

BETA READER
Joni Lavery

EDITING
Ellen Campbell http://ellencampbelledits.com/

COVER DESIGN
Streetlight Graphics http://www.streetlightgraphics.com

ABOUT THE AUTHOR

Mark Sarney has been writing science fiction since he was a geeky, contrarian kid in Rochester, NY. He once converted his garage into an actual forest for Halloween, has stuck his head inside the Oval Office, and converts sencha tea and long commutes into fiction.

You can follow him at: marksarney.com or twitter.com/marksarney.

The Obesity Conspiracy Trilogy
The Obesity Conspiracy
The Obesity Pandemic
The Obesity Apocalypse

The Kagent Trilogy
Crashpoint (Kagent Series: #1)
Twistpoint (Kagent Series: #2)
Chokepoint (Kagent Series: #3)